Ghost's Beauty

A Dublin Falls Archangel's Warriors MC Novel #6

By Ciara St James

Copyright

Graphic Designer- Niki Ellis Designs, LLC

Editor- Maggie Kern @ Ms. K Edits- https://www.facebook.com/Ms.Kedits

Dublin Falls Archangels' Warriors MC Novels:

1- Terror's Temptress
2- Savage's Princess
3- Steel & Hammer's Hellcat
4- Menace's Siren
5- Ranger's Enchantress
6- Ghost's Beauty

Disclaimer: This book contains sexually explicit scenes. It is intended for audiences 18+. There may be graphic description of sex acts some may find disturbing. There may also be descriptions of physical violence, torture, or abuse. Some strong themes are found in this series. While the characters may not be conventional, they all believe in true love and commitment. The book is a HEA with some twists and turns along the way.

Dublin Falls MC Members:

Declan Moran (Terror)- President
Grayson Sumner (Savage)- Vice President
Dominic Vaughn (Menace)- Enforcer
Chase Romero (Ranger)- Sergeant at Arms
Jaxon Quinn (Viper)- Treasurer
Slade Devereaux (Blaze)- Secretary
Logan Priest (Steel)- Road Captain
Mason Durand (Hammer)
James Johnson (Tiny)
Talon Adair (Ghost)
Galen Duchene (Smoke)
Dane Michaelson (Hawk)
Jack Cannon (Devil Dog)
Eric James (Razor)
Quin Thomas (Torch)
Gage Lambert (Storm)

Blurb

Ghost:

I'm a Navy corpsman turned Archangel's Warrior.
I spend my days creating beautiful custom bikes.
At night, I yearn for a woman of my own.
Then my club rescues a group of women from a terrible fate.
One woman immediately captures my attention.
But she's scarred and needs time to heal.
I'm determined to wait as long as it takes to have her for my own.
And do whatever I have to in order to keep her.

Wren:
I had been through a horrific ordeal.
A nightmare no woman should have to endure.
I don't think I can ever fully trust a man again.
But I feel safe with the Warriors, and Ghost in particular.
He's my savior.
I just have to ignore my attraction to him.
Why would he want me?
There are other women who are always showing up with him, and I'm afraid to be touched.

The lifeblood of an Indie author is reviews and ratings on websites like Bookbub, GoodReads, social media, a retailer of your choice, etc. Please take a moment after reading and leave a review please. Every single one counts and is so appreciated! Thank you- Ciara.

Dedication: This book is dedicated to the women, men and children who have lived through the terrible trauma of being taken and abused. There is hope and life out there. Stay strong. There are those who understand and love you.

Acknowledgment: Characters Birdie Grant and Hayes Ellison are courtesy of author, E. R. Whyte and her book Remember Me available at major retailers. She also publishes lighter, sweet books as Elle Rae Whyte. Check out her series and other information about her at https://www.facebook.com/elleraewhyte

Chapter 1: Ghost

The hard-top road was flashing by under my wheels as my brothers and I sped down the winding country roads. Today was a great day for a ride. It was early October and the leaves had started to change in eastern Tennessee. Reds, golds, oranges, and browns exploded on the trees everywhere you looked. The temperature had dropped out of the terrible ninety-plus degree ranges of summer. Today was a nice seventy-five degrees with a breeze. Though what made it a perfect ride was the woman on the back of my bike. Something that had never happened before with me.

Wren Masters had finally gotten on a bike to take an actual ride with the club and was hugging tightly to me as we took the curves on this winding road. She'd been with us since May when we rescued Ranger's old lady, Brielle, from a group of human traffickers. Wren had also been held captive by the same people. The two women had bonded over their shared ordeal and since Wren had no family back in South Carolina where she was from, she stayed in Dublin Falls with Brielle and the club.

Even in her prison cell that day, dirty and bruised, she'd been so beautiful. She hadn't let what they did to her break her. She was fierce and stood up for herself. I'd felt my heart stop when I saw her there and every day since, I'd been enthralled with her. I knew she had a lot to heal from both physically and mentally. The traffickers had raped her. I knew that much. She'd talked to Brielle and Regan about it in more detail. She'd talked to Brielle and Regan about it in more detail and one day soon after they were rescued, I overheard her telling Brielle that she felt like she was dirty, undesirable to men and unsure if she could ever be with a man again. I'd told her she wasn't dirty, and it hadn't been her fault. If a man didn't want her because of what happened, then he wasn't a real man. I'd also let her know that when she was ready, I would be the man claiming her. I intended to be the man she finally trusted to love her. She hadn't believed me.

I'd spent the last several months showing her she could trust me. She'd become more trusting as she stayed and worked with our club. She seemed okay with our guys but was leery of other men outside the compound. Not that she showed fear, just caution and a readiness to defend herself. She'd gotten her concealed carry permit a couple of months ago at the club's shooting range. All the women in our club had them. We defended and protected our women, but they had to be able to defend themselves if needed. More than one had to do so in the past much to our dismay.

I wanted to join my seven club brothers who had found their old ladies over the last couple of years. Hell, we now had children in our club—something else I'd been thinking about since I'd met Wren. To date, we had six babies with two more due in December and Rowan, Brielle's daughter, who was turning four years old this month. Ranger had adopted her as his own. She was now Rowan Elise Romero. He had completely accepted her as if she were his own biological child. She was our princess and ruled every one of us tough, badass bikers. God help the boy who tried to date her when she got older. Well, God help any boy trying to date any of the Warriors' daughters.

Steel, Hammer, and Regan had twin daughters, Sierra and Sienna. Savage and Janessa had Kenna, and Menace and Alannah had their little girl in July, Savannah Rose Vaughn. The boys needed to catch up. Terror and Harlow had Hunter who just turned one in August. Tiny and Sherry's son, Samuel would be one in January. Luckily, it looked like Viking and his old lady Trish as well as Ranger and Brielle were going to have boys. That would get us close to even.

You'd think being an MC we'd hate having so many babies around, but it was the opposite. It made us an even tighter family. We loved our women and children fiercely. We would do anything to protect them. Wren was in that group even if she didn't know it. I'd told my brothers when she came to the clubhouse after her rescue, that she was going to be my old lady. I laid claim immediately so no one else got any ideas. Wren was a beautiful woman. Men couldn't help but look at her and be interested.

She stood about five foot five compared to my six foot three. She had long auburn hair that hung to her waist. Her eyes were blue-green. She had the curves of a woman, not a stick figure like what you see on television these days. She had full breasts, a tucked in waist and full hips for a man to hold onto when he made love to his woman. She wasn't fat but had meat on her bones so you wouldn't worry about breaking her when you took her hard. That's what I wanted in a woman.

I laid in my bed at night dreaming of taking her. I'd taken her slow and easy and fast and hard in those dreams. I'd taken her in every position imaginable and in every way I could. I was in a constant state of arousal, but I didn't go to the club bunnies to get relief even though they were there and offered often. As soon as I'd seen Wren, all desire to fuck another woman was gone. I wanted only her. I took care of my hard cock myself. I knew she needed time and I would give it to her. I wouldn't rush it. My brother Ranger got impatient with Brielle and he almost did something disastrous. It had almost cost him his woman. She'd been attacked and left for dead. He still blamed himself. Brielle was like Wren. She'd been raped four years before Ranger met her, but she hadn't been ready yet to trust a man when they first met. He'd warned me not to rush it like he did.

I brought my mind back to the ride. I needed to concentrate on the road. I had precious cargo onboard. We were riding today to see our associate club, the Iron Punishers, up in Bristol, Virginia. It was a great ride a couple of hours away. They'd been to our compound several times and now it was time for us to go visit theirs. They were our greatest ally against the Black Savages and Satan's Bastards MCs. The two MCs that wanted our territory in order to run their guns, drugs, and prostitutes through to North Carolina and beyond. We'd been warring with them. We'd taken out some of their drug houses and hopefully we'd take out a few of their gun storages soon. The Punishers had an informant who fed us information on what those two clubs were planning. They were dumb enough to talk about it in a local bar. It wasn't until several months ago, we found out who the

Punisher's informant was. It was Reaper's, the Punisher's president, sister, Harper.

When Viper and a few of the other Warriors went to help the Punishers hit our enemies a few months back, he'd met Harper. Well, more like she'd almost kicked his head off when he'd been sent to fetch something at Reaper's house and he came upon her in the shower. I'd noticed since then he was preoccupied a lot of the time and stayed away from the club bunnies and barflies too. I think he was fascinated by Harper. The rest of us would get to meet her for the first time today. The reason we were visiting is because they were having a party. Reaper was celebrating her graduation from college and had invited us.

I squeezed Wren's thigh and shouted, "Are you doing okay back there, sweetheart?"

She shouted back, "Yes." Her mouth was near my ear so I could hear her. I wanted to be sure she was fine since she hadn't ridden but once before around Dublin Falls with me. I'd gotten her to do it a couple of weeks ago.

I saw Steel, our road captain, signal we were pulling over. He planned the rides and ensured we got to where we were going safely. We were pulling into a gas station. We'd fill up our tanks even though some might not need it since we had done it before leaving Dublin Falls. This would give all of us a chance to stretch our legs, use the bathroom, and get something to drink if we wanted. Riding was very dehydrating due to the wind wicking the moisture out of your body. As we pulled in, I looked over my shoulder at Wren.

"We're gonna gas up. Why don't you stretch and

use the bathroom, sweetheart? Maybe get a drink. Here, will you grab me a water? Use this for our drinks." I handed her twenty dollars, and she took it reluctantly. I wasn't going to allow my woman to pay for anything. She nodded and swung off the bike. I held onto her hand to be sure she was steady on her feet. As she headed to the station, I shouted, "Be sure you get yours with it too, Wren." She frowned, and I laughed.

I got off and waited my turn at the pumps. This station had four pumps to our eighteen bikes. Everyone had come except our two newest prospects, Adam and Nick. We'd left them to watch the compound. This would test them. Our older prospects, Finn and Tyler, who had been with us since February, had come along this time. We wanted to see how they acted away from the compound. Also, they deserved to have some fun. Both so far had been solid prospects. Both were ex-military. Tyler was a cousin to Viking's old lady, Trish, and Finn had been in the Marines with our brother, Devil Dog, and Terror's old lady, Harlow.

All the old ladies went inside to use the bathroom. Finn had gone in to watch over them. When it was his turn to fill up, Tyler would take over. We didn't like to let our women out unprotected, especially with this not only bringing us closer to the Punishers' territory, but also to the Savages and Bastards. You couldn't ever be too careful.

This trip we hadn't brought the children. They would have been accommodated and welcomed, but we decided it was too much, especially with Savannah being so young. In fact, Alannah had stayed behind with her. Menace had argued he would stay too, but she told him he needed to be with the club for this. He was our enforcer.

He'd reluctantly given in to her. She, her grandma—Ms. Marie, and one of Brielle's employees, Cindy, would watch the babies and Rowan.

Cindy had started to help out with the babies back in April or May. We'd found she was very good with them, we trusted her, and she respected the club. In addition, we always paid her for helping. She needed extra money to send to her nieces and nephews. Apparently, her two sisters had a bunch of kids with different baby daddies and couldn't care for them without help. The prospects would also be able to help the women. Prospects were expected to help do anything and everything the club told them to do. In our club, that included helping with the babies and kids. If they didn't have exposure to babies and kids before they joined, we made sure they got it afterward. We were lucky. They all seemed to like them and did well with them.

I'd gotten my tank filled and was going to go hit the restroom before we took off. Wren was still in there. With our ladies and only a single women's toilet, there was a line since other people were stopping here too. Finn was standing toward the front of the store by the cashier so he could view the whole place. His back was to a wall. He was definitely prior military. Always protect your back. As I came in, I gave him a chin lift which he returned. I saw a couple of the old ladies looking at drinks and the others were in line to use the bathroom. I headed toward the bathroom. A guy was just ahead of me, going the same way. We got to the men's room to find the door locked. He cursed and I just relaxed against the wall to wait my turn. A minute later, the door opened and out came Wren. The man got in her face as soon as he saw her.

"Can't you read bitch? It says men not split tails. Use your own bathroom," he snarled. Rage shot through me. Who the fuck did he think he was talking to? No one was going to talk to my woman like that! I'd stepped up to latch a hold of him when Wren got back in his face.

"Listen, asshole, there were no men in here, so I used it. There were like ten women needing the bathroom and no men. Step off and shut up. It's all yours now." His face got red and he went to get in her face again. I grabbed him by the back of the neck this time and shook him like a rag doll.

"I expect you'd better shut your mouth and listen to the lady. There's nothing to get pissed about. You weren't here. You've been waiting a fucking minute just like me. And another thing, you're talking to my lady. I've killed for less. Don't make me ruin our day. She doesn't like blood." He'd gone pale and had started to shake when he looked over his shoulder and saw me standing there in my cut. I'd seen a few of my brothers out of the corner of my eye, come up behind us.

He started stammering. "I-I-I'm sorry. No disrespect." I shook him again.

"Don't tell me sorry, tell her. And never refer to a woman by that disgusting name again. That's so fucking wrong." He stammered out his apology to Wren. When I let him go, he headed for the door foregoing the bathroom. The guys were laughing. Wren was looking at me, stunned. I dropped a quick peck on her mouth. "Forget him, sweetheart. Go get our drinks and I'll be out in a minute." I went into the bathroom with her still staring at me. I'd staked my claim again with that kiss. It wasn't much of a kiss, but it was the first one I'd given her. She hadn't pulled away or hit me. I took that as progress. I was gonna start testing where she was in her recovery. If I could at least hold her and kiss her, it would be wonderful. I needed to be able to do at least that much.

When I came out, Terror was next in line. He grinned. "I see you decided to lay more claim to Wren. I've got my fingers crossed, brother. I know she's attracted to you. See where it goes and just keep it slow." I nodded and wandered out into the store. She was next in line to pay. She had two waters in her hands. I grabbed a Snickers bar. I'd noticed she seemed to eat those the most. I went up and put my arm around her shoulders handing her the candy bar. She just looked at me.

"I didn't know you wanted candy. Sorry," she apologized. I leaned down and kissed her cheek.

"It's not for me, it's for you. That's your favorite right? You should eat it. We won't get there for a little while and the barbeque isn't until later. You didn't eat before we left." She appeared startled that I knew she hadn't. I watched her every move when she was around. I knew she hadn't eaten. She needed to take care of herself. She'd lost weight after her capture and was still gaining it back. I knew this because I'd overheard her telling Brielle, she had. She still looked gorgeous, but I wanted her healthy.

When we got to the cashier, he was eyeing her with interest. She was oblivious and put the items down on the counter. He was chatting, trying to get her attention as he rang up our three items as slowly as possible. I shot him a glare and he finally shut up. Back outside, she was trying to hand me the change. "Keep it." I told her.

She argued with me. "Ghost, take your damn money. I don't need it. Thank you for paying for the water and candy bar, but I do have my own money." I pulled her into my arms. She stiffened a little but didn't struggle to get loose.

"I pay whenever we go anywhere. Get used to it. And keep the money. We'll probably stop other places over the next day or so. Now stop arguing, eat your candy bar and drink some water before I have to paddle that gorgeous ass in front of everyone." She gasped. I wanted to see how she reacted to that. I would never hurt her, but I was dominant in bed and I wanted to test how she'd react to orders. I would be paddling that ass one day, until she screamed in ecstasy. I liked to play around with B&D—bondage and domination. I hoped I could make her like it too. If not, I wouldn't force it on her. It just would change how I was in bed. For her, I'd do it.

She closed her mouth and stepped out of my arms. "Try it, Ghost, and you may find your ass paddled too." She walked off swinging her hips while eating her candy bar. I laughed. Yeah, she would be fine. She hadn't shrunk away from me in fear. My Beauty was strong and feisty. I hurried to gulp down my water as I saw the rest of the guys finishing topping off. She was now chatting to Brielle at the SUV. Since Brielle and Trish were pregnant, they weren't allowed to ride on the bikes. No one would ever endanger them or the babies that way. They were being driven by Tyler.

A minute later, Steel shouted for everyone to

saddle up. She came back and swung up on the bike behind me. She wrapped her arms around me as I started the bike. I reached behind me to pull her closer to my back and tightened her grip around my waist. She was holding on fine; I just wanted to feel her sexy body against me more, her pussy rubbing against my back. Even though we were clothed, the thought of her pussy being that close made me hard. Not the most comfortable way to ride, but I'd gotten used to being hard around her.

We took off. The next hour was spent enjoying more of the sun and warmth. We were pulling into the Punishers' clubhouse outside of Bristol, Virginia in no time. This was a funny town. Half fell on the Tennessee side and half in Virginia. So, people in the same town could live in Bristol, Virginia or Bristol, Tennessee. State Street in its historic downtown is the official state line for Tennessee and Virginia.

Chapter 2: Ghost

The Punishers' clubhouse was on land outside Bristol on the Virginia side. They had fifty acres from what Reaper had said. They'd recently enclosed a large portion of it like we had ours. They also liked our setup of having houses built within the walls when a brother took an old lady and started a family. This ensured they were better protected. I planned to have a house built for Wren and me soon. I had the spot picked out. She just didn't know it yet.

There were numerous bikes and a couple of trucks in the parking lot. I could see people outside the clubhouse milling around the yard. A prospect had opened their gate for us, and we swung in beside the other bikes. I had Wren jump off so I could back my bike into place. She was chatting with Regan and Harlow. Reaper and his VP, Maniac, came over to greet us. We were all shaking hands or giving each other back-slap hugs. It was great to see them again.

They escorted us to meet the rest of the club and their guests. The Punishers were all single, so I knew there would be bunnies around later. Right now, it was just them and a few friends of the club. Most seemed to not have women with them either. I saw many eyes looking at our women with keen interest and even desire.

Who could blame them? Our women were gorgeous and sexy. Even when they were pregnant, they lost none of their beauty or attractiveness. Trish and Brielle were heavily pregnant and attracting as many looks as the others. I could see Viking and Ranger holding their women close. All of them had on *Property* cuts except Wren. I hadn't gotten her to the point I could officially lay claim to her with one. I'd have to keep an eye on her and make it plain to all these slobbering wolves she was already claimed, even if she didn't wear a cut. Anyone messing with her would have to answer to me.

Reaper was introducing us to his sister, Harper, who was the honoree for the party. She was gorgeous and I could see Viper watching her. He had a hungry look in his eyes. He'd better be careful or Reaper might castrate him. Harper, was about five foot six or seven with long dark brown hair that hung below her shoulders. Her eyes were hazel but looked greener rather than brown. She was beautiful. No wonder she'd captured Viper's attention. I could see she had other men's attention not only in my club but Reapers. I was amazed he let her work in a bar. Wren and the ladies were chatting away with her. Reaper and his guys pulled us away to talk nearby. I made sure we weren't too far from our women. Reaper seemed to know we wouldn't want them out of our sights.

He was razzing some of the guys. "Damn, I see you're up to your usual shit. Finding gorgeous women, claiming them before anyone else has the chance and then knocking them up. What the hell? What chance does that give the rest of us? But I see you brought someone without a property cut. She's gorgeous. How is she related to the club?" I could hear the interest in his voice. A couple of his brothers were nodding. Terror jumped in before I could say anything.

"I'm sorry, brother, but Wren isn't available. Yes, she doesn't wear a cut, but it's only a matter of time. Ghost has already claimed her."

Reaper looked at me. "You've claimed her? Why isn't she in a cut then? I'd be careful with that one. Someone could try to steal her," Reaper told me.

I stepped up. "Then someone would be dead. She doesn't wear one because she's still recovering from her ordeal several months ago. She came to us when she got friendly with Brielle during their captivity." His guys got silent. Reaper was looking pissed now.

"You mean she was one of the women you rescued from that human trafficking bastard, Cochran? Fuck! Then that means she was..." he trailed off. They knew most of those women had been raped and beaten before they were to be sold. I nodded. They all groaned.

Maniac spoke up. "Man, brother, that fucking sucks. I'm amazed she's able to be around so many men, even in your club."

I nodded. "She's comfortable with us but she'll be leery and careful with all of you until she knows you. She doesn't back down though. They didn't break her. I just need to take my time with her. But make no mistake, she will be mine when she's ready." They all murmured their understanding of the line I had just drawn. They would keep their hands off of Wren, and no one would make a serious play for her. That didn't mean they wouldn't flirt. All of us would have before we found our women.

We talked a bit before the women decided to rejoin us, then we broke off into groups with various Punishers to be introduced to their other guests. Some were friends of the club while others were family or friends of Harper. I noticed Viper made sure to be in whatever group Harper was in. I noticed a few Punishers checking him out. I excused myself to go talk to him.

"Hey, brother, just a warning, you've got some of the Punishers watching you. They see how you're looking at Harper. Man, don't go there. If you try to 'hit and quit' that, they'll kill you. And then we'd have to declare war." He looked around making eye contact with those watching him.

"Let them try. And I'm not planning to 'hit it and quit it,' brother. I plan to have that riding on the back of my bike just like you have Wren. I've been waiting for the right time. This is it." I laughed and wished him good luck. Viper was a scary bastard. They'd better watch out. He'd been a Navy Seal with Savage. That man knew more ways to kill then you could probably think of in a lifetime. I'd picked up a lot from my days as a Navy corpsman attached to marine detachments, and he knew way more than me.

I went back to Wren and our group. I'd kept her close the whole time, and she didn't seem to mind. She was nice and polite to all the Punishers and the other people she met, but I could see she was alert to any man who seemed to get close. She scanned her environment constantly. Her hypervigilance was something that may never go completely away. And it shouldn't. You couldn't be too careful these days.

A while later we'd moved into the group which Harper was part of. Regan, Hammer, and Steel were in that group as well. She was talking about the degree she earned, the one we were celebrating her graduation from today. "I finally finished my master's in psychology."

Regan perked up. "Psychology. What was your focus?"

Harper smiled. "I plan to do behavioral counseling with mental health patients. Maybe in a hospital or prison." I saw Viper stiffen when she said prison. He didn't like that at all. Regan was becoming more excited.

"Really! I work as a nurse practitioner in a psych unit at Dublin Falls General Hospital. We're looking for a behavioral counselor. Where have you applied?" Harper went on to tell her. Regan was urging her to consider applying at Dublin Falls. I figured her brother wouldn't be happy to have her a little over two hours away, but she'd definitely have us to look out for her. And if Viper got his way, she'd be there eventually anyway. She also apparently had her bachelor's in criminal justice since she also loved forensic psychology.

Damn, she had two degrees and I knew the master's level had to have taken her six to seven years. I had to ask. "Damn, Harper, that's impressive. How old are you to have done all that work?" She laughed.

"I'm twenty-four. I had my associate's degree almost completed by the time I graduated high school. It helped a lot then I took both programs at the same time. Whenever I wasn't doing classes I worked. I like to stay busy." Her face showed wasn't being prideful about her accomplishments. She acted like it was just what anyone would do. I looked at Viper. He was thirty-four. Ten years wasn't too much of an age gap. He'd prospected with his best friend, Savage, after his time in the service.

We'd been there almost two hours when Wren and a couple of the ladies asked where the bathroom was. Harper said she'd show them. They headed off to the compound with her. I stayed with the guys drinking my beer. Crusher was telling a hilarious story about this one time they got into a bar fight. Suddenly, I heard female voices yelling. Whipping around, I saw Harper and the ladies by the clubhouse door as if they'd just come back out. A guy had Wren wrapped in his arms. She was struggling to get loose and I could see she was fighting hard. I took off running with my brothers and several Punishers not far behind.

As I got closer, she finally connected with his balls. He screamed out in pain, dropped his arms, and doubled over. She went all Xena on his ass. She kneed him in the face and then kicked him in the gut when he fell to the ground. I could hear what she was screaming. "Keep your fucking hands to yourself! I told you I wasn't interested. Leave me alone." She was shaking so hard, I thought she might collapse. I went to her. I made sure she could see it was me before I touched her, then pulled her into my arms. She had started to sob.

"Shh, sweetheart. It's okay. He won't bother you again. Come on. Let's go somewhere quiet."

Maniac was gesturing for me to follow him. He took us to a room and softly said, "Take her in here, Ghost.

This is your room for the night. No one will bother you. Let us know if you need anything." He threw a worried look at her as he left.

When we'd walked away, I'd seen Reaper had a hold of the guy. He and my brothers would take care of him. Though I wanted to be the one to do it, she needed me more. She was curled up on the bed crying and rocking side to side.

"Baby, you have to stop crying. You're gonna make yourself sick. Please," I pleaded with her. Seeing her like this tore me up. I eased down on the bed beside her and pulled her into my arms. Her face was now lying on my chest, and her tears had slowed down. I held her for another ten minutes while she cried. When she'd shed enough tears, she stopped and looked at me.

"I'm sorry I made a scene. When he grabbed me, all I could think about was when those men kidnapped me and when they'd come for me," she whispered. I knew she'd been raped by more than one man. The rest I had no idea. I kissed her softly on the lips.

"Tell me. You need to talk about it. Talk to me, please." She shifted so she could look at me better.

"They grabbed me late at night on my way into my apartment. I'd stayed late at school doing my lesson plans. I found out later they'd been watching me for a while. They used something to knock me out before I could put up a fight. When I came to, I was in that basement in a cell. They had one other woman at that time. She'd been there a couple of days before me. The rest came over the next week and a half. It wasn't until the following day, one of them tried to come into my cell and rape me. I fought back and he left. No one came around for a couple more days. The other woman had been raped a couple of times during those two days. She never tried to fight them. Two days later, another one tried his hand at raping me. We fought and I was eventually able to make him go away. By then they were getting really pissed." She paused and took a deep breath.

"So, one night, two of the others came after me. I fought but I couldn't beat both of them. They eventually got me down where they could hold me, and they took turns raping me." I felt my gut twist hearing this. I knew it had happened but to hear her tell it was worse. I could see she wasn't really with me but back in the memories.

She continued, "It was the next day when the fifth one made his try. I fought him until he gave up and told me I was too much trouble. By then, they had three other women. He raped one of them instead. The two who raped me came back three days before you guys came to rescue Bri. They did the same things again, but it took them longer to get me down. I'd learned how they worked the first time. They did the same thing and laughed as they left saying they'd be back for more. I waited in dread to see when that would happen. Then Bri came and we talked. You all came and rescued us soon afterward. It didn't seem real when it happened. I thought my mind had finally started to play tricks on me." She closed her eyes at this point and shuddered. I pulled her closer.

"Wren, you have nothing to worry about again. We will protect you. I will protect you for the rest of your life." Her eyes opened and she searched mine. I decided to lay it out to her and see what she would do. "Sweetheart, you must have realized by now, that I want you." She stiffened. "Don't. I want you but not just to fuck and play with and then walk away. I want you as my old lady, Wren. I want you like Ranger has Brielle. All my brothers know I've claimed you. I'll wait until you're ready. Tell me there's a chance you feel the same." I was hoping she felt the same way. I thought she felt more but I had to be certain. It would kill me if she said she had nothing but feelings of friendship for me. I couldn't continue without knowing.

She rolled so she could sit up and lean against the headboard like I was. She took my hand and rubbed it while looking at it. She sighed. "Ghost, I won't lie and say that I'm not attracted to you. I do feel something. I just don't know if I can let a man touch me again. I do have sexual thoughts," she glanced at me and back down, "but I don't know if I could carry through with them. And, I'm still waiting to be sure one of those bastards hasn't infected me with HIV. So far, the HIV test has been negative. Thank God all the other STDs have been cleared. I won't know for sure until November which would be the six-month mark. I would never put you at risk until I know that I'm okay even if I was ready to try and be with you." I kissed the top of her head. She looked up.

"Baby, that's all I need to hear. As long as you're willing to try, I'm happy. We'll wait for the test to be finalized as negative then see where it goes. I know it will be fine. Until then, I want us to spend time alone. We can go to dinner or watch movies, whatever you want. I just want to have time when it's you and me, and no one else. Can we do that?" She gave me a little smile and nodded. She snuggled back in my arms and eventually fell asleep. I knew she needed to rest after that emotional outpouring so I relaxed and enjoyed holding her.

Chapter 3: Ghost

She'd been asleep about an hour when she jerked awake. I soothed her and then asked, "Do you want to stay in here or maybe go back to the party. It's up to you."

She glanced around. "I'd like to go back but I need to fix myself up. I know I have makeup all over the place. How you can even look at me, I don't know."

I hugged her. "Baby, you're beautiful even if you had mascara to your knees. Let me go get your stuff from the SUV and you can freshen up. I'll lock the door so no one can come in." She nodded. I got up and grabbed the key on the nightstand. Maniac had laid it there before he left. All the rooms like ours had locks, so the person who claimed it could keep others out. I went out, locked the door, and headed to the parking lot.

Outside, some of the guys saw me and headed over. Reaper and Maniac were right behind them. Terror was the first to speak. "How is she doing, Ghost? Does she need anything? One of the women can go in if she doesn't want to come back out."

Before I could answer Reaper jumped in, "Fuck, I'm sorry, Ghost. We sent that little fucker out of here. He was one of the guys who works for us at our garage. He won't be anymore. I told him he'd better hope we didn't see him again anytime soon. A couple of the guys escorted him home and will reinforce the message. Does Wren need anything?" I knew he meant the two would beat the hell out of him to "reinforce" as he mentioned. I was happy he was gone but disappointed I couldn't beat him myself.

"Thanks, man. She's better. He made her have a flashback to her kidnapping and rapes. She fought her captors more than once. She cried for a good while but now she's ready to come back out. She just wants to freshen up, so I'm gonna get her bag out of the car." They nodded and said they'd be waiting for us. As they headed back to the groups, I got in the SUV and grabbed her bag. I stopped at my bike and got my stuff out of my saddlebags. As I walked back inside, a bunny from the Punishers' club came up to me.

"Hello, handsome. I see your name is Ghost. I'm Paula. You wanna find someplace to get better acquainted?" She tried to rub up against my arm.

I shook her off. "No thanks, Paula. I have an old lady. I'm not interested." I went to walk away, and she latched onto my arm.

"Oh, that's okay. She doesn't need to know. We can keep it our little secret."

I shook her loose. I was starting to get pissed. She was acting like some of the bunnies at our club had when some of my brothers settled down with their old ladies.

"It wouldn't be okay with me. I don't cheat on my woman. Now get lost and a word of advice, stay away from any of the Warriors with an old lady. They won't take you up on your offer and their ladies will likely kick your ass." She huffed and stomped off. I turned to head down the hallway and there stood Wren, watching.

I walked up to her. "Sorry it took so long, babe. I got caught outside by the guys wanting to know how you were doing."

She nodded. "It looks like you got caught inside too. I heard what you said. Is it true? You wouldn't cheat on your woman?" she asked as we walked down the hall and back into the room.

I nudged the door closed and threw the stuff on the bed. I took her into my arms. "Dead serious. None of us will ever touch another woman when we have one."

She frowned. "But Ghost, we're not having sex. I'm not officially your old lady. You have to have needs and have had them all these months."

I backed her to the wall and leaned down to kiss her cheeks, forehead, and then her mouth. "Yes, we're not having sex and I do have needs, but no one will satisfy those needs but you. To put it bluntly, I take care of them myself. My hand has been seeing a lot of action. It will continue to see it until you're ready."

She gasped. "You can't mean you haven't touched a woman since I've..."

I nodded. "That's exactly what I mean. Since the day you came to Dublin Falls, I've not touched a woman in any way. I won't, baby. It's you I want and you I'll wait to have."

She pulled my head down and sealed her lips to

mine. She was kissing me with a hint of hunger. I groaned and kissed her back. The kiss went on for a while. When we broke apart, both of us were a little dazed. I gave her a wicked grin while she blushed.

"Go get ready, woman, before I lose my good intentions and try to convince you to get naked with me. I'll wait for you outside in the hall." She gave a quick nod and went to grab her bag off the bed. I went out in the hall to calm down and get my throbbing hard-on under control. I'd seen her glance down when I said we needed to stop. She had seen my cock pressing against my zipper trying to get out. I wanted to lay her down on that bed and make love to her until we both were exhausted. Her mouth had been so sweet and hot. I could kiss her for hours. I loved to kiss. I pushed down and against my crotch trying to get my cock to settle down. I was out there maybe fifteen or twenty minutes before she opened the door.

She'd repaired her makeup. Her red hair had been in a braid from the ride. She'd taken it out and it hung long, down her back. She was still in her boots, tight jeans and a Harley shirt one of the girls had convinced her to get. It was tight and molded her full breasts perfectly before skimming down to her waist. She had decent cleavage showing but not so much she looked trashy. I whistled and she blushed. I shut and locked the door and wrapped my arm around her shoulders. We walked down the hall and back outside.

She was instantly surrounded by our women and Harper. From then on out, we moved from group to group again. Everyone made sure to not mention the incident and to act normal. She had relaxed but stayed watchful.

I could see her looking around. I leaned over and whispered to her. "He's gone. You have nothing to worry about, babe." She sighed in relief.

It was now going on five o'clock. The Punishers had the grills heated up and the meat cooking. As for other food, all of our woman had cooked and we'd brought it in the car. All of them were excellent cooks. In addition, I knew Reaper had said they would have food from a local restaurant and his sister, Harper would cook as well. I'd heard her talking about cooking even though her brother had tried to insist she didn't. Terror had warned him not to buy much or have Harper cook herself to death since our women tended to cook enough to feed an army.

By six o'clock, the chicken and steaks were done. The ladies had been in the kitchen warming up things while the meat cooked, and now they all helped to carry out the food and set it on the tables set aside for it. The tables were heavily laden with food. Everyone settled down to do some serious eating. There were compliments all around. Our women had brought homemade rolls, fresh butter and homemade jams, potato salad, coleslaw, some kind of green bean dish, street corn, lasagna, a pasta dish in Alfredo sauce, au gratin potatoes, several different kinds of pies and Alannah, even though she couldn't come, had made a tiered cake for Harper's graduation.

She'd had Ranger tell Reaper she'd make the cake and to ask him what Harper's favorite flavors were. He'd tried to say it wasn't necessary, however she insisted. It was three tiers and her favorite fruit flavor of raspberry. It was pink with raspberries and flowers decorating the top and edges of each tier. On the front of the tiers is where she had written *Congratulations Harper*. Alannah had said it was a Raspberry Pink Velvet Cake with Raspberry Cream Cheese filling. It was beautiful and looked like a professional had made it. Harper had gone crazy seeing it. The restaurant had made baked potatoes with all the fixings, baked beans, broccoli casserole and mixed fruit. In all, they had about sixty or so people here today.

I kept an eye on Wren. She was eating which made me happy. I didn't want her to lose any weight. Brielle had a problem with losing weight when she got stressed. I was hoping Wren didn't. After the food had been consumed like locust had descended, the prospects cleaned up. The music was turned up and the firepits and a big bonfire were lit. The drinks were flowing more. Some of the non-club friends they had invited were well on their way to being drunk. None of the bikers had consumed enough yet to be near that stage. Wren wasn't drinking. She'd told us before she didn't often and I knew here with people she didn't know, she'd never drink. I'd been drinking a few beers and water in between. I kissed her ear. "Babe, do you need something else to drink. Your water is almost gone."

She smiled. "I'll get it. I think I'll have a soda."

"I'll get it for you."

"No, I can get it Ghost." The ice chests with drinks were near us so I could keep an eye on her.

She was coming back when I was patted on the ass. I swung around to see Paula standing there. Jesus, didn't the woman listen? I'd seen her around the various guys rubbing up on them. She'd looked at me more than once but never came into our group. I was standing with Ink, Ratchet, and Crusher from the Punishers. Ink and

Savage were talking about tattooing and piercing. Both of them did it for a living. "Paula, I told you before, I'm not interested. Get lost." The guys had gone silent.

She pouted. "Please, Ghost. I know we could have so much fun. I know you said you have an old lady, but I checked out all the cuts, no one has one saying *Property of Ghost.*"

Before I could respond, Wren was beside me handing me another beer. She looked at Paula. "That's because it's tattooed on my ass and my fists. If you don't want to see it up close and personal on my fists, I suggest you move on and stay the hell away from him. I heard him tell you no in the clubhouse. Don't make him have to tell you a third time. Bunnies in our club get sent packing if they keep after a brother who tells them to get lost."

Paula stood there with her mouth hanging open. The guys were laughing their asses off. Paula snarled, "Bitch."

Wren smiled and said, "Slut." Paula stomped off, throwing dirty looks over her shoulder at Wren. I was about to tell Wren thank you for the rescue when Ink piped up.

"Hey, Fists, can I see that tattoo on your ass? Might want to display what it looks like at the shop." He said it with a devilish grin on his face.

She looked at him with a deadpan expression. "I could but then I'd have to kill you before Ghost did." He roared with laughter. She gave him a wink. Soon the whole place heard about what she had said to Paula and Ink. The Punishers all started to call her *Fists*. She took it in stride with a smile on her face. I was fucking proud of her and to be honest, turned on by her feisty attitude.

It was getting late. The friends and family members had left. Only us and the Punishers remained along with their bunnies. We'd left ours back at in Dublin Falls. The Punishers had seven and they were looking like they would be working hard tonight. Eight of our members and our two prospects were single. All twelve of the Punishers and their three prospects looked to be single. I didn't think Viper would be hooking up. He was sticking close to Harper. Not everyone would hook up, however, most would. The party had turned more risqué. Open fondling was happening—hands down pants on both sides. I knew Wren had seen some of this back home but normally she left before it got really crazy. I pulled her aside.

"Sweetheart, things are gonna get crazier now. Do you want to go back to the room?" She surprised me.

"No, I want to see what it gets like. I know I usually leave about this time, however, I'm curious. If it gets to be too much, I'll leave. I'm not sure I want to see some of your brothers doing the deed. Do they all have sex out in front of everyone and do they get completely naked?"

I shook my head. "Not all of them do it in front of people. I don't know for sure about the Punishers. And usually no one gets totally naked except maybe the bunnies. Babe, you have to be prepared, some girls take on more than one guy at a time," I warned her. I was surprised she wanted to stay but also interested to see how she reacted. I hadn't cared if anyone watched me when I had sex in the past. With Wren, I wasn't sure I'd want anyone to see her even partially naked. And after what she went through, she probably wouldn't want them to anyway.

I kept her under my arm. Over in one spot, I could see a bunny on her knees taking turns sucking off two Punishers. In another, Hawk had his hands down a bunny's pants. In yet another spot in the shadows, Torch had another one riding his lap. She had her clothes off, but he just had his pants down. Over on the picnic table was another bunny. She was sucking a Punisher's cock while Blaze fucked her from behind. I glanced at Wren. She was watching with interest. Her cheeks were pink, and her breathing was a little labored. I pulled her into a dark area against the side of the clubhouse. She glanced at me.

"Do you like what you see? Does it turn you on?" I whispered as I caressed her face. She blushed more and gave a little nod. "Do you want to play a little? I can give you some relief."

She moaned. "Ghost, we can't. I have to wait for the test and besides, I don't know if I could even though I want to."

I kissed her.

"Let's see if I can get you off. I promise I'll only use my hand. Please, babe, let me try. We can go to the room so we can be alone." She shook her head no. Damn. I had hoped I could touch her, but she surprised me with her next words.

"Not inside. Right here. No one can see us." I jerked

back in surprise. Seeing she was serious, I groaned and kissed her. I was devouring her mouth while she did the same to mine. She was sucking on my bottom lip. I slipped my tongue into her mouth and dueled with her tongue. We were panting hard.

While she was distracted by our kissing, I slide my hand under her top to touch her breast through her bra. She moaned and thrust it into my hand, hard. I pushed her bra up and wrapped my hand around her naked breast. Her nipple was hard. I teased it with my fingers, and she gave a whimper. I broke our kiss and yanked her top up so I could taste her full breast. It was overflowing in my hand. I sucked on it and bit down gently with my teeth. She was rubbing against me, panting. I freed the other one and took turns licking, sucking, biting, and tweaking both of them with my fingers. She was now almost sobbing. My cock was so hard, I felt like it could rip through my jeans. I was fucking on the brink of losing my mind.

I pulled back. Her eyes were glazed with passion. I slowly slid my hand to the waistband of her jeans and stopped. She nodded hesitantly then with more confidence. I unsnapped and unzipped them so I could slide my hand down under her panties. When I did, I felt a tiny landing strip of hair and then naked lips. I pushed between them to find she was soaking wet. Her juices covered my fingers, and I moaned. "Babe, you're so wet. Fuck! Let me make you come." I went back to kissing her and sucking on her breasts as I fingered her nether lips and clit. She was hanging onto me and moaning. Her juices were increasing. I carefully slid one finger inside of her. She tensed for a second and then slowly relaxed. She was fucking tight. I thrust in and out. She was getting close. I could blow just touching her.

As I thrust again, I felt her hand on the buttons of my jeans. I stopped and looked at her. "I want to touch you, Ghost. Please." I nodded and she unbuttoned my jeans and I helped her to push them down below my ass. She looked down. It was dark but there was enough light to see my cock. She gasped. I knew I was bigger than a lot of men. My cock was standing at attention and smeared with precum. She wrapped her hand as far as she could around it then ran her thumb over the head of my cock, smearing the cum more. I moaned. Her hand felt so good. She gave an experimental pump, and I shuddered.

I went back to fingering her toward her release while she pumped my cock up and down. It didn't take long before we were both breathless and about to climax. I thrust into her with two fingers and used my thumb to press on her clit. She was squeezing me harder and playing with the sensitive spot under the head of my cock. I felt the tingling coming up my legs. I was about to blow. I bit her earlobe and rasped out, "Please be close, baby. I'm gonna come." She moaned and I thrust a couple more times. We'd timed it so she was pumping in time with my thrusts. She clenched down on my fingers and came screaming with her head thrown back. I growled and shot my load all over her hand. She kept pumping until I stopped coming while I kept thrusting in and out of her pussy until her spasms stopped.

I laid my head down on the top of hers. "Wren, that was perfect, babe. Thank you."

She raised her eyes and smiled. "I should be the

one thanking you, Ghost. I didn't know if I could do it for sure."

I kissed her. "Babe, when we're alone, call me Talon. That's my real name, Talon Adair." She nodded. "Okay, we need to get cleaned up. I assume you're ready to go inside." She agreed. I used my tee shirt to clean her hands and my cock before tucking it back in my pants and buttoning up. She got her bra back in place with her shirt pulled down. I helped to button and zip her pants.

I led her to the clubhouse. No one paid us a bit of attention. I knew some had heard her cry out when she came, but no one bothered us or remarked about me being shirtless. I led her to our room. Inside, I told her to use the shower first. I wanted desperately to shower with her but decided to not push any more. She'd pleasured me while I did the same to her. I was surprised she'd done that much. There's no need to spook her. When she came out fifteen minutes later, I went to take my shower.

She was in bed under the covers when I returned from the bathroom. I had on a pair of shorts. I usually slept naked but would keep these on for her tonight. I was happy she hadn't balked at sharing a room and bed. Her nightclothes were a tiny pair of shorts and a tank top. I pulled back the covers and slid under them. She shifted. I kissed her ear. "Wren, can I hold you tonight?" She scooted over into my arms laying her head on my chest. Her arm went over my stomach and one leg was thrown over my hip. I pulled her even closer so she was plastered to me. I gave her a deep kiss which she returned. When we broke apart, I told her, "Sleep tight, beauty. I'm here." She gave me another quick peck and was soon asleep. I laid there for a bit after she'd fallen asleep thanking God, she'd let me in a little. I only hoped she'd let us keep advancing our relationship once we were back home. Tonight, had only reinforced to me she was the one.

Chapter 4: Wren

We had been back from the party at the Punishers' clubhouse for a week. It had been fun, but the best part was allowing for Ghost and me to pleasure one another. I wouldn't try to go farther until I knew for sure he would be safe. I would know after my test on November thirteenth. That would be exactly six months since the first exposure to those men. Since the party, we'd spent time alone every day. One night, we went to dinner. Another night, we watched movies in my room at Brielle and Ranger's house. They'd insisted I stay with them once their house was done, which they'd moved into soon after their wedding. Another night, we watched television in his room at the clubhouse. All normal things most dating couples do to get to know each other.

Today, we were having a birthday party for Rowan. She was turning four. She just got under the wire by a couple days for being a Libra. Her birthday was October twenty-first and Scorpios started on October twenty-third. She was excited. Bull, Demon and most of their other guys from the Hunter's Creek Warriors chapter were coming over for the party. She'd wrapped their club around her little finger just like she did the Dublin Falls chapter.

Alannah had made her a Disney Princesses cake

in her favorite flavor of chocolate. Since Rowan loved the food from this Mexican place in town, we all worked on recreating some of her favorite things. I'd had grown up with a best friend who was Mexican, and her mom had taught both of us how to cook authentic Mexican food. Unfortunately, Maria had been killed when we were sixteen by a drunk driver. After that, her family had moved away and I'd lost contact with them. It was too hard for them to stay where everything reminded them of her, but I still recalled those lessons from her mom. Come to think of it, I hadn't really had a close friend again until Brielle.

The clubhouse was an explosion of pink, white, purple and turquoise. There were streamers everywhere, tablecloths, paper plates and cups as well as a princess themed décor in those colors all over the place. We'd had opened the daycare at the beginning of September and in addition to the Warriors' seven kids, which included Rowan, we'd kept two spots open for the two coming in December. It was likely Trish wouldn't go back to the Fallen Angel, so she might work at the daycare with some of us. I was running it as the director since I was a licensed teacher and had child development certifications. Ms. Marie was on staff but refused to be paid. We needed to have at least four staff to be able to care for a max of twelve under school age children plus an additional three school age ones. So, we had room for six children.

As time passed, we might have some of the Warriors' children stay separate in the farmhouse with our volunteers, so they aren't part of the group childcare home we were licensed to operate. This would allow us to bring on more children with paying parents. But right now, they were fine. We had taken on a three-year-old and two five-year-olds, plus one in kindergarten, one in first grade and one in second grade. Our oldest was seven. We'd hired two ladies from Dublin Falls with years of daycare experience to be the other staff. However, with many of the ladies volunteering, we had way more than the four-to-one ratio required if the children were six weeks old to eighteen months, which is when it jumped to a six-to-one ratio. I'd had to help them navigate all the rules in the state of Tennessee pertaining to a daycare. Then I outlined for them an educational plan. It would still be fun for the kids, but they would start learning things they would need to know when they went to school.

Rowan was such an extrovert, she had made fast friends with the three, five, six, and seven-year-old children from the daycare. A few had been in the weekly "Mommy and Me" group she'd attended at the rec center. As soon as the daycare opened, the moms had beaten the door down trying to get admitted to the MC's daycare. We had a waiting list a mile long and growing. Those six were coming to her party today. It would be interesting for the club to be exposed to more children around her age rather than babies and toddlers.

I was putting the finishing touches on one of the tables when I felt arms wrap around me. I knew it was Ghost. His natural scent gave him away. I couldn't describe it, but it was Ghost—kind of woodsy with underlying notes of musk. He kissed my neck.

"Hi, baby. You got a minute?" I nodded and he led me down the hall to his room. I was curious to see what he needed to talk about in private. Once we were inside, he shut the door and had me pushed up against it, kissing me like a hungry man. I groaned.

We'd pleasured each other a few more times since that first time last week. Every time it had been wonderful. I was enjoying his touch and looking forward to being able to see if I could stand to do more. The desire was there for sure. I broke away. "Talon, we can't. The kids and their parents should be here soon. God, you're making me crazy." He nibbled on my ear and down my neck.

"Not as crazy as you're making me. Shaking that ass all over the common room. God, I want to peel these clothes off and throw you on that bed. Just let me get a couple more kisses, then we'll stop."

We spent the next fifteen minutes devouring each other. I finally called it to a halt. He moaned but nodded. I straightened myself up as much as possible and headed out. He said he'd be out soon. I knew he was going to relieve himself. Ghost had told me he masturbated all the time to thoughts of me. I hadn't admitted to him I was doing the same, thinking about him at night.

I headed out to run back to the house and repair my makeup. I saw a few of the guys grinning as well as the ladies and pretended not to notice them. They knew we'd been fooling around. After I repaired my makeup and brushed my hair, I went back outside. I could see unfamiliar cars in the parking lot now. It looked like the kids and their parents had arrived.

The Hunters Creek crew had come in last night. Rowan had loved having them to herself for the evening.

It was amazing to see these tough bikers reading with her, playing games, and even playing tea party or dolls. Bull called her his granddaughter like he did the other babies. Only Hunter was truly his grandchild. He had told Rowan she could call him grandpa and she'd taken him up on his offer. She didn't have any grandparents.

Inside, I could see the others all talking to the various parents. I'd of course met all the kids and their moms. The dads I had not. They didn't come to interview or do the drop off/pick up of the kids. I got the impression none of them were very hands-on. They were nothing like the Warriors. The Warriors were that way even for kids who weren't their own. The single ones even did it.

The parents were being introduced to the Warriors and the other ladies they hadn't met yet at the daycare. I saw them looking at the bikers a little wearily. I slid into the group. I said hello to the moms and got introductions to the dads. The kids were already playing with Rowan in the kids' room. She'd taken them down there to show it off is what Harlow told me.

Cassie was the mom of one of the five-year-old kids, Hannah. She introduced her husband, Dan, while explaining to him I was the director of the daycare. He kind of gave me the creeps to be honest with the way he was staring at me. I shook his hand really quick. "Wren, we were telling the others how surprised we were to see the kids' room and I hear there's a big playground out back. Wow. I never imagined they would have all this for the kids," Cassie said, and I laughed.

"Yeah, they did most of it before they even had any from what I was told. They expanded the playground once they started having kids," her husband Dan piped up. "Do you have any kids?"

"No," I told him. He was eyeing me and the other old ladies like we were a buffet. About that time, Ghost came out of his room and headed straight over to me. He gave me a kiss and then was introduced to everyone.

We weren't going to eat yet, so Ms. Marie went to see if the kids wanted to play inside or out on the playground. It sounded like a herd coming when they ran into the common room ready to go outside. It was a warm October day, so they had no need for a jacket while the sun was out. We moved everything and everyone outside so we could keep an eye on them. The prospects took out the chests with drinks in them. One was set up for the kids and the other had adult drinks. There were chairs and picnic tables all around the area. We sat down to talk. The babies were with us and passed around between us, the Warriors, and the other moms. I could see the other parents' surprise at how the Warriors handled the babies. The guys were talking to the dads and finding out what kind of work they did. Everyone was getting along and other than a beer here and there, no one was drinking much other than Dan. He seemed to be hitting the alcohol pretty hard.

We spent over an hour outside with the kids running wild on the playset. Rowan had just come over to say she was hungry. All the women and I went inside to get the food set out. We'd cooked it earlier and kept it in chaffing dishes over a flame so it would stay warm. We set everything out on the two tables we had off to the side so everyone could go down both sides to serve themselves. Cassie and one of the other mom's, Sue, asked where we'd gotten the food. We told them we'd made it. I could see they were surprised. I got the impression none of them cooked much.

After everything was set out, we called in the kids and men. The Warrior guys helped the kids get their hands washed up. We organized it so the children got served first then the guys and women went through the line. I was going to wait until everyone had gotten their food before getting a plate. Ghost drew me in line with him. "You need to eat. You've been going all day. Everyone is fine. Relax." We filled our plates and took a seat.

The next half hour was filled with people eating, talking, and everyone seemed to enjoy the food. Once the food had been consumed, Rowan decided she wanted to open her presents. There was a table weighed down with gifts. Everyone got her something, even the single guys. She got beautiful clothes, shoes, too many toys to count, books and dress-up clothes, some movies and in one box, she had her own cut. It had *Property of the Warriors* on the back. On the front her name was *Little Princess*. She squealed when she opened it. At first, I thought Ranger got it for her, but he said no it was Bull. He'd thought about it, but Bull had beat him to it.

When she'd opened everything, she was beyond delighted. Her and the kids played with her stuff for another hour. As we kept an eye on them, I could see Rowan and all the other kids were getting tired. I nudged Brielle. She saw where I was looking and nodded that she understood. We didn't want to have any meltdowns today. Brielle asked Rowan if she was ready to eat cake. Cheers were heard all around as the kids raced inside to the cake. Her beautiful cake was brought out to be admired and her candles to be blown out. Everyone dug into the delicious chocolate cake Alannah had made. After they were done eating, we got all the kids wiped up and they decided to go outside and play just a bit more on the playground. Everyone headed back outside with them. I told Ghost to go ahead, I needed to use the bathroom. He went out with everyone else.

When I'd finished using the bathroom, I decided to pop the cake in the fridge. I was in the kitchen making room for it when I felt a hand on my ass. Assuming it was Ghost, I turned around smiling. It wasn't Ghost. It was Cassie's husband, Dan. He'd been drinking hard all day and was drunk. I'd seen her giving him pissed looks a couple of times. I stood up and tried to move away from the fridge and out in the open so I wouldn't be trapped by him. He blocked me.

"Hey, baby, no need to run off. I've been watching you all day. Fuck, you're hot. I see the others all have those vests on, but you don't even though that guy, Ghost, seems to hang on you all the time. What are you, one of those bunnies I've heard MCs keep? Those fuck toys. Man, what I wouldn't do to fuck you. Why don't we go in one of those rooms and have a little fun while the brats play?" His voice was slurred, and his face flushed. I glanced down and could see the erection tenting his pants. The feeling of being closed in started to overtake me.

"Move. I'm not a bunny. I'm with Ghost. You lay a hand on me and he'll kill you."

He laughed. "Not if he doesn't know. It'll be our little secret." He lunged at me, grabbed my shoulders and shoved me against the fridge. I cried out as my back hit the handle. He was trying to kiss me. I struggled to get him off me. I was about to knee him in the balls and scream when he was jerked away and went sailing across the kitchen. Standing there was an enraged Ghost. This version of him was scary to see. He went after Dan and started to beat the hell out of him.

"Please, Ghost, stop. You're going to kill him!" I begged. He kept going. I ran to the door and shouted for the guys. They all seemed to come running. Savage was first through the door.

"What's wrong, Wren?"

I pointed to the kitchen and then they heard the fighting. He took off with several behind him. The women and many of the other guys came inside. I was crying. Brielle had me in her arms. Ranger was standing guard over both of us. Out of the kitchen came Savage, Ghost, Devil Dog, Terror, Bull, and Demon. Devil and Terror were dragging Dan between them. He looked half-conscious with bruises and cuts visible on his face. Savage and Bull had Ghost between them holding onto his arms. Luckily, Ms. Marie and the prospects had kept the kids distracted outside. Ghost looked half crazy. I ran over to him. He shook the guys loose and wrapped me in his arms.

Cassie cried out, "What did you do to my husband?"

Ghost raised his head and glared. "I beat his fucking ass for attacking my woman, Wren. He had her cornered in the kitchen and was all over her," he spit out between his clenched teeth. She paled and looked at Dan. He was now looking around.

"She came on to me! I wasn't attacking her. She's just an oversexed whore." I held onto Ghost as Savage, Bull, and Demon also grabbed him to keep him from attacking Dan again.

Terror shook Dan. "Shut the fuck up. We know that's not true. You're lucky we saved your sorry ass. Ghost was in the Navy and knows a lot of ways to hurt or kill someone. You never touch an old lady of the Warriors. She might not have had a cut on, but it was clear she was taken. And she would never have come onto you. You need to get your shit and leave." He looked at Cassie. "It's up to you if you want to stay or not. If you do, we'll be sure you and Hannah get home safely. And I'd think long and hard about staying with a piece of shit like this."

She was crying. She glared at her husband and said, "I'd rather stay."

They got two prospects to take his ass home in one of the club's SUVs.

Chapter 5: Wren

Ghost took me to his room. Inside he was running his hands all over me. "Baby, did he hurt you? God, I'm so sorry. I didn't know he'd be dumb enough to try something. I saw he was interested in you. Fuck! I should have kicked his ass when he kept staring." He was rambling while his hands roamed over my body. He touched my back and I flinched. He froze. "Wren, what's wrong with your back?"

I caressed his face. "It's nothing. He shoved me back and I hit the handle on the fridge."

He turned me around and said, "Let me see." He pulled up the back of my shirt and swore. "Fuck, you have a big bruise already. Let's get some ice on this. You need to lie down."

I tried to reassure him I was okay. "Talon, I'm a redhead. I bruise really easy. I'll be fine." He insisted I lie down. I did so he'd calm down. When I did, he ran out of the room. He was back in under five minutes with an ice pack which he put on the bruise. He slid into bed with me.

"Can I get you anything, sweetheart? Are you in pain?"

I shook my head. "No, I'm fine. He scared me but

other than the bruise, I'm okay. Please don't fuss." He kissed me.

"I'll always fuss. It's my job to protect you and I failed." I hushed him and gave him a kiss. We laid there together for about a half hour. I sighed.

"We need to get back out there. Rowan is going to wonder where we went. I don't want this to spoil her birthday party." He reluctantly agreed. I brushed my hair with his brush, and we went outside hand in hand.

The kids were now quietly playing. They all looked ready to take a long nap. The others greeted us. I saw that Cassie and her daughter had left. The remaining parents were looking at Ghost and I leerily. We acted like we were fine. Another thirty minutes and the rest of the parents and kids packed up to go. Once they were out the gate, the rest of us headed back inside. Rowan went with Ms. Marie to her house to get ready for bed and watch a movie so she could relax to sleep. Ranger and Bri told her they'd be there soon. She gave everyone hugs and kisses and thanked them for her gifts. She really was a very smart and well-mannered kid.

As soon as they were out of earshot, the others started to question me about Dan. I told them what he said and did. The guys wanted to go beat on him more. I told them he was a creep and I wouldn't probably see him again. It wasn't like he ever dropped off or picked up his daughter. Ghost told them about the big bruise on my back.

Steel and Hammer spoke up. "He's an ass. He runs that new construction business in town. He's been trying to take business away from us for months. From what we heard, his guys do shoddy work, and very few people want to do business with him. He also runs over budget and over schedule. He and his family moved here a couple of years ago. The wife and daughter seem like good people, but he's a piece of shit. Don't worry about him, Wren."

I gave them each a smile. I really loved the whole club. They were like the brothers I'd never had. Well, all except Ghost. What I felt for him wasn't sisterly at all. The old ladies were like sisters with Bri being a sister and best friend. I didn't know what I'd done to deserve them.

The ladies headed to their various houses, those with babies to get them settled though they had napped on and off today. For Brielle and Trish, they left to rest their pregnant bodies. Bri was lucky Ranger let her stay up this long. The man tried to make her rest almost all day. Thank goodness she had good people cleaning for her business. He wouldn't let her clean the compound houses. Cindy had taken those over.

Ghost and I helped the others tear down the party decorations. The prospects said they'd do it but I insisted. It didn't take long. Afterward, the other guys were all playing pool or darts, watching television, or playing cards in the common room. I wasn't ready to turn in for the night, so I joined the guys playing cards. I was still too wound up and needed a distraction. They were playing poker. I joined a table which had only Hunter's Creek guys at it. The Dublin Falls guys just grinned. I couldn't get them to play with me anymore. I was crazy good at poker. They swore I cheated or had magic. I'd taken a lot of money from them until they quit playing against me.

They agreed upon a certain amount everyone had to have for buy-in. You put the money into a pot and were issued poker chips. This time they were doing one hundred dollars as the buy-in. It was steep. Ghost pulled it out of his wallet. I told him no. He leaned down. "I know you're good for it. And I also know you're gonna kick their asses. Now play." I took the cash. Then the game was on.

For the next two hours we played. Some dropped out when they lost all their money to be replaced by others. Others just bought more chips. At the end of the two hours, I was the clear winner. I had six hundred dollars in front of me. We'd bet in increments of five. I'd lost some hands, but overall, I won. They were all moaning. The Dublin guys were laughing their asses off.

Demon sighed and asked, "Okay tell us what you're doing. Damn, they need to take you to Vegas."

I grinned.

"I have an eidetic memory. I remember every card played and calculate the odds." He laughed and shook his head ruthful.

I stood up and thanked them for their money. They all tried to get me to play more but I told them another time. I was ready to relax at the house. Ghost went with me after we said goodbye to everyone. Ranger and Brielle had been at the house for a while, and greeted us when we came in the door to go to my room. They were used to seeing us together. Bri knew Ghost and I had fooled around some but hadn't gone all the way.

Rowan was in bed sleeping like the dead. She didn't hear anything once she fell asleep. I took a quick shower and crawled into bed with Ghost. He pulled me onto his chest.

"Finally, I have you alone." He ran his hands all over me being careful to avoid the bruise on my back. I was wet for him in just a couple of minutes. We were kissing and rubbing against each other. I was panting. God, the next few weeks couldn't go quickly enough for me. I knew ninety-nine percent of people who had HIV showed positive within those first five months after exposure. I just wanted to be sure about the last one percent. Dr. Hunter told me the possibility was nil. Ghost and I had talked about it over the last week. I knew he was clean because he told me about getting tested regularly and always using condoms anyway. He'd gotten his last test two months ago and per his admission, hadn't been with anyone since he met me.

Ghost was panting. He licked up to my ear. "Baby, I want to see all of you. Are you okay with that? If not, that's okay. I just want to look at this gorgeous body." I moaned. He'd seen my breasts. So far, I'd kept my pants on when he pleasured me. I'd seen him with his shirt off and his pants down.

His cock was huge and intimidating. It had to be over eight inches and thick. He had muscles all over including huge arms and thighs. His tats were mostly tribal in nature to go along with his Native American heritage. He'd told me his mom and dad had both been fifty percent Apache. His blue eyes came from his mom. His skin was the color of bronze and his hair was black as coal and hung below his shoulders. He usually wore it with the top half pulled back in a man bun while the rest hung long. I wanted to see all of him. I was just nervous for him to see all of me.

He was patiently waiting for my answer. I swallowed and nodded yes.

He groaned. "Do you want me to keep mine on or take them off. You tell me what you're most comfortable with doing. I promise we won't do more than you want." I leaned forward and kissed him.

I gather my courage and told him, "I want both of us naked, all the way." He closed his eyes and took a deep breath. When he opened them, I could see such heat and desire burning in them. He stood up and began to peel off his shirt. His boots and socks he'd taken off while I was in the shower. When he got to his jeans, he undid them and worked them down to his knees where he paused. I looked at his delicious cock. He never wore underwear. Seeing I wasn't protesting, he took them the rest of the way off throwing them on the floor.

Ghost crawled onto the bed and hovered over me. "Now, it's your turn. If you want to stop, just tell me." I nodded. He reached down and pulled my sleep tank over my head. My breasts were bare underneath. He sighed and took one of them into his mouth. He was always telling me how beautiful they were, and I teased him about being a breast man. He'd said he was more of an ass man usually, but my breasts were perfect. He also had said he thought my ass was perfect even if he hadn't seen it naked yet. He kept up the attention to my breasts for several minutes. Finally, he pulled away and slid his hand to my shorts. He stopped and looked up at me. "Okay?"

I sat up and told him, "Yes, I'm fine."

He began to pull them down my hips, past my thighs and over my calves until they joined his jeans on the floor. He stood up and looked down at me. He ran his eyes from my head to my toes and back. I could see his cock twitch. He growled, "Turn over." I did. I felt his hands on my ass. He caressed and massaged my ass cheeks before squeezing them. He leaned down and kissed my back and breathed into my ear. "Just as I thought, every inch of your body is perfect. This ass was made for me."

He slid into bed and helped me to turn back over. He inched down the bed and gently pushed my thighs apart so he could get the full view of my pussy. I was nervous having him inspect me so closely. He groaned. "Shit! So pretty and perfect. God, baby, I've never seen such a pretty pussy." He ran his fingers lightly up and down my slit gathering my juices on his fingers. He petted me over and over. I was squirming on the bed. Usually, we pleasured each other at the same time. This time he was too far away to reach him. I moaned.

"Talon, honey I can't reach you when you're all the way down there."

Ghost grinned. "I know. I want to enjoy this first. You don't know how badly I want to taste you." I shook my head no. He nodded. "I know, not until after the last test. But I am warning you now, woman, as soon as that comes back negative, I'm gonna eat your sweet pussy until you scream. Fuck!" He went back to pleasuring me. He slid his fingers up and down my slit, pinched my clit, and thrust his fingers in and out of my entrance. I was mindless with desire and lifting my hips off the bed thrusting back on his fingers. He sped up and all too soon I was cresting, yelling out my pleasure as my pussy clamped down on his fingers. He kept thrusting throughout my whole orgasm. I was limp when I came down from the high.

He crawled up the bed to lie next to me and was kissing me. I kissed him back and then pushed him on his back. He settled back to allow me to get him off. I had other ideas. He couldn't taste me yet, but nothing said I couldn't taste him. I'd been thinking about it. I didn't know much about oral sex. I'd only ever been with one guy before the rapes and he'd been a guy from my freshman year of college. All he had worried about was getting his rocks off.

I leaned over Ghost and kissed down his chest, running my hand down to his cock. It jumped in my hand. I lightly pumped up and down as I kissed farther down to his stomach. His breath hissed out. "Babe, what are you doing?" I could hear the excitement in his voice.

I raised up. "I want to see what you taste like. I've never done this before. Can I try?"

He moaned. "Fuck, yes. Play. Are you sure you want to?" To answer his question, I slid down and licked the head. He jerked and moaned. I spent time licking all around the head, down his shaft and even his balls. He was groaning more and more. He pulled gently on my hair. "Suck my cock before I die, woman."

I laughed and then engulfed his head in my mouth. His hips lifted off the bed. He was stretching my mouth to capacity. I worked to take as much of him as I could. I increased my suction and wrapped a hand around the base. I began to move up and down his shaft. I found a rhythm which he seemed to like, and I kept it up. I made sure when I pulled back to suck on the head to lick, too. I played with his balls and stroked his base.

I found the longer I did it, the more I could get in my mouth. He was moaning and shifting around on the bed. I sped up and tightened my hand and mouth just a bit more. He growled. "I'm close. I'll tap your shoulder when I'm about to come so you can pull back." I kept bobbing my head up and down. I knew I wasn't going to pull back. I needed to taste him. The little I had tasted from the precum had been delicious. Less than a dozen strokes later and I felt his tap. I kept going. He moaned. "I'm coming baby, pull back." I shook my head and kept up the suction.

He came, roaring and bucking his hips in and out of my mouth. His hot, salty cum filled my mouth and ran down the back of my throat. I swallowed as fast as I could. As he stopped jerking and coming, I pulled off his cock and lightly licked up his whole shaft and around the head. He grabbed my arms and pulled me to his mouth where he proceeded to ravish my mouth. He whispered. "Wren, that was incredible. I can't even describe it. Baby, you didn't have to swallow. I know most women don't like that."

I kissed him. "I wanted to taste more of you, and I love the way you taste."

He groaned and pulled me to lie half on top of him.

When he'd calmed back down, he pulled away. "I want to ask you something. I want you to consider moving into the guest house with me. I want to have more privacy so we can spend more time together. No one is in it. Would you consider that?"

I gaped at him.

"You want to live with me?"

He nodded. I was speechless.

He went on, "You don't have to decide now but think about it, please."

"I will," I promised him. It wasn't long after he stunned me by asking me to move in with him that I fell asleep. This would be the first night we'd stayed together like this the whole night. Wonder what Ranger and Brielle would think?

Chapter 6: Ghost

Today was the day. Wren went to see Dr. Hunter to get her final HIV test. He said he would be able to do a rapid test in the office and she'd know within twenty minutes. I couldn't wait. The last month had been so good but so frustrating. We had pleasured each other in so many ways, but I hadn't gotten to taste her yet or have my cock deep inside anything other than her mouth. I wanted both but would settle for tasting her. She had been doing great in trusting me with her body. After being raped, we both had worried she wouldn't be able to handle it. I did get her to finally agree to move in with me at the guest house a little over a week ago. Being able to be alone with her was fantastic. The next step would be to get her to agree to us building a house of our own on the compound. I'd wait and ask her about doing it next month if things continued to progress.

Her appointment was at the end of the day. She had been up early and nervous all day. She hadn't gone to the daycare either. She was hugged up against me on my bike as we drove into the parking lot of Dr. Hunter's office. She got off and smoothed her hair. We walked inside holding hands. She was tense. The waiting room was empty since she was the last appointment. She signed in and we waited. About ten minutes later, the nurse came out escorting a pregnant woman and called us back. They took her blood and we waited some more. Wren fidgeted the whole time and never said a word. She was lost in her thoughts. Just over twenty minutes later, Dr. Hunter came in. He greeted Wren and introduced himself to me. He looked down at his laptop.

"Well, Wren, as you know, today marks six months since your exposure. The results show you're HIV negative, my dear. No worries. You're in the clear." He smiled as she thanked him and then burst into tears. He patted her shoulder as he left us alone. I rocked her.

"Baby, it's okay."

She nodded.

"I know, I'm just so relieved." Once she got herself back together, we headed out to my bike.

I took her to dinner so we could celebrate and relax. Afterward, we took a short ride. It was getting cooler, so I didn't want to keep her out too late. Back at the compound, we stopped at the clubhouse. Most everyone was there. It seemed like they were waiting for us. Wren came in smiling and they cheered. They knew what that meant. We were both congratulated and we stayed long enough to have one drink. I was anxious to get her back to the house. As soon as we were through the door, we attacked each other. She was practically climbing me, and I was kissing her and trying to shed my boots. She laughed and let me get them off, finally flinging them in the corner. I carried her to our room.

We'd been sleeping together every night in each other's arms. I laid her down on the bed, shed my clothes, then stripped her naked. Her perfect body was lying there like a feast. I groaned and went straight for heaven. I pulled her thighs apart and put her legs over my forearms. I licked her from bottom to top of her slit. She was already wet. I moaned as I tasted her for the first time. She was a little sweet, tangy with a hint of musk. "Fuck, Beauty, you taste like heaven."

I dived back in to eat her sweet pussy. She was moaning and writhing on the bed. She was flooding my mouth with more of her juices. I lapped while working my fingers in and out of her tight pussy. Jesus! I couldn't wait until we got to the point of having sex. I wanted to be buried as deep as possible inside of her, to feel her clamped tight on my cock, milking me dry. I groaned and sucked on her clit. She came screaming her release. She squeezed my fingers over and over while flooding my mouth with more juices. I crawled up beside her when she'd relaxed. I kissed her. She moaned and devoured my mouth. My cock was hard as a rock. I needed relief. I laid back.

"Baby, I need you. Suck my cock. I need to come. Eating that pussy of yours made me so fucking hard." She sat up and looked at me and then down at my cock. She seemed a little uncertain. I sat up.

"Babe, what's wrong?" She hesitated. Now I was getting worried. Had I done something wrong when I went down on her. "Did I hurt you?"

She shook her head no and cleared her throat. "I want to try having you inside of me, Talon. I want you to make love to me."

I felt my heart stop.

"Are you sure, sweetheart? I mean, I want to more than you can know, but I don't want you to rush into anything."

She nodded. "I want to try. I just don't know if I'll freak or something. I'm worried about that."

I pulled her in for a hug.

"If you do freak, we'll stop and either do something else or wait until you're ready to go on. You're in charge."

She slid her hand up my neck and kissed me.

I spent time sucking on her nipples and playing with her pussy to be sure she was nice and primed. Once she got lost again in the sensations, I rolled over to get into my nightstand drawer.

She stopped me. "What are you doing?"

I kissed her.

"Just getting a condom."

She shook her head.

"I want to feel you inside of me. All of you. If you're okay with us going bare. If not, we'll use the condoms. I'm protected. I went on birth control after what they did. I just couldn't stand the thought of someone doing that again and getting pregnant. I'm not sure I could be like Bri, though Rowan is precious." She stopped. I eased back.

"Nothing would make me happier. I'd love to go bare. I've never done it. I didn't know you were on anything." I kissed her just a bit longer to be sure she was fully back in the mood. I was gonna be a lot to take. She had to be wet and ready for me. She was moaning when I pulled her thighs apart and settled between them. I felt her tense a little. I stopped.

She caressed my face.

"No, don't stop. Please."

I placed my cock at the top of her slit and ran it up and down her wet lips to get it lubricated. Then I positioned it at her opening and eased the head inside. Shit! She was tight. She would have to really stretch to take me. I inched in a bit more and then pulled back. She stayed with me. I could tell she was a little uncomfortable but not in pain. I worked back and forth for several minutes until I had all of my cock buried inside of her. I was sweating and shaking. I'd stopped a couple of times, not because of her, but so I wouldn't shoot my load. She was the tightest, wettest pussy I'd ever felt, and the sensation of being bare was amazing. I rested once I was all the way inside.

I blew out the breath I'd been holding. "Beauty, you feel amazing. Like nothing I've felt before. I want to make this last as long as I can. I promise I'll make sure to get you off. But God, I'm so ready to come."

She laughed and I groaned as the shaking made her clamp down on me. I couldn't wait any longer. I pulled out a little and then pushed back inside. She whimpered and grabbed my shoulders. I watched her face as I began to thrust in and out to be sure I wasn't hurting or scaring her. Thankfully, all I saw was pleasure. I sped up a little, going just a bit harder and deeper. She wrapped her legs around my waist and raised her hips off the bed to meet my thrusts. I moaned and thrust harder and even faster.

I slid in and out over and over. She was panting and moaning, her nails biting into my back. She leaned up and licked my nipples. I lost it. I started to pound in and out going deep. She was thrusting up against my every stroke. I was feeling the burn and tingle in my legs and balls. When the two met, I knew I'd blow my load. I panted into her ear, "You're so perfect." I ran a hand up to tweak her nipples and then slid down to rub her hard clit. After a couple of rubs, she came screaming.

"Talon, oh God! Don't stop."

She was strangling my cock. I had to work to thrust two more times while she was clamped down and then I was coming, grunting and growling out my long release. It felt like I just kept coming and coming.

"Fuck, your heaven, baby. Pure heaven and perfection. So good." I kept thrusting until she had relaxed, and my cock was starting to go soft. I reluctantly pulled out and flopped down on the bed beside her to pull her into my arms.

I puffed out my breath. She was rubbing my chest. When I could think, I looked at her. "Are you alright? Did I hurt you or get too rough? I tried to control it, but you felt too good. I kind of lost it."

She grinned.

"Yes, I'm alright. No, you didn't hurt me or get too rough and I love that you lost control. Feel free to do it anytime. I never knew it could feel like that."

I hesitated and then asked her a question. "Before you were taken, how many guys had you been with? I know you told me you'd never given a blow job before."

She looked a little embarrassed.

"I had a boyfriend in college. We dated my freshman year and we ended up having sex for a couple of months before he dumped me. All he ever worried about was himself."

I looked at her incredulously. I knew from talking to her she was twenty-five to my thirty-three.

"You mean to say you never had anyone but that asswipe until those bastards? Jesus, why didn't you tell me? I would have taken more time to make it better."

She burst out laughing.

"Talon, if you made it any better, I'd be unconscious. I saw fireworks."

I grinned and blew on my fingers like I was hot.

She laughed and smacked me in the chest. "Don't get a big head."

I got up, then picked her up and took her into the bathroom. I started running water into the tub. "You need to soak. I don't want you to get too sore."

She sank into the hot water as I pulled some Epsom salts out from under the sink. I used it when I worked out too hard. I poured some in the water and then slid in with her. She sighed and leaned back in my arms. When the tub was full, I washed her sexy body. Once she was clean, including me thoroughly washing her pussy which caused her to moan, and I felt she'd soaked long enough, I got us out and dried off. We hit the bed. I kissed her. "Baby, I love you," I whispered.

She gave me a surprised look then got a huge smile on her face. She whispered back, "I love you, too, Talon."

My heart sped up in joy. I'd been wanting to tell her that for a while. We fell asleep holding each other.

The rest of the week flew by for me. Overall, it had been a good one, except one night when things had gone horribly wrong for a poor couple. I'd been riding back after dark to the compound. It was rainy which made it a miserable ride, even though I had rain gear. I was riding along one of the more remote roads outside of town, when I saw up ahead a car fishtail on the road then careen down over the embankment. Another car directly behind it, came to a stop. I hurried to pull over and placed a quick 911 call.

Once I did, I ran over to the side of the road. A man from the other car was on his knees in the mud. Looking down the embankment at the Mustang wrapped around a tree. Shit, that didn't look good. The whole front end was demolished. "Hey. Hey, man. Are you hurt?" I asked.

He looked up at me dazed and then scrambled to his feet. "I'm fine. We have to help my girlfriend. She..." He paused and I saw him swallow hard before turning to slide down the decline to the car.

I slid down with him, not wanting him to see what might be his dead girlfriend. The wreck was serious. I forestalled him getting to the driver's side. "I've already called EMS. Why don't you let me check on your girlfriend? I'm a paramedic and was a Navy corpsman. What's her name?"

He stared at me for a moment before he asked me. "What's your name?"

"Ghost."

"Ghost. She's Birdie. Help her?"

I gave him a nod and hurried to the driver's side. I had to give the door a sharp tug in order to get it open after I peered inside. She was slumped over the steering wheel not moving. Blood was running from a large cut on her forehead. Glass was shattered all around and over her. I couldn't tell what other injuries she might have without moving her. I placed my fingers on her carotid, praying I'd feel a pulse. It would destroy this guy if I had to tell him his girlfriend was dead. Just like it would destroy me if something happened to Wren.

I could hear the scream of sirens in the distance. I breathed a sigh of relief. I turned to look at him. "She's alive." I saw him sag in relief. Now came the real work. They were going to have a time getting her out of this. Maybe even needing the jaws of life. I did what I could to staunch the bleeding without moving her. He stood there watching looking helpless.

The next half hour was a busy haze. I knew some of the crew. They welcomed my help as the firefighters and police worked to get her free, so she could be taken to the hospital. I found out from her boyfriend his name was Hayes Ellison and he was a professor nearby. His girlfriend was Birdie grant. He hinted at them having some kind of misunderstanding and her being upset as the cause of her speeding in the rain and him following behind her. I took pity on him when they loaded her in the ambulance and followed them to the hospital. No one should be alone during something like that.

Thinking back on that night, I sent up another prayer for Birdie. She was in a coma the last I'd heard. I'd been checking in on her. I felt some kind of connection or responsibility for her and Hayes. When I'd gotten home that night, I'd unloaded to Wren about them. About how much it would kill me if that had happened to her. She'd held me all night as I relived seeing Birdie in that car, so still and pale.

Shaking off those thoughts, I got back to the present. It was now Friday night. The ladies had all decided they wanted to go dancing. Well, everyone but Brielle and Trish. They were only a few weeks from their due dates. They would stay at home with Viking and Ranger. Ms. Marie was helping them to watch all of the kids. I knew I needed to let loose and relax. Watching Wren have fun would do it.

Wren came out of the bathroom dressed for our night out. I groaned. She looked up. "What's wrong, Talon?" I walked over and pulled her into my arms.

"You look too fucking sexy to take out in public. I'll be beating men off with a stick. Let's stay home and make love."

She laughed and gave me a kiss.

"No, I want to go dancing, and besides, I spent time to look like this. I want others to see me." I growled but let her go. She was dressed in a pair of high-heeled black boots that went up over her knees and molded her legs. They screamed *"fuck me."* Her jeans were black and molded her ass like a glove. Her ass was so perfect. It was like an upside-down heart. I had fantasies about what I wanted to do to that ass. One day, I'd tell her. Though we'd had sex every night since our first time on Monday. I wanted to be sure she was comfortable with me sexually.

Her top was one that had long sleeves with large open slits down the whole length of the arms. It was low in the front showing off the tops of her breasts and her cleavage. It was tight all the way down to where it tucked into her jeans. She had on silver hoops and a necklace which were set off by the purple color of the top. She wore dark purple and gray shadow on her eyes and her lips were a pale rose. Her eyes were made up with dark purple and gray shadow and her lips were a pale rose. Her high cheek bones stood out. Her hair was hanging loose to her waist with the ends curled. She grabbed her leather jacket. We were all meeting in the clubhouse first. She had no idea there was another reason we were all meeting other than just to make sure everyone was ready to roll out.

At the clubhouse, everyone was gathered in the common room. I saw Terror counting heads. He nodded to me indicating everyone was there. I looked over to Viper and he nodded toward one of the tables. On it was a box wrapped in silver gift wrap with a bow on it. One of the ladies must have wrapped it. I tugged her over near it. The gang got silent which made her look around. They were staring at us. She looked at me.

"What? Why is everyone staring?"

I kissed her.

"Because they're waiting for this." I grabbed the box and handed it to her. "Baby, I've had it for a while and have been wanting to give this to you for six months. I waited until you knew everything was clear This is the real reason, we wanted to go out tonight."

She slowly opened the box and cried out when she saw the leather with our patch on it. She pulled it out to look and ran her hands reverently down the leather. It had *Property of Ghost* across the top rocker on the back. On the front was her road name, *Beauty*. She was tearing up.

One of the guys yelled, "We were gonna put *Fists* on it, but Ghost vetoed it."

She burst out laughing. She took off her jacket and slipped it on. It was a perfect fit. She gave me a deep kiss which didn't end until the gang had whistled and teased us so much, she had to laugh.

We were soon on the road. It was cold so I wrapped her in her jacket, putting her leather cut over it, and made her put on a scarf, gloves and tucked a throw over her legs. It was only about fifteen minutes to the bar, but I didn't want her getting too cold. She snuggled up against me.

She whispered in my ear, "Thank you for my cut. I love it. I'll show you how much later when I fuck your brains out." She nipped my ear, and I growled.

"Keep talking like that and I'll be fucking you right now on this bike."

She laughed and we took off. Exactly fifteen

minutes later, we pulled into the Fallen Angel. As usual for a Friday or Saturday night, they were full. Most of the dinner crowd was gone. We headed inside and were seated at our booths.

Sabrina, one of the waitresses, came over to take our order. She'd been Trish's roommate for a while. Trish had stopped working last month when Viking had gone off on her being up on her feet too much. He'd tried to get her to quit before that, but she refused. She'd had a few contractions and that was the end of him letting her work. We ordered our drinks and settled back to listen to the music. People were up dancing and the waitresses were busy. Savage's old lady, Janessa, had worked here too when she first came to town. This is where he first saw her and fell for her.

The music was great. The band played music you could fast dance to, some line dancing songs and of course, slow dances. I planned to have her in my arms tonight for some of those slow dances. All our women seemed to love to dance, and they had rhythm too. It wasn't long after we got there that all of them were on the dance floor. They were shaking it and having a great time. We kept an eye on them as we drank and talked. We'd been there an hour or so and I'd danced one slow song with Wren. They'd taken a brief break to have a drink and were back up on the floor. I could see a group of ten other women who all seemed to be together. They kept eyeing our old ladies and then looking over at our table. They had some men with them who were up on the floor acting like fools. None of the guys could dance and the women didn't hold a candle to ours.

The floor was crowded. One of the guys bumped

into Wren. I saw him say something and she nodded, saying something back. They both went back to dancing. I stayed in my seat since it looked like it had been an accident. I looked away to say something to Savage, who was facing the dance floor. I saw his eyes dart to the floor and get wide. I turned around and saw a couple of the women from the other group up in Wren's face. The other five Warrior ladies were standing with her. Wren was shaking her head and pointing toward the table where the guys now sat. I got up to go see what was going on. I wouldn't hit a woman, but I also wouldn't let one hurt Wren. Not that she probably needed my help, she was full of fire to go along with her red hair. As I got close, I could hear Wren yelling to be heard over the band.

"Listen. I told you. We bumped into each other accidently. He apologized and I did the same. We didn't say anything else. I wasn't coming on to your man. I have a man."

The other woman sneered. "You biker whores are all alike. Think you can have any and all men. Well, you're not getting mine."

I saw when Wren snapped. She stepped up and got toe to toe with the other woman. "Like I'd want your scrawny ass man. I have a fucking man in my bed who looks like a god and fucks like one too. I wouldn't let your man sniff my dirty underwear."

The other woman gasped and then swung her arm up to slap Wren. Wren stepped away avoiding the slap and came back with a punch to the chick's mouth. She grabbed her mouth and started to scream. Her friends were yelling and pushing in toward Wren. The other old ladies stepped up and were backing them down.

I was busy watching the show when the guys with those women came pushing up. The one who had bumped into Wren was holding the one she punched, asking what happened. She was bawling about Wren hitting her. He gave Wren an ugly look.

"Why'd you hit my girlfriend, bitch?"

Wren sneered back. "Because your stupid girlfriend jumped my ass thinking I was after you because we bumped into each other on the dance floor. I told her all we did was apologize to each other. She thinks it was more than that. She got insulting so I told her how it was. She tried to slap me, so I punched her in the mouth. You should take her home."

He looked at his girlfriend. She was crying saying she didn't say anything to Wren. He was looking more pissed and he stepped closer to Wren. I'd seen and heard enough. I pushed in until I was standing between him and my woman. He looked up at me. His buddies were throwing worried looks around and then got pale when they saw my brothers behind me.

"Buddy, I recommend you take your girl and leave. I heard what she said. She did start it."

He swallowed and backed up. His girlfriend saw it and began to shriek at him. "You're gonna let a biker whore talk shit to me and hit me then just walk off. Hit him."

He swung around to look at her.

"Do you not see these fucking bikers? They'd kill us.

Shut your damn mouth. You started shit again." We were all watching the two of them and I didn't notice one of the other women with her sneak up on Wren and slap her. The other patrons just sat there in shocked silence. The next couple of minutes saw fists flying. Except, it wasn't any of the guys. It was the women. Ours never threw the first punch, but they sure finished it. All ten of those women thought they'd get in on the fight. A few tried to do a two on one and got their asses handed to them. Me and my brothers stood there making sure no one else jumped into their fight. We finally thought they'd had enough punishment and pulled our women back.

I could feel the tension running through Wren. She finally relaxed. The other guys not holding one of the old ladies, helped the others to get their women and leave. Terror, Savage, Steel, Hammer, Menace, Tiny, and I took our women into the office. They didn't look much worse for wear. I didn't know other than the one slap if anyone else had landed anything on them.

Wren looked at me. "So, are we here so you make sure we're okay or to get a lecture? Because if it's for a lecture, save it. She started it. I finished it."

I laughed.

"No babe, I just wanted to check you out." She gave me a kiss. The others were satisfied that their ladies were fine. They gave them each a hard kiss. We went out to continue our night. We stayed another two hours without further incident. Most of the other customers went back to their enjoyment after throwing us nervous looks for a while. A few did get up and leave as soon as the fight was over. No one approached us to say anything about the fight. I think they were too scared to do it. When we got back to the compound, it was after one o'clock in the morning. Telling everyone good night, I swung Wren up in my arms and headed for the house.

She was laughing at me. "Talon, put me down before you hurt yourself."

I snorted. "Yeah, like you weight enough to hurt me. How much do you weigh, one hundred fifteen?"

She huffed. "I'm one hundred and twenty-five."

I laughed. "Whoa, that much? Just kidding. Babe, I weigh two hundred and thirty and can bench press over four hundred pounds. I can lift you without breaking a sweat."

I laid her down on the bed and bent down to take off my boots and socks. When I had those off, I unzipped her boots to slide them off her sexy legs. Her socks came off next. Then I peeled those tight-ass jeans off of her while kissing down her legs. Now she was lying there in just her bra and panties. They were silk and lace and sexy as hell in a pale pink. She sat up.

"I need to take a shower after all that dancing. Want to join me?" I stripped off my clothes while she laughed and took off her bra and panties. I picked her up and threw her over my shoulder to carry her into the master bath. I turned on the shower. She was struggling to get down. I smacked her ass.

She froze.

"Hold still. I don't want to drop you."

She huffed. "Did you just smack me?"

I chuckled. "Yep. And there's more where that came from. You'll like it, I promise." She went silent, and I lowered her to the floor. She was staring at me, so I kissed her. "Babe, I tend to be dominant in bed, in all sexual play in fact. This, I consider sexual play. When you're ready, we can explore what you like and don't like. Now, let's get cleaned up so I can get you dirty again." I pulled her into the shower with me.

She was quiet as I washed her body. I grew concerned I'd upset her. I raised her chin with my finger. "What's wrong? Did I scare you?" I hoped like hell I hadn't. I'd been trying not to overwhelm her. It had just sort of come out.

"No, not scared. Just a little surprised. I know people are into things like that, but I've never really thought about it one way or the other," she said softly.

I sighed. "Babe, I'd never do anything that really hurt you. Not to say you can't have a little pain that turns into a lot of pleasure. I would never do anything you absolutely didn't want. If we try something and you don't like it, just tell me. I like soft bondage and domination. But if you turn out not to, I don't have to have it. All I have to have is you."

She nodded and then proceeded to wash me like I'd done her.

When I got her back to the bed, I laid her down and I kissed back up her legs making sure to skip over her pussy. She moaned. I licked up her stomach to her chest where I circled her nipples over and over without touching them. They were like hard beads. Then I kissed up to her mouth without kissing her lips. I kissed all around. She was growling now. I went back to teasing her by licking, touching and kissing close to but never touching her hot buttons.

She finally burst out, “Why are you torturing me?”

“This is to show you how good it can be when you put off gratification for a while. It makes the orgasm so much more intense when you finally have one.” She frowned but didn’t say another word. I worked her to a fever pitch. She was squirming all over the bed. I smacked the side of her ass. “Lie still. Close your eyes and feel.” She settled. I teased her for another ten minutes. I knew she was close to cracking. Some nights I’d push her that far, but tonight was just to test her boundaries and see if she could play. I dropped my mouth to hers and kissed her. She moaned. While kissing her, I tweaked her nipples, and she drew in a shuddering breath. After playing with her nipples for a bit, I slid my hand down and ran my fingers through her folds. She was soaking wet. I stroked her clit and sank my fingers into her pussy. She was lifting her hips off the bed, whimpering.

I left her breasts and slid down between her legs and took her hard clit into my mouth and sucked. She came, shrieking. Her pussy clamped down so hard, I thought she might break the fingers I’d slipped inside. While she was still coming, I pulled out my fingers, jerked her legs over my shoulders and plunged my cock into her pussy. She sobbed and kept coming. I powered through her tight fist of a pussy. She finally let up enough so I could much more easily thrust in and out. God, she felt so fucking good! I pumped in and out faster. Playing with her had excited me. I pulled out and ordered her, “Get on your hands and elbows."

She scrambled to do it. I slammed back into her from behind. Shit! I could go deeper this way. I fucking loved doing it doggie style. I started to ride her harder, faster, and deeper. She was sobbing into the pillow. Her pussy was starting to quiver around me. My release was almost there. I pulled her hair to bring her head up and back. I leaned over her back to whisper in her ear, "You're so fucking hot. Take it. Take my cock and milk every drop out of me."

She thrust back on my cock hard and then kept doing it. I was seeing stars. She slammed back three more times and then I came. She screamed her release as I grunted every time I shot more cum into her pussy. I collapsed over her back taking her to the mattress without putting my full weight on her.

After I could talk. I tugged her into my arms and kissed her. "How did that feel, Wren? Did you like it? Is there anything you didn't like? Did I do anything to scare you?"

She opened her eyes.

"It was scary because I didn't know if I could stand it. You had me so strung out. It felt wonderful and I loved all of it."

I smiled.

"So, does that mean you're willing for us to play more and see what we both like?"

She nodded, and I gave her a gentle kiss. I went and got a washcloth so I could clean her up. Afterward, she snuggled into my chest. I knew I'd found the perfect woman for me.

Chapter 7: Wren

Today was Thanksgiving Day. All the ladies of the MC had spent a large part of yesterday and half of today cooking a huge Thanksgiving feast. Bull and his guys weren't coming this year, because of a problem at one of their businesses. They would wait to come for Christmas. We'd finished dinner and most people were watching the football game.

Terror's phone rang, and he answered it. "Hey, man, what's up?" He listened and then shouted, "They what? Fuck." He listened longer. "Okay, we'll expect you in about three hours or less." He hung up. We were all looking at him. He glanced around.

Harlow finally broke. "Well, what is it?"

"That was Reaper. He's pretty sure the Savages and Bastards just tried to blow up his clubhouse. He thinks they were targeting Harper." He didn't get any farther. Viper came ripping up out of his chair.

"What did you say? They were after Harper? Is she fucking okay?" he shouted. Terror nodded to him reassuringly.

"She's fine. She was moving food to the clubhouse.

When she was done unloading the food, she parked her car but not in her usual spot against the side of the clubhouse. She wanted to have it out of the way. So, they moved it toward the back part of the front acreage. Not long after five o'clock when they usually eat, they heard a huge explosion. It blew some windows out of the clubhouse. Her car was nothing but a ball of flames. Reaper's freaked the fuck out. She's the only female attached to their club. He thinks they finally figured out she was his sister and knew she'd overheard shit at the bar." Viper was headed down the hall. Terror yelled after him, "Where are you going, brother?"

Viper stopped and looked at Terror.

"I'm going to Bristol to get her ass and bring her down here. We can protect her better. We have more men and better security."

Terror shook his head no. "There's no need. Reaper said he was bringing her down here. He feels the same way. He wants her here until they figure something out, and she has an interview next week at Dublin Falls General Hospital."

I watched as some of the tension left Viper's body. He did seem to really care about Harper. I'd heard about their first run-in and then had seen them at the party. He looked at her like he'd never seen anything like her. I saw she had a spark of interest too. It would be fun to have her around the place. Viper reluctantly eased back down in his chair.

The next couple of hours were tense. I knew we were waiting for the Punishers to arrive. Two and a half hours after Reaper's call, we heard motorcycles. All of us went outside to greet them. Viper was the first one out the door. A car pulled in with the bikes. Viper rushed over to the car. Harper swung open the back door and Viper was pulling her out of it. I could see Reaper eyeing Viper and his sister.

We took everyone inside. He'd come with five of his guys. The rest stayed to watch the compound. They were thinking the bomb had been put on her car when she had it in at another garage a couple of days ago. She'd run into car trouble when she was out of the area. She had it taken to the closest one to get it checked then planned to have the club work on it if it needed more work.

We showed Harper around while the guys all went into church with Reaper and his guys. She sighed. "He'll never let me out of his sight again. He's bad enough on a good day. But now, I'll be confined to the compound until I'm a hundred."

We laughed. "Don't worry, we'll save you if he tries that here."

"I am excited to get to see all of you. I have an interview next week at Dublin Falls General for a counselor position. I was going to call tomorrow to see if you'd be okay with me coming down for a few days and staying here."

"That's wonderful, Harper! And of course, we would have said yes to having you stay. We wouldn't have taken no for an answer." Regan assured her.

When the guys came out an hour later, it looked like Reaper and Viper had been through the wringer. I saw them throwing each other intense looks. The guys offered to have them all stay tonight and head back in the morning, but Reaper wanted to have a meeting tonight with all his guys. He took Harper aside to talk to her. After he was satisfied, they said their goodbyes. While they were in church, the prospects had brought in her bags. Since we had no idea where Terror wanted her, they had left her things sitting in the common room. Viper went over and picked up her bags heading for the door. Harper was up and after him. I could hear them arguing as they left. I looked at Ghost.

"What's up with that?"

He shrugged. "My brother, Viper, is getting his head on straight. Reaper was pretty direct with him in church. He told him to stay away from his sister because she's not a booty call. Viper got pissed and told him he'd never considered her to be one. He basically told him his intentions were serious. Reaper didn't know how to take it. She's going to be staying with Terror, Harlow, and Hunter. They should be back soon."

We all sat back down, and some were playing pool while others just talked. When Viper and Harper came back, I could see her lips were red and her hair a little messy. I think Viper had been putting some moves on her. She came over to sit with the women while Viper joined some of the guys. The next couple of hours were fun watching Viper look at Harper and Harper sneak looks at him when he wasn't looking. I finally had to say something.

"So, you and Viper, huh."

She jumped then sighed. "No, not really. He says he wants to get to know me, but I'm not into the biker free-love shit. I've seen enough of it to know how they are. He says he isn't thinking that. I haven't seen any bikers not be that way."

Harlow jumped in, "It's true, most bikers are into quick hookups and then leave, but the Warriors here who have women, don't do that. They don't cheat. Viper sees that here. I suggest if you like him, to give him a chance."

Harper sat there with a considering look on her face. She shook it off when we talked about going Black Friday shopping the next day. The guys weren't happy about it, but we all wanted to go and had convinced them we would be fine. They were sending half the damn club with us it seemed. We all agreed to meet at the clubhouse at six tomorrow morning. I heard the guys going with us groan. It would be Adam, Finn, Tyler, Nick, and Blaze. Brielle and Trish weren't going because they were at the miserable stage of their pregnancies. That left seven of us including Harper. Not long afterward, we started to break up and go our separate ways.

Back at the house, I got ready for bed. It was already midnight and I had to be up at five-thirty to get ready. Ghost crawled into bed, and pulled me into his arms. "Listen, I want you to be really careful tomorrow. Stick with the guys. Don't any of you go off on your own. Stay aware, and make sure you carry your gun."

I gave him a kiss.

"Don't worry, babe. I will. I promise. You try not to worry all day tomorrow."

He sighed. "I wish I could go but I have to finish that damn bike tomorrow. I'll see you when you get home." He held me as we both fell asleep. That damn alarm would go off in no time.

We were all at the clubhouse by six the next morning as planned. The guys looked way more bleary-eyed than we did. We loaded up into two SUVs and one guy drove each of them, while the other three would ride their bikes as our escort. We were heading to some of the bigger stores up around Knoxville. We hit the first one at seven and it was a madhouse. The guys were not happy with the crowds and I could see their point, but it would make it harder for any of the Bastards or Savages to spot us in these kinds of crowds. We spent over an hour in the electronics store. The guys at least liked it in there. Our next stop was a big clothing store. This one they liked a whole lot less. I was trying to decide what to get Ghost for Christmas. He claimed there was nothing he wanted or needed.

We went into the Harley dealership and we were finding things in there for the guys. I found several more vintage-looking shirts I thought he'd like. I looked at the riding gloves, belts and a whole lot of things. As I was looking at bikes, I had an idea. Ghost's saddlebags on his bike were worn. I'd heard him muttering about one of them that gave him a hard time closing. I'd ask one of the guys to help me figure out how to get him new ones and the best place to buy them. Our next two stops were a baby/ toddler clothing store and a toy store. In those we were doing damage. I found gifts for all the kids and babies. I was busy looking at a playset for Rowan. Harlow and Regan were in the same aisle. I felt a presence and turned. There stood Dan, Hannah's dad, the one the guys had thrown out of Rowan's birthday party last month. He was glaring at me. I looked around to see if one of the guys was nearby. I could see Finn at the end of the aisle. He was looking at something Harlow was showing him. I eased in their direction. Dan stepped between me and them.

"I've been waiting to see you, bitch. Your fucking biker boyfriend and his crew have been blackballing me. I can't get any business. I know it's them doing it. All because I touched one of their whores. I mean, all I barely touched you. I should at least get to fuck you for this kind of trouble." He grabbed for my arm, and I jerked out of his reach. The aisle was full of people, but they were all in their own little worlds not paying attention. I decided I'd yell.

"Keep your hands to yourself. I don't know what you're talking about, but you need to get out of here." I saw Finn's head whip around and look at us. He was pushing through the crowd toward me with Harlow and Regan hot on his heels. Dan snarled at me.

"You fucking know what I'm talking about! Don't play dumb. Your fucking MC is ruining my life." He went to grab me again. I stepped back but couldn't get away since a woman was standing behind me. He latched onto my arm and yanked me toward him, hard. His grip was crushing my arm, and I cried out. I kicked him in the knee. His leg buckled and he swore. That's when Finn reached us. He got a hold of him and backed him up against one of the shelves.

"What do you think you're doing, asshole? You never lay a hand on a Warriors' woman. You have a death wish. You should've learned the first time." I could see security making their way down the aisle. I grabbed Finn.

"Let him go. Here comes security. I don't want you to get into trouble. We'll handle this another way." I could see he didn't want to do it, but finally he let him go. Dan scurried away. When security got to us, we pretended not to know who the person was that grabbed me, and they soon left.

Finn was apologetic. "I'm so sorry, Wren. I stopped to look at something for Hunter. I should've never taken my eyes off you. Ghost is going to kill me." I was trying to soothe him while Harlow hugged him.

"Finn, I distracted you. If anyone is at fault, it's me." I tried to calm both of them down. By now all the ladies had found us along with the other guys. Blaze was pissed and had a frown on his face. We decided to take a break from shopping and went to have lunch. They took us to a little pizza place. We were talking and relaxing when I heard bikes roar up outside. I looked at the others in confusion. None of them seemed to be concerned or surprised. In the door came Ghost, and all the other ladies' men. I stood up as Ghost came charging straight toward me.

"Honey, what are you doing here?" I asked.

He pulled me into his arms. "Where else would I be when I find out a man tried to attack my woman?" My mouth fell open. I looked at him and then the others.

"Who told you?"

He had a pissed look on his face.

"Blaze texted me what happened and so did Finn. That's the first thing you should've done, Wren! Anyone touches you or threatens you, you call me immediately!" he half-yelled.

I felt my temper start to rise. I jerked back out of his arms. "Don't you dare yell at me! I didn't get hurt. I planned to tell you when we got home. There was no need to call in the National Guard. And it seems I didn't need to tell you when your brothers run straight to you and tell anyway. If you'll excuse me, I need to use the bathroom. I feel the need to murder someone. It's best you leave me alone." He stood there stunned as I stomped off to the restroom. Inside, I locked the stall door and sat on the toilet. I had tears in my eyes. How dare he yell at me in front of everyone. I didn't think it was that big of a deal. He treated me like I was his little, not-so-bright kid. The outer door opened, and Regan and Harlow called out my name. I pretended to flush the toilet. I wiped at my eyes to make sure none of my tears had escaped.

Pulling the door open, I nodded at them and went to wash my hands. I checked out my image in the mirror. My face was still pink. I turned to them to find them watching me closely.

"Where to next? Another store or are we commanded to return to jail." They gave each other a worried look.

Regan spoke up. "We're going to head home. We're sorry, Wren."

I cut them off. "There's nothing to be sorry about. Is everyone ready?" She nodded. I headed out with them following me. I could see everyone else was in the parking lot. Ghost was on his bike beside the car. I headed toward the one I rode in.

He called out, "Babe, you ride with me."

I turned to look at him. "No, I don't think so. Don't push me right now, Ghost. I'm riding back the way I came. So, either I go in the car or I walk but I will not be getting on that bike." I could see he was pissed. Well, let him. He never even gave me a chance to say a word before he jumped all over me in the restaurant. He finally shrugged. I got in the car with Finn, Harlow, Janessa, and Harper, and we took off. The ride back was quiet. I could see Harlow and Janessa wanted to say something, but I gave them looks telling them to let it be. As soon as we pulled into the compound, I got out and started to pull my bags out of the car. Ghost walked over and took them out of my hands. I ignored him and told the others I'd see them later, then headed for the house. He followed behind.

Once we got there, he dumped the bags by the front door while I headed toward the bedroom to change. He caught my arm and swung me around. "Want to tell me what the fuck that was all about? You're acting like a pouting child," he said.

I saw red. I jerked my arm, but he wouldn't let go. I looked up at him.

"Oh, really? And you coming into the restaurant ranting about me not calling you wasn't childish? I must be acting like a child because you treated me like one. Like I was a brainless twit. How dare you?" I yelled.

"I was fucking worried! Some man, who basically attacked you once, tried again. You didn't even bother to call me. I'm responsible for you, Wren!" he shouted back.

I froze.

"Responsible? Why? Do you think because you rescued me, you have some responsibility to now take care of me?"

He nodded.

"Of course, I'm responsible for you. I have to be sure your protected."

I felt my gut clench. Was he with me out of some stupid sense of responsibility rather than because he really loved me? I could feel the vomit moving up my throat. I jerked again and he let go of my arm. I ran into the bathroom and locked the door. I kneeled by the toilet as he pounded on the door telling me to let him in. I heaved and vomited. I did it three times then laid down on the cold tiles. He'd finally stopped pounding. I closed my eyes. A few moments later, I heard a click. Opening my eyes, there stood Ghost. He had picked the lock. He was frowning and came over and dropped down beside me.

"Baby, what's wrong? Why'd you lock the door? Wren, I don't want to fight. I'm sorry."

I shook my head.

"I need you to leave, Ghost. I need you to leave me to think."

He looked puzzled.

"Why?"

I pushed up off the tile. The room spun for a few seconds.

"I need to think about what you said, and I can't do that with you here."

"That's bullshit! What do you need to think about? You should have called me, Wren. Let's talk about this like two adults." He argued.

I ignored him and laid down on the bed. He left in a huff when I wouldn't talk. I laid there thinking about what he said. I was a responsibility. I must have fallen asleep because when I opened my eyes it was dark outside. A light was on at my bedside and Harlow was sitting in a chair.

"What are you doing here, Harlow?" I asked, pushing my hair out of my face. I felt like crap.

She sighed.

"We're worried about you. Ghost came back to the clubhouse saying you wouldn't talk to him and you'd been sick. What's going on, Wren? Are you that upset over him coming to the restaurant today?"

I clenched my fists and looked over at her.

"Yeah, I'm upset how he treated me. But more than that, I'm upset to find out I'm a responsibility for him. I thought he was with me because he loved me but now, I don't think he is. I think he feels he's responsible for me since he rescued me. I don't want someone who's with me for that reason. I needed to think."

She was now sitting on the edge of the chair with her mouth gaping open.

"You think Ghost doesn't love you? Wren, no, we can all see how much he does. You need to talk to him. I don't know what he said, but I can't believe he meant he was with you because you're a responsibility, honey. Why don't I go and get him so you can talk?"

I shook my head.

"No, I can't talk right now. He needs to leave me alone tonight. Please, tell him I need this. I don't want to see or talk to him yet."

"Fine, I will. But don't lie there stewing all night. Go talk to him." She told me before leaving.

I took a shower and then settled back into bed. I sat there for hours thinking. Finally, around three in the morning, I knew I needed to talk to him. He hadn't come to the house so he must have stayed at the clubhouse in his room. I got dressed and headed over there. Inside, the place was dead. I slipped down the hall to his room trying not to make any noise and wake up the other guys. I grabbed the doorknob and opened the door. The sight in front of me took my breath away, causing me to gasp and cry out.

Ghost was in bed, naked, with one of the bunnies. It looked like they had been sleeping, and my cry had woken them up. He sat up bleary-eyed and blinked.

"Babe, what are—?" He stopped when he saw my face and where I was looking. He looked over and saw Becki. His eyes swung back to me and I could see them fill with panic. I wanted to vomit again. He'd run off to fuck a bunny. I was just a responsibility. He jumped out of the bed.

"Babe, it's not what it looks like."

I couldn't stay and see this anymore. I looked at Becki who was smirking.

"You can have him. I'm done." I swung around and ran down the hall. I could hear him yelling my name telling me to stop. As I passed the bar, I saw the keys to one of the SUVs. I grabbed them. I knew they went to the blue one. I hit the parking lot, ran to the SUV, opened the door and jumped in. I took off for the gate. Luckily it was programmed to open automatically from the inside. For the next few hours, I just drove.

When I got too tired to drive, I pulled into a hotel in Sevierville. The club always kept a stash of cash in the cars. Ghost had showed me the hiding spots one day. I used it to buy gas and the room. I fell into bed and dropped into a restless sleep. I would worry tomorrow on where to go. One thing was for sure, I wouldn't be staying at the compound. I never wanted to see Talon Adair again.

Chapter 8: Ghost

I stood there frozen as I watched my woman run away from me. I yelled at her to stop, but she kept going. I was trying to find my clothes. Hawk, Blaze, and Devil Dog ran into my room and stopped dead in their tracks. They watched as I fumbled for my clothing, stunned to see Becki in my bed... I growled.

"Get this bitch out of here. She must've crawled in here after I fell asleep. Fuck! Wren just came in here and saw her. I need to go after her!" They jumped into action and dragged Becki out of my room. I was throwing on my boots when Nick came running into the room.

"Ah, Ghost, man, your old lady just raced out of here in one of the SUVs."

I swore. She had left the fucking compound. I ran into the common room. Several guys were now up. I headed for the door, and Viper got in front of me.

"What's wrong? The guys are talking about you being in bed with Becki and Wren saw it. What the fuck, Ghost? You didn't fuck Becki, did you?"

I swung around and got in his face.

"No, I didn't fuck Becki! I love Wren. I stayed here because she was upset last night. Sometime after I went to bed, Becki must have crawled into it with me. I was half drunk and passed out when I went to bed at eleven. I didn't know she'd come in my room. Wren came in and I woke up to see her standing there and Becki naked in the bed. I have to find Wren. She thinks I cheated on her, Viper. She left the fucking compound alone!" I was yelling by this time. Terror and Savage walked in the door. Someone must have called them. They came over.

"Sit, brother. We'll find her."

I paced around the room.

"I don't want to sit. I need to go find her. Goddamn it! She thinks I cheated on her. She was upset earlier and now this. She's going to fucking leave me. Do you understand? She's going to leave me and if she does, you might as well just kill me right now. I can't live without her." I was ranting now. The fear was eating away at my insides.

One of the guys went to get Smoke. He walked in the room shaking his head.

"I'm sorry. We didn't put trackers on those vehicles. Since everyone got the implants, I never thought to do it. Fuck, I'm so sorry."

I knew he couldn't track her because she didn't have the tracker implant. I'd mentioned she should get one but never pushed for it to be done. I was beginning to hyperventilate.

He went on, "I did look at the video feed from the camera outside the gate. She headed west when she left. We can start searching that way."

All the guys seemed to be here now. We headed out, splitting into two groups. One to look around Maryville and the other to head more toward Knoxville. We rode around for the remainder of the night. We didn't see the SUV anywhere. She didn't have her cell phone with her, so I couldn't call her.

By seven in the morning, we all met back at the clubhouse. I was sick to my stomach. I kept imagining Dan or the Savages and Bastards getting ahold of her. She didn't know the area that well. Where could she have gone? The old ladies were up and, in the clubhouse, now. Harlow came over and sat down with me. I looked at her.

"What am I going to do, Harlow? Even if we find her, she'll probably never want anything to do with me again. Why didn't I lock the door? Shit, I don't even know what set her off earlier yesterday. She said I treated her like a child and then she got even more pissed when I tried to talk to her at the house."

Harlow sighed.

"Ghost, she told me when I went over there last night that you said she was a responsibility. That made her start wondering if you loved her or just saw her as that. She needed more time to think. I tried to get her to talk to you then, but she said not yet. She asked me to tell you to wait which is what I did. I'm sorry. I never imagined this happening. Terror told me what happened with Becki. He's banished her from the compound."

I was stunned. Wren thought she was just a responsibility to me. I thought back to what I said and groaned. She had asked me if she was really one and I had said yes. Fuck! I didn't mean it the way she obviously took it. I looked at Harlow. I knew I had tears in my eyes, but I didn't care.

"Harlow, what will I do if she refuses to believe I love her and didn't touch that slut, Becki? If I lose her, I'll…" I couldn't go on. She was hugging me when Terror came over.

"Ghost, we'll find her. Smoke has been pulling up video feeds all over. It will take a bit to comb through, but he'll find her. I've banned Becki for now. I want to have the club vote tomorrow. We'll have church then rather than today. I know the vote will pass but we'll make it official. Now, tell me what happened. I've heard a bunch of jumbled up shit."

I told him what happened yesterday at the house and then last night. I'd gotten drunk because I missed her and was upset, she wanted to be alone. I'd crawled into bed around eleven, half lit from the alcohol. That's the last I remember until I heard her cry out and woke up to the nightmare. When I saw Becki in the bed naked next to me, I could have hurled. I knew exactly what it looked like. I could kick my own ass for forgetting to lock the door. I told him what Harlow had said about being a responsibility. He was rubbing his head and swearing when I got done.

"Shit, Ghost. That sucks man. But I know we'll find her, and you will get her back. She'll come around. You remember how pissed Regan got and then the time Alannah got mad at seeing that bunny on Menace's lap. Our women get feisty." Harlow smacked him on the arm. He laughed. "See what I mean. They get that way. You sure she's not pregnant, because if I recall, Regan was when she got so pissed? Harlow wanted to kill me more often when she was."

I sat up in the chair. She couldn't be pregnant. We'd only been having sex for less than two weeks and she was on birth control. However, the thought she might be did something to me. It made me want it to be true. I wanted her to be carrying my baby. I wanted to marry her. Shit, I needed to find her.

We spent the rest of the morning riding around looking for her. By four o'clock in the afternoon, we still hadn't found her. She'd been gone just over twelve hours. Smoke had caught glimpses of the car in the various video feeds, but they were all over the place. She must have been aimlessly driving. I was about to head out for another run when Brielle came into the common room. She looked beat. She was due in six days. She came toward my table. I was sitting with Ranger, Terror, Viper, and Savage. Ranger had said he left her at the house to rest. He jumped up and hurried over to her.

"Baby, are you okay? You should have called me. Do you need something?" She shook her head. He sat her gently down in the chair like she was made of glass. She looked at me.

"Ghost, I just got a call from Wren."

I leaned forward.

"Where is she? Is she alright?" She held up her hand to stop me.

"She said she's fine. She wants me to get someone to pack her a bag. She said she doesn't want to cause anyone any extra work. She wants to make this transition easy and asked if one of the prospects would bring her stuff to her."

I looked at her in amazement.

She looked away and then back at me. I saw sadness in her eyes. "She doesn't want to see you, Ghost. She said she has no desire to see or hear from you. It was all a mistake to get involved with you. She never should have believed you loved her. She's so messed up, Ghost. Nothing I said got through to her. She has convinced herself you only felt responsible for her, never loved her, and you slept with Becki. According to her, you probably never had stopped fucking the bunnies and you lied to her about not being with anyone after you met her."

I laid my head down on the table feeling despair. Jesus Christ! It was worse than I thought. She wasn't even going to let me explain. She planned to leave and never see or talk to me again. I picked my head up.

"Where is she, Bri?"

She shook her head.

"I don't know. She wouldn't say. She just asked to have her stuff packed and she'd call me again on what to do with it. I'm sorry. I tried to get her to tell me."

I jumped up and ran to the hall bathroom. I puked up the small amount of lunch I'd forced down. As I flushed the toilet, I heard someone come into the bathroom. I swung around to find Terror and Savage. I shook my head as I grabbed the mouthwash under the sink to rinse out my mouth. I stood hunched over staring at the sink. Two hands landed on my shoulders. I shuddered.

"She's never going to forgive me or let me explain. She's gone. What do I fucking do now?!" I felt like sobbing like a baby. I didn't care. I couldn't find my usual calmness. It had deserted me. I saw a lonely life out in front of me. I'd never love another woman. She was it. She was my life, my everything.

Savage kicked the door shut.

"Get a hold of yourself, Ghost. She isn't gone. You'll find her and you will make her listen. Even if it takes a year, you keep at it until she listens. Then, you do anything and everything in your power to show her you do love her, want her, and never touched another woman. I refuse to believe you can't make this right. She's upset. For all we know, its other shit causing her to react like this. Don't lose faith."

It took me a few more minutes to get myself under control. Back in the common room, Smoke was sitting with Bri and Ranger. He had Bri's cell phone. My heart jumped. I rushed over.

"What are you doing?"

Smoke was grinning.

"I ran a reverse check on the phone number Wren called Bri from. It isn't a blocked number. It belongs to a Hampton Inn out in Sevierville. Here's the address. I was about to call and ask to be connected to her room, so I could confirm she was there."

I nodded, and he placed the call.

He hung up quickly. "She's there. They asked me to

hold while they connected me to her room. I didn't want to chance her picking up."

I jumped up. I was off to get my woman. Terror, Savage, and Viper all said they'd come with me. None of us had been riding far from home without at least being paired up. We were on our way five minutes later.

Chapter 9: Ghost

She was less than an hour away and it wasn't long before we pulled into the parking lot. I hoped she didn't hear our bikes. I rode around the building and found our SUV parked in the back lot. I left the guys there to guard it in case she ran. I walked around to the front, opened the door and walked to the front desk. A young girl in her late teens was on duty. She stared at me in awe. I smiled.

"I'm looking for my wife. Her name is Wren Masters. She checked in late last night. I was to meet her, but she forgot to tell me what room we were staying in. She has her phone off so I can't call her. She tends to do that when she takes a nap. Can you tell me what room she's in so I can head up?"

She looked hesitant but I kept up the smile. She gave in and looked in the computer.

"She's in room three forty-four. I can ring her if you like."

I shook my head.

"No thanks, love. I want to surprise her. We haven't seen each other for a week."

She directed me to the elevators and told me to turn left when I got off them on the third floor. When

I got off the elevator, I saw a cleaning lady. I asked her to go ahead and take more towels to room three forty-four. I knew if I knocked and Wren saw me through the peephole, she'd never open the door. She agreed and grabbed some. I stood off to the side while she knocked and called out housekeeping. I heard Wren call out for her to come in. The housekeeper used her master key to open the door. I stepped inside taking the towels from her. She gave me a puzzled look but left. I shut the door and latched it. Turning around, I heard water splashing in the bathroom.

Wren called out, "You can leave them on the bed. Thank you."

I stepped into the bathroom. Her back was toward the door due to where the tub was. She had the water as high as it would go. Her skin was pink from the heat. I felt my cock jerk in my pants. Even with all the shit that was going on, I wanted her. But that would have to wait. I stepped closer and she turned letting out a scream. I dropped down on my knees beside the tub.

"Baby, it's alright, it's just me. I didn't mean to scare you. Calm down." She was staring at me like she couldn't believe her eyes. Her eyes darted from me, to the door and then down to herself. She reached up and grabbed a towel hanging on the rack over the tub, then stood up wrapping it around herself.

"How did you get in here, Ghost? What are you even doing here? Get out. I want you to get out right now!" She was now half shouting.

I shook my head.

"No, babe, I'm not leaving until we talk. So, get dried off and come out to the bedroom." I turned and left her.

She finally came out wrapped in a robe, looking tired with dark circles under her eyes. She sat down as far away from me as she could get. She didn't say a word and wouldn't look me in the eye.

"Wren, I need you to listen to me. Don't interrupt, just listen. Please." She didn't say anything. I sighed. "I'm sorry I upset you yesterday when I came to the restaurant. I was scared when the guys texted me. All I could think about was what if he'd hurt you or taken you. I admit, I was at fault for not telling you what to do if something like that happened. I assumed you'd automatically call me. Then when we got home after you wouldn't ride with me, I should have let you explain. I saw you were mad, but I honestly didn't know why what I did and said upset you so much. When you asked if I thought you were my responsibility, I told you yes. Because as my woman, you are. I'm responsible to see that you're happy, safe, and loved. I didn't know you took it to mean I was only with you because you were a responsibility. How could you think that, babe? Where have I gone so wrong that my woman can doubt I love her? When you got sick, I was worried, but you sent me away. Do you know how much that killed me to walk away when you were upset, angry, and on top of it, sick? God. I sat in that clubhouse worrying for hours. Then Harlow came and told me you didn't want to see me or talk yet. I admit it pissed me off a bit but it worried me more. Again, I ignored my gut and stayed away. I decided to get drunk. I drank until about eleven. By then, I was half drunk. I went to bed in my room at the clubhouse. Alone." Her eyes flickered to mine and then she looked away. "I did not invite Becki to share it with me. I know what you saw when you came in, but I swear nothing happened. She must have come in after I crashed. I didn't lock the damn door. The next thing I knew, you were standing in the door. Jesus, babe, you can't believe I'd fuck around on you. You can't. I love you. I've been going crazy for the last fourteen hours looking for you. God, please talk to me," I pleaded.

She was sitting there shaking her head no. My heart sank. She looked up and she had tears running down her face.

"I don't know what to believe, Ghost." My heart seized. She was calling me Ghost not Talon. "You were in bed with another woman, naked. How do you know you didn't fuck her? You said you were half drunk. Maybe you don't remember." I went to protest, but she held up her hand. "Let me finish. I cannot and will not be with someone because his sense of honor makes him feel like he is responsible to take care of me after he rescued me. I don't need or want that. While I was at the house last night, I looked back and was thinking about it for hours. I tried to recall if anything you ever did or said made me believe I was just a responsibility. I didn't think so. I also thought about what I'd feel like if you had been the one in my shoes and I never called. I knew I'd be upset. I realized I needed to go tell you what I thought and to apologize for not calling you and for getting so upset. But, Ghost, when I saw you with her, I couldn't take it. That sight gutted me. It got me to thinking again." She got up to pace. It took everything I had not to get up and go to her.

"I don't think we went about this right. From

the day you brought me to the compound, I've been essentially thrust in your face and life. You saw me every day. That kind of thing could make someone think they had feelings when they really didn't. You may think you love me, but I'm not sure you do. I believe it's for the best if we don't see each other for a while, maybe indefinitely. Maybe you didn't invite her to your bed, but you left the door unlocked. Isn't it possible, somewhere deep down, you wanted to see if someone would come in.? I don't blame you. You deserve to do what makes you happy. I thought it was me. Now I think it's better if you go back to your old life. One where you can sleep with someone new every night and not have to take responsibility for anyone but yourself. Take the time to see what you really want and who you want. Now, I think you should leave. I'll talk to Brielle and have one of the prospects drop off my things."

She turned her back on me. Did she think I was going to leave? Fuck that. I stood and rushed toward her. She swung around in surprise. I grabbed her and backed her up to the wall.

"I'm not fucking leaving now or ever. I will not lose you over this! We went about things just perfect. You were in my face every day and I loved it. I wanted you from the second I saw you. I never doubted it for a minute all these months. I waited for you to be ready. I didn't lie about not being with other women that whole time. I'm not lying about Becki and I left the damn door unlocked because I was drunk. But I wasn't so drunk, that I didn't know what I was doing. I would remember fucking someone. I didn't. No one is bringing your clothes. You're coming back to the compound with me. We're going to fix these doubts you seem to have."

She was struggling to push me away. I leaned down and captured her mouth. She tried to keep her mouth still and her lips closed but I didn't stop kissing her. Not until she half kissed me back a little, then I pulled back.

"Do you hear me? I love you! I love you and I want to spend the rest of my life with you. If you ever left me, Wren, I couldn't go on. I'd wither away and die. You have my heart, mind, body, and soul. I practically cried in front of some of my brothers today when I couldn't find you and thought of what I'd do if you never took me back. I'll do anything to prove to you I love you. I didn't cheat on you now or before. You want me to take a lie detector test, I'll do it. Just please, for the love of God, don't leave me. If you do, I have nothing to live for." I pleaded with everything I had.

She was staring at me in disbelief. I eased away from her and took her to sit with our backs against the headboard and my arms wrapped around her. I kissed her forehead, cheeks and nose. She ran her hand down my face.

"Talon, I want to believe you love me like I love you, but it's hard to believe a man like you, who could have picked any woman, would want someone like me. Someone damaged and used. Jesus, we had to wait six months to be sure I didn't have HIV."

I jerked and looked at her incredulously.

"Baby, do you think because you were raped that you're less desirable or even dirty?" She was avoiding my eyes now. I gave her a very gentle shake. "Shit, woman. I told you months ago, you're not dirty and any man who thought so wasn't a real man. You're not responsible for what those men did to you. If I have to spend the rest of my life saying it, you will realize it's true. You are beautiful, smart, and sexy as hell. Men drool just seeing you. I could tell you well over a dozen who'd beat a path to your door if I was ever dumb enough to let you go. Some of them my own brothers!" I moved her off my lap and slid off the bed to my knees at the side of the bed. "Now I'm begging you, please, please, come back with me. Let me love you for the rest of my life."

She burst into tears and crawled down onto my lap. I don't know how long I held her, rocking her and whispering in her ear. When she finally calmed down, I lifted her face. "Will you come back to the compound? We can talk more there. I just need to have you safe and back home." She gave me a small nod. I eased us up off the floor. I sent the guys a text while she got her things together and put on her clothes. When she checked she had everything, I led her to the elevator and then outside. She stopped when she saw the others. I pushed her toward the SUV, and she got in. I buckled her in. "Baby. You drive and we'll follow you." She nodded. I got on my bike and we were soon on the road. The drive back was uneventful.

Less than an hour later, we were pulling into the compound. She parked the car while I parked my bike. The others got off their bikes and slapped me on the back as they headed inside. I opened her door and led her toward the house. Once we were inside and took off our shoes, I led her down the hall to our room. She seemed a little nervous. I suggested she soak in the tub since I'd interrupted her last soak. She agreed. I took her into the bathroom and started running water in the tub. As she stripped, I stripped off my clothes. She gave me a surprised look, so I kissed her.

"I want to join you. Is that okay? If not, I'll jump in the shower. I've been out riding most of the day."

"Yes, I'd like that," she said.

We both got in the tub and just relaxed. After about fifteen minutes, I kissed up her neck to her ear. "I love you. I need to hold you tonight in our bed. I promise I'll do nothing else. I know you need time. Just promise not to lock me out or leave again. Please."

She turned her head and kissed me.

"I promise. Let's go lie down."

Back in the bedroom, we got under the covers. She snuggled into my chest and I blew out a sigh of relief. I rubbed her back until she fell asleep. I laid there thinking about what had happened. I would never again let her think for a minute I didn't love her or that I wanted someone else. I fell asleep thinking about what I was going to do next.

It had been a couple of days since everything blew up between Wren and me. We'd talked a lot and I think she believed I did love her. She also told me last night she believed I hadn't invited Becki to my bed, or that I had touched her. Becki had been voted out of the club permanently. She'd been pissed. I watched her go without a bit of pity. She knew I was with Wren. She knew what happened when you messed with a committed member.

Today was Tuesday and I planned to surprise Wren at the daycare. I had her favorite food from the local Italian place for lunch. I pulled into the parking lot with our lunch safely packed in my saddlebags.

It was almost the beginning of December. The air was cold at night and got up in the low forties most days. I headed inside the daycare. It had been built in a separate building on the farm. I punched in the security code to get into the building. I could hear a couple babies fussing in the one room. Wren came out.

"Honey, what are you doing here? Is everything okay?"

I gave her a kiss.

"Everything is fine. I brought you lunch. Trish said you usually eat something around one after the kids go down for a nap. Is this still a good time?"

She grinned.

"Yes, perfect. Let's go to my office." Her office was on the second floor of the building. They had supply rooms and such upstairs. She pulled me inside and shut the door. I began to lay out the food. She was overjoyed to see her favorite and we were soon eating. I spent more time watching her enjoy her food than I did eating. She noticed.

"What? Do I have sauce on my face?"

I laughed.

"No, I was just enjoying watching my woman eat. You even make eating look sexy."

She shook her head. "You're crazy."

I just grinned. Once we were done, I cleaned up the boxes. She pulled me over to sit on the couch and teased me it was time for our nap. I held her and we just kissed until it was time for her to go help get the kids up from their naps. I followed her down holding her hand. At the door, I gave her a deep kiss and told her I'd see her at six. She usually got off around five and one of the others stayed until six for the last few kids needing to be picked up. However, today everyone had to leave by five, so she stayed over until closing time.

I went back to work on the bike, Blaze and I were working on. At five-fifty, I headed down the road to the daycare. I took her in this morning and would pick her up, like I usually did unless I had to go out for club business. I pulled into the parking lot and shut off my bike. There was one car in the lot. I headed inside and could hear raised voices in the back. I hurried down the hall into the main play/ living room.

Standing in the middle of the room was Dan Peters. Wren was across the room with his daughter, Hannah. Hannah was crying softly. Wren looked pissed off.

"Listen, Mr. Peters. There is no need for such language. I suggest you take Hannah and head home."

He sneered. "You don't tell me what to do, bitch. I know your boyfriend and his club are blackballing my construction company. Another project we bid on went to them today. You tell them, if they keep it up, they'll be sorry. All this over a piece of ass."

I'd heard enough. I charged in and grabbed his arm.

I told Wren to get Hannah ready and meet us outside in five minutes. I pulled him out of the room. I didn't want his little girl to see me threaten him. I dragged him out to the parking lot and shoved him away from me.

"Listen here, you piece of shit. Don't ever come around my woman or any of our places and spout a bunch of threats and bullshit. You have something to say to the Warriors, then say it to a Warrior. It may surprise you, but you're not significant enough for us to bother blackballing your company. I heard you do shitty work and people are talking. We have more work than we know what to do with. We have no need to take it away from you. However, if people come to us rather than you, we won't turn them away. Now, stay the fuck away from Wren. I hear one more threat or she has another run-in with you, you won't like what happens. You don't want the Warriors as your enemy. Get out of here."

Hannah had come out the door with Wren. She looked apprehensive. I hated to allow her to get in the car with him. She got in while he glared at us the entire time. I made sure to smile at Hannah and tell her I'd see her soon. He roared out of the parking lot.

I pulled Wren into my arms. "Did he touch you? What was he saying before I got here?"

She shook her head.

"He didn't touch me. He was ranting the same thing he was when you walked in—about the club taking his business. Threatening me if it didn't stop."

I got her on the bike after she locked up, and we zipped up the road to the compound. Inside the common room, I went over to Terror with her on my arm. He glanced up and smiled.

"What's up you two?" I went on to explain what happened. Terror was frowning when I got done. "Terror, I think we need security at the daycare. I know we thought with the locked doors, needing either the code or for someone to ring you inside was enough, but what happens when it's someone who has the right to be there and they get mad or violent. He came to pick his daughter up. By the way, babe, how often does he pick her up?"

She frowned.

"Today is the first time he's ever came to get her. It's always Cassie who drops her off and picks her up."

That made me worry more.

Terror was nodding. "I agree, we need to have someone there. Do we think it needs to be all day or during the main drop-off and pick-up times?"

Several others had come over and were listening. We had a debate for the next twenty minutes or so. Finally, we agreed to start with just the peak drop-off and pick-up times. If we found him or anyone else was dropping in earlier, we'd adjust. Smoke had come out and talked about installing a panic button. It would be easy to tie into the current security alarm system. We told him to get it done as soon as possible.

I took Wren home. Dinner was a simple steak on the grill, a baked potato and salad. After cleaning up, we watched television then we headed up to bed around ten. I stopped her in the middle of stripping for her shower. "Hurry up and take your shower. I'll be in the bedroom."

She gave me a wide-eyed look. While she showered, I waited in the bedroom. I'd decided to show her some more of my dominate side in bed. So far, she'd responded well to my light demands. I planned to increase those tonight.

She came out showing her sexy, naked body. I grabbed her and devoured her mouth. She wrapped her arms around my neck and kissed me back equally as hard. I pulled back. "Lie on the bed on your back with your legs spread, legs hanging over the side of the mattress." She looked a little startled but did as I commanded. I kneeled down and began to run my hands up her legs. Her skin was so soft and pale. Against my bronze skin, she appeared even whiter. She didn't have freckles all over like most redheads. Her skin was creamy. I licked as I caressed her, making her moan.

I worked my way to her center. When I got there, I skipped her core and kept kissing, touching and licking my way to her mouth. I stopped along the way to lap at her breasts. When I got to her mouth, she was trying to kiss me. I shook my head.

"No. No kiss yet. You'll only do what I tell you to do. Remember, I'll not do anything to hurt you and it will always lead to more pleasure for both of us." I nipped her ear. She gasped and her hips jerked. I knew she was aroused. I'd seen her glistening juices and I could smell her arousal. My cock was already hard and ready to play, but I wanted to prolong it as long as I could stand it.

"Roll over," I ordered her. She did. I worked my way down the back of her body like I did up her front. When I got to her ass, I kissed it and then I slapped her ass cheek.

She reared up in surprise and looked over her shoulder at me. I smacked her again. "Do you like that?"

She nodded. I proceeded to spank her until both cheeks were pink. She was moaning and rubbing into the mattress. I pulled her up.

"None of that. Get on your knees." She dropped to her knees on the floor, then looked up at me. Her mouth was at the perfect height. I caressed her face. "Suck my cock." She smiled and then she had her hot little mouth all over my cock. She sucked and licked until I thought I'd go crazy. She played with my balls and stroked my length. I was now the one panting. She was moaning the whole time. I saw her run her hand down her belly toward her pussy. I grabbed her hair and pulled her off my cock. I made sure not to do it too hard. I didn't want her hurt.

"I didn't say you could play with that pussy, did I?"

She shook her head.

"Since you tried to be a bad girl, get back on the bed. I'll have to make sure you don't do that again." She scrambled onto the bed. "Lie down with your head over the edge and put your hands under your ass. I'm going to feed you my cock and you'll take what I give you." I was soon pushing my cock back into her mouth. With her head like this, it opened her throat up more, and I found I could slide deeper. Soon I was pumping my cock in and out of her mouth. I'd hold it deep until I knew she'd be running out of air, then I'd ease back so she could breathe. She never complained and she tried to swallow my cock every time.

When she did this, it would massage the head of

my cock so much, I wanted to scream and come down her throat. God, it felt so good. As I was pumping in and out, I reached down and played with her breasts, causing her to moan and squirm. I was starting to get close. I pulled out of her heavenly mouth, and she pouted. I turned her around so her legs were now hanging off the bed. I got down on my knees on the floor and spread her legs. Her pussy was dark pink, swollen and covered in her juices. I dove right in. She yelped when I attacked her. I ate her pussy like a starving man. I licked, sucked, and nibbled all the way up and down her slit.

I thrust my fingers in and out of her entrance. She was moaning and begging. I kept it up until she was about to blow, then I rubbed my pinky around and over her asshole while I sucked her clit and thrust my fingers deep. She came screaming. Her pussy clamped down hard on my fingers. Her juices were running down her thighs, and I lapped it all up. When she came down from her orgasm, I pulled her off the bed and walked her to the sliding door. It went out on the back porch. It was dark outside and none of the other houses were behind us. I led her out to the chaise sitting on the porch. “Get on your hands and knees. I need to fuck that hot little pussy.” She whimpered but got down on the end of the chaise so her ass was facing me. I rubbed the head of my cock up and down her slit. As I ran it back down, I came to her entrance and pushed inside fast, without stopping. She cried out. It wasn’t a cry of pain; it was one of pleasure. As soon as I hit her cervix, I eased back and proceeded to fuck her like a man possessed. I rode her hard and deep. She was begging and crying for me to make her come. I smacked her ass. Her pussy clamped down and more juices flooded her depth.

I knew I wouldn't be able to last much longer. I grabbed her hair pulling her head back and around to the side. I licked her ear as I pumped in and out of her perfect pussy.

"Who does this pussy belong to?"

She panted and faintly said, "You."

I slammed into her again.

"Who is the only one that'll ever be inside this body?"

She whimpered, "You."

I pounded in again.

"Who fucking loves you more than anything in the world?" I growled.

She blinked and sighed. "You Talon, you do."

Her words set me off. I gave her a hard kiss and then holding onto her hair I thrust in and out of her tight, wet pussy over and over. She came a few strokes later and I rode her the whole time until she was almost done and then I came, thrusting deep and holding my cock there while I filled her with my cum. I kept jerking and spilling my load. I leaned forward and whispered in her ear. "I love you Wren."

She sobbed. "I love you too, Talon. So much."

When we finally recovered, I carried her in the house and into the shower, where we spent time soaping and washing each other. By the time we were done, the water was getting cold and I was hard again. I sat her down on the sink counter. I felt her folds and she was as wet from our playing in the shower as I was hard. I pushed her knees up and back and sunk my cock into her hot pussy. I proceeded to ride her fast and hard until we both came again. She was as good the second time as the first. We fell into bed exhausted.

Chapter 10: Wren

It was Sunday and everyone was having breakfast at the clubhouse. The ladies, minus Brielle and Trish, had made breakfast for the gang. They didn't because they were miserable. Bri was two days past her due date and Trish was due in three days. They hadn't been sleeping well. We'd just finished eating and had sat down to watch some television in the common room. It was a football game. Brielle told Ranger she needed to go to the bathroom. He went to help her up. She couldn't get up on her own these days. She took one step and then gasped. Looking down at the floor, you could see the puddle of water forming at her feet. Ranger looked stunned.

She whispered kind of stunned, "My water just broke." Those words sent Ranger into commando mode. He barked orders for Finn to go get her bag from their house. It was packed in the front closet. He yelled for Tyler to bring the SUV to the front door.

Brielle smacked his arm. "I'm not going anywhere until I change into dry clothes." He tried to protest but she glared at him. He quieted down. Finn came in with her bag. She took it and Ranger took it away from her and carried her down the hall to the bathroom. While she was getting changed, we were settling on who was staying and who was going to the hospital. She came back and we headed outside. Ranger got her inside the SUV and was about to close the door when Trish cried out and doubled over. Viking grabbed her hand.

"Trish, babe, what's wrong?" he asked her anxiously.

She blew out her breath. "The contractions have suddenly gotten worse. I think we should go. My bag is inside the clubhouse. I had Regan get it earlier."

He looked at her stunned. "Earlier? You mean..."

She nodded. "I've been in labor since about three this morning. I texted Regan and she said it could take a while. I had her get the bag when everyone was distracted cooking. But now they're getting more intense. I'll ride with Brielle." Viking helped her into the SUV with the stunned look still on his face. They were only twenty-two or twenty-three. From what I heard, they'd had a bumpy road when they first got together and had been married for over a year. I went to get on the bike with Ghost. I was going into the birthing room with Brielle. She'd asked me already.

In no time, they had both ladies in the labor and delivery rooms. Only so many could be with them at a time. Brielle had Ranger and I with her full time and then other ladies trickled in and out. I heard Janessa was in with Trish. They were close friends. Viking was in with her as well and looking really nervous, or so I was told.

The rest of the day into evening went this way. We'd gotten to the hospital around nine-thirty in the morning. While Trish had been having contractions longer, Brielle's water broke which sped up things, plus this wasn't her first baby. That evening at nine-fourteen, Brielle gave birth to their son, Gabriel Zane Romero. He weighed in at eight pounds ten ounces and was twenty-two inches long. She had to have him via C-section since Bri was so tiny. Both Ranger and I were in there when they operated. He was nervous as hell about something going wrong. He had been worrying about a C-section the whole pregnancy. She was five foot two to his six foot four.

After she was out of surgery and back in her room, everyone could take turns to see them. At ten-thirty, Trish gave birth to their son, Saxon Kade Youngblood. He weighed in at eight pounds even and was twenty-one inches long. Everyone was cheering and happy. Months ago, Trish had kidded about how funny it would be if she and Brielle had their babies on the same day. Who knew it would really happen and just over an hour apart?

The club now had four boys and five girls. As I was sitting with Ghost, I wondered who would be next. He had me wrapped in his arms, sitting on his lap. I told him what I was thinking.

He licked my ear and whispered, "Maybe us. What would you think about us having one of those? A little girl maybe, who looks like her momma. We could go home right now and practice."

I looked at him with my mouth hanging open. He laughed and I punched him.

"It would serve you right if I took you serious and said let's do it."

His face got serious. "Beauty, I'm dead serious. I want a baby with you, and I want it as soon as you're ready for one."

I sat there stunned, thinking about what he said. Not long afterward, we all headed home so the moms and babies could rest. Back at the house in our bed for the night, I rolled over to look him deep in the eye.

"Were you serious at the hospital about wanting to have a baby with me?"

He nodded. "Babe, I was absolutely serious. I would love nothing more than to plant a baby in my woman's belly. To watch you grow round with our child, and to hold that baby in my arms. I love you, Wren. I want it all with you. I know things seem like they're going fast but when you know, you know."

I sighed. "Don't you think we need to do other things first. We don't have a house of our own."

He scooted up in the bed.

"We can. I was waiting to ask you about us building one, but now since you've brought it up... I have the perfect spot to build the house here in the compound. All I need to know is what kind of house you would like. You tell me and we can get Steel and Hammer started on it. And I plan to marry you, Wren. So be prepared, I'll be asking you one day. But that's for another day. Let's get back to the whole baby and house part. Do you want to start having them build us a house? If so, what do you like for architecture? I like the idea of a one story, and I don't really want a bunch of siding. Other than those two things, I'm open," he said eagerly.

I stopped to think. What did I like? I liked the idea of a one story and agreed on the siding part. I really liked the stone on Ranger and Brielle's cabin. A whole house like that would be cool. I slid up to sit beside him.

"I agree with the one-story idea, and I'd love a house made all out of the stone like Ranger used on his and Brielle's house."

He smiled. "I like that a lot too. What about number of bedrooms, kinds of rooms, those sorts of things?"

Again, I had to think.

"I would want at least four bedrooms and three full bathrooms. Open concept in the living room, kitchen and dining room. I don't think I'd want a formal dining room unless the breakfast area couldn't be made big enough for large group meals. An office would be nice as well." We went on to talk about the things we liked and types of décors. When we were done it was one o'clock in the morning. As we snuggled down to sleep, I said to Ghost, "Oh, by the way, I'd love to have a baby with you, too. Tell me when."

I drifted off to him telling me, "I love you too, and I want a baby now. Let's start tomorrow."

It was Wednesday, Trish's original due date. Trish got to come home late Monday evening, but Brielle had to wait until she had been there for forty-eight hours after her C-section. She got home last night really late. I took today off from the daycare so I could help her if needed. Ranger was there but he needed to rest as well. He was downstairs working on something, and I had gone to check on her. Brielle had laid down for a nap while Gabriel napped, and she was now feeding him. I told her what Ghost had said the night she had the baby. She gasped and then laughed.

"Well, he's a true Warrior. Find your woman and get her knocked up and in a house as soon as possible. Oh, and then marry her sometime in the middle of all of it."

I had to laugh.

"What did you say to him," she asked.

"Well, I told him what I liked for a house and then right before we fell asleep, I told him I wanted a baby as well. He said we'd start the next day."

She smiled. "I'm so happy for you. Just so you're prepared, you'll be married before the house is done. It's a toss-up if you'll be pregnant before the wedding. To date, only Sherry and Tiny along with Viking and Trish did the wedding before the baby. Of course, Tiny married Sherry straight out of high school, so they waited ten years before they started a family."

It was close to five when I left to head to the house to finish preparing dinner. Tonight, I was doing a jambalaya with crusty homemade bread. The bread I had made and froze a week ago. I was in the kitchen when Ghost came in. He pulled me back in his arms and kissed my neck. "Something smells really good. I can't wait to eat it." He laid a folder down on the counter. I glanced down at it.

"What's this, Talon?"

"The house plans. Hammer brought them to me today. I'd told him and Steel what we wanted, and they pulled plans they think we'll like. I want to look at them after dinner to see if we can find what we want. If we do,

I'll give it to them to start. I also want to show you where I would like to put the house. Can you leave the food for a few minutes?"

I nodded. All it needed to do was simmer and then I'd add the shrimp the last few minutes. I grabbed my coat and followed him outside. He took me past the other houses and showed me a spot which backed up to the woods like Ranger and Brielle's did. In fact, right now, they'd be our closest neighbor. I told him I loved the spot.

Back at the house and after a dinner, we looked through the plans. They'd given him a dozen different ones all having the required rooms and stone exteriors. My eyes kept going to one made out of river rocks. It had a lovely front porch as well as a covered patio in the back. We'd been looking and discussing them for an hour. Ghost finally asked which one my favorite was. I didn't want him to just go along with mine to make me happy, so I recommended we lay them out and assign them numbers. Then each of us would write down the number and hand it to the other. He agreed so I grabbed paper. I handed him my folded paper and he did the same. I opened it and looked at him. He was looking at me. We both laughed. He'd chosen my favorite! We put them all back in the folder to give to the guys with our choice on top.

I went over to check on Brielle again and Ghost went with me. She was resting and Ranger had baby Gabriel in his arms. I teased him he was going to spoil him. He just grinned and then handed him over to me. He was so cute. You couldn't tell what color his eyes would be, but I agreed with Bri he looked like his daddy.

Ghost nudged me. "Stop hogging that baby. Give him to me."

I mock pouted as I put him in his arms. He was a big baby but looked so tiny in any of the guys' arms. Ranger went to check on Brielle.

We were busy admiring him when Ranger came back with Brielle in his arms. He gently put her down in a chair. I knew she hurt from the C-section. She was protesting. "Damn it, Ranger, I can walk. You have to stop carrying me. The doctor said to walk so I get over being sore."

He growled. "Bullshit, you hurt too much to walk. You can try walking in a couple of days. Now sit there and behave. I'll be right back." He went to the kitchen to get her iced tea. He'd already served us drinks when we came. I went to kneel beside her chair.

"How're you feeling, little momma? I see Ranger is spoiling you. Do you need anything? Did you eat tonight?" Before she could answer, Ranger did.

"She didn't eat enough," he growled, and she shushed him.

"You never think I eat enough. I'm producing milk so I'm eating fine."

He shook his head and went to stand by his son. Ghost was busy admiring him. Brielle gestured for me to come closer. "You're definitely in trouble. Look at that expression on his face. Baby-making fever right there. Watch out."

I smothered a laugh.

Once Gabriel was settled in his crib, I showed them the house plans. Both of them were excited for us. We talked a bit longer and then left them to get some sleep.

In bed, we talked about the house. He began to kiss me. I could feel the passion in those kisses. I stopped him. He looked at me with worry. "What's wrong baby?"

I gave him a kiss.

"Nothing's wrong. I just wanted to ask you something." He nodded for me to go ahead. "Don't take this the wrong way, please. I love everything we do together. I know you're a dominate in bed. Does that mean I'm never allowed to be the one to direct our lovemaking? I ask because I don't know how this works when your partner likes to dominate."

He slid up to sit. "Babe, yes, I like to lead in bed. I get pleasure from not telling you what to do but from stretching boundaries. To give up total control to another heightens your pleasure which in turn heightens mine. I've never had a woman try and take charge. To be honest, I think I'd like to see what that would be like. Why don't we find out? Tonight, you tell me what you want." He laid back down and spread his arms wide.

I swallowed nervously. I wasn't sure I could. He laid there patiently. I decided to start with kissing. I crawled up and straddled his torso so I could reach his mouth. I slid my lips lightly across his while tracing the seam between with my tongue. He responded. I pushed my tongue into his mouth to duel with his. Again, he responded.

Feeling emboldened, I began to kiss my way down

his chest. I circled his nipples with my tongue and then flicked them. He groaned. I tweaked them between my thumb and forefinger like he would do mine. Leaving my hands to play with them, I slid down farther to lick and suck on his hard, muscled stomach. I grazed my teeth along his muscles. He hissed and put his hand in my hair to direct me down more. I stopped. "No, put your hands above your head. No touching unless I tell you to do it." His eyes widened and then got more heated. I took my time there just to torture him. I knew he wanted me to suck his cock. It was nudging up between our bodies trying to get my attention. I was starting to see the attraction he had to being in control.

After I thought I had tortured him enough, I slid the rest of the way down and licked the head of his cock. He moaned in relief, but I wasn't ready to give him any more relief. I teased him up and down and all around his balls but did no more than lightly suck on the head of his cock. He was trying to thrust it further into my mouth. I slapped the side of his hip. He froze. I waited until he relaxed then I went back to teasing him. I now had my hands all over his thighs and balls. The precum was oozing out of his slit, and I lapped it up.

Suddenly I engulfed his cock with my mouth, taking as much of him as I could. He shouted out his pleasure. I proceeded to suck and lick him until he was a quivering mess. He was moaning and grunting, begging me to suck harder and let him come. I teased until I knew he was right on the brink and then I stopped.

He yelled, "Fuck no! Don't stop, baby."

I smiled and shook my head.

"Roll over onto your stomach," I commanded him. He groaned but did it. Once he was in place, I proceeded to tease him by licking, sucking, biting, and caressing him from his neck to his feet and back up. He ground his cock into the mattress. I knew he was rubbing it to get off. I smacked his ass cheeks. He growled.

"No, I didn't say you could come. No rubbing one off using the mattress. Delaying will enhance your pleasure. That's what you tell me. Well, we're delaying it, baby," I teased, and he swore.

I kept up the torture for a bit longer. By then, I was dripping wet and couldn't stand it any longer. I told him to roll back over. He did so eagerly. When he was flat on his back, I slid my hand down and through my folds. I pulled back my hand covered in my juices and held it up so he could see. He moaned. His eyes were devouring me. I decided to reward him. I know it was especially hard for him to allow me this much control. I offered him my fingers.

He licked them clean, groaning and muttering, "You taste so good, baby, so fucking good." His cock was so red, almost purple with his need.

I straddled him and grabbed his cock. He moaned as I lowered myself slowly down on him. I made sure to circle my hips. When he was fully embedded, I rose up slowly and then came back down. I took it as slow as many times as I could. His fists were clenched. I know he wanted me to ride him hard. I leaned up and kissed him. His mouth responded eagerly. "Tell me what you want, Talon. Tell me."

His eyes were sparkling.

"I want you to ride my cock hard and fast. I want to fill that pussy full of my cum. I want you to slam up and down on me until we both come. Fuck me hard, Wren. Fuck me hard."

His last words broke me. I started to ride him harder and harder. I was slamming myself down on his iron-hard cock. It felt so good. I could feel my release rising. I leaned up and latched onto his mouth and pulled his long hair. He hissed and I kept riding him until I felt the tingling coming up my legs. I tore my mouth away from his.

"I'm gonna come," I moaned. I slammed back down two more times and then I came with him, grunting and shouting his release. He kept jerking while I spasmed, milking him dry. Finally, I collapsed onto his chest.

He brought his arms around me and rubbed my back as he murmured into my ear, "Wren, that was fucking amazing, baby. So, fucking amazing. I never imagined this. Only you. Only with you could I do this. Shit!" I smiled. Finally, he fully softened, and I slid off him. He pulled me into his arms and caressed me while praising me over and over. I was so sleepy. He carried me into the bathroom to clean up. We fell back into bed exhausted but very sated. I drifted off held tightly in his arms.

Chapter 11: Ghost

Today was Saturday and a big day at our range. The club was hosting a three-gun shooting competition. This is the first we'd done, and it was mainly due to Alannah. She had done those competitions when she was younger and still had contacts. We were due to make a nice profit off the event. Everyone was out to help, including Bull and some of his guys. They were considering maybe building a range themselves in Hunter's Creek.

This competition was being held by a Tennessee sporting group. In three-gun the participants are put through a set of courses in which they shoot three different guns—a rifle, a pistol and a shotgun—at different stages and engage in various short and long-distance targets from various positions. This competition would have a total of thirty competitors. Not the largest, but it was a good beginning. Ranger was acting as the host since he ran the range and was a certified instructor, range master and such. A lot of us had been in the military so we would be able to help. I, Janessa, and Regan would be providing medical care if anyone needed it. Trish, Brielle, and Ms. Marie were at the compound with a few of the guys and prospects to take care of the kids. The newest babies were only six days old. Cindy was helping out as well.

I was explaining the three-gun competition to Wren. She had never heard of it and was excited to see one. My woman had such energy. She was dressed warmly since it was only a high of forty-five today. We were lucky it was sunny with no rain in sight. We'd opened up a concession stand. It would serve hot coffee, hot chocolate, water, and sodas. No alcohol at one of these competitions. In addition to drinks, the women had pitched in and made all kinds of desserts to sell. They'd done shopping at Sam's Club and bought candy and individual bags of chips along with hot dogs and hamburgers. Ms. Marie had made a huge vat of chili to sell along with it.

The turnout was wonderful. The Tennessee sporting group had advertised but we made sure to do so as well. We posted it to our webpage where we did all our fundraisers. Each of our businesses displayed flyers and most of the other businesses in town had happily put up flyers. We'd let our associates, the Iron Punishers and Pagan Souls as well as the other two Warriors' chapters know in case they wanted to come. Wren was helping in the concession stand with Harlow, Alannah, Sherry, and Harper. We were expecting Reaper soon. He wanted to check on his sister.

The day was progressing well. Finn and Nick had come to the competition to help watch the ladies and fetch for them if needed. No one from our group was competing except Alannah. At first, when we'd talked about hosting, she'd declined to do it, but Menace had talked her into trying it. He knew she missed it. She'd been practicing for the last few months. That was when she wasn't working and taking care of Savannah. Little

Ms. Savannah was four and a half months old. She had plenty of people willing to babysit her when mommy needed to practice. However, to be honest, Alannah had always kept up her skills and didn't need to start from scratch. We made sure all of our women could shoot, had their concealed carry permits, and practiced at least monthly.

I was patching up a guy who'd cut his hand on his gear. Regan was taking a break and Janessa was working on a little boy who'd fallen and tore up his hands and knees. He was only three and needed the more feminine touch. I'd just put on the final piece of tape on my guy's bandage when I heard a commotion outside the medical tent. I excused myself and ran out. I could see a big crowd over by the concession stand. I started to run toward it. I saw my other brothers and some of the Punishers and Souls headed that way too. I pushed my way through the crowd.

Harper, Wren, and Sherry were surrounded by several guys. They looked to be a bunch of country boys. I recognized one of them. It was Dan Peters. He was up in Wren's face. Finn and Nick were dealing with two of his friends. I reached them just as Tiny and Viper got there. We pulled the women behind us. I could see the rage in both their eyes. Viper felt for Harper what Tiny and I felt for our women. No one was going to fuck with them. I stepped up and got into Peters' face.

"What the hell do you think you're doing, Peters? This is a public event. No one came here to see you acting like a fool. This is the third time you've felt the need to confront my woman. This is the last time I'm going to say it. Stay the hell away from her and our club."

He sneered. "You goddamn Warriors think you're so tough—riding around on your bikes, flaunting your whores. People think you're a bunch of good guys. Well you're not. All of you are a bunch of dirty bikers. You've been ruining my business because of that bitch right there. All I did was take her up on her offer. She came onto me then acted like I did it. Now my business is dying. You guys have been blackballing me. I know it! I want it to fucking stop," he ranted.

People were just staring at him like he was crazy. Anyone that knew us in town, knew we wouldn't do that or have to. I wanted to plant my fist in his face, but there were too many witnesses. I had to appear the calm one just so everyone could see how unhinged he was. My biggest worry was I didn't want him to impact our ability to host these kinds of events.

"Listen, Peters, no one is blackballing you. We haven't said a word about you or your construction company to a soul. If you're losing business, it's because of your reputation. People have been telling us about you doing shoddy work, going over schedule and budget. That kind of thing can ruin a business. We can't help if they hear this and decide to come to AW Construction. Now why don't you calm down and take your friends and leave. Everyone is here to have a good time, not watch this. There're kids here man." I could see he was getting madder and madder. He had to be the first one to get physical. We could only be seen as defending ourselves and not initiating anything. Over his head I saw more of my brothers, Reaper, Maniac and Bull with Payne. A sheriff was pushing his way through the crowd.

Just as the sheriff reached us, Peters threw a punch. I ducked and came back with a punch to his gut. He doubled over gasping for air. I could see the guys with him had taken to throwing punches when he tried to hit me. My brothers had taken each of them down to the ground and had them in submission holds. The sheriff was looking around in amazement. He was just about to talk when I heard a yell behind me. I swung around to see a guy had come up behind Tiny and Viper who were standing in front of Sherry and Harper. The man had grabbed Harper by the hair which was the yell I heard. She swung around and punched him in the face. Viper gave a roar and went after him. She was hanging onto him to prevent him from killing the guy. Her brother had pushed up to them and had the guy on the ground, pressing his face into the dirt.

Terror stepped up and shouted for everyone to let them up. They did so, but I could see Reaper especially didn't want to and Viper wanted to beat him until he couldn't move. The witnesses were shouting, telling the sheriff and his deputies who had joined him, that Peters and his guys started it. They told them we only defended the women and ourselves after they threw the first punch. In less time than you would think, he had them in cuffs and were transporting them to jail. We promised to come down and give our statements after the competition was over. We tried hard to make it the least disruptive as possible. Luckily, the sponsors understood it was out of our control.

A couple of hours later and the competition was over. Alannah had placed second which she was happy about since she'd been out of the circuit for so long.

We got things cleaned up and then headed down to the sheriff's station. Sherry, Wren, and Harper had to go with us to give their statements on what happened before we showed up. By nine in the evening, we were finally done and back at the compound. We didn't press any charges since none of us had gotten touched other than Harper having her hair pulled. The ones we hit all ranted they wanted to press charges, but the sheriff told them to shut up and go home.

Back at the clubhouse, we all sat around talking about Peters in the meeting room. Reaper and his guys along with the other clubs had stayed. Reaper was livid. "I fucking sent her here thinking it was safer. Shit! What's up with this Peters person. Why does he have such a hard-on for the Warriors?" Terror and I explained what had happened at Rowan's birthday party. He sighed. "Shit, all this because he's jealous and wants your woman. Damn, I wish I could say I'd take Harper back with us." I saw Viper stiffen. "But we still have the Bastards and Savages sniffing around. The other day a couple of them tried to run a couple of my men off the road. I almost didn't come down today in case they realized she was here."

Terror growled. "Damn, Reaper, why didn't you tell me? Do you need us to send any of our guys up to your clubhouse? You're attracting them because of your association with us. They haven't been around making any trouble down here which worries me. We think we might have a lead on a gun storage facility, out between us and Cherokee. It's in what we consider neutral territory. Neither us nor the Souls have it within our territories. There's an old shipping complex with storage warehouses. A couple are used for long-term storage of truck parts. We think those are used to hide the guns. We just found it and Smoke has set up cameras for surveillance. Once we find out for sure if the Bastards and Savages have been seen going in and out of there, we'll set up a run."

Reaper grunted his agreement. He looked at Viper. "You still watching my sister and keeping your hands to yourself?"

Viper swung around. "I've been keeping an eye on Harper. And as for my hands, I told you before, I would never do anything your sister didn't want me to do. I have no intention of playing games with Harper. I don't see her as some piece of ass. I just want time to get to know her and let her get to know me. I want to have her as my old lady." His last remark had every one of the Punishers looking around and murmuring. We weren't surprised, we all knew he was head over heels for her.

Reaper scowled. "What makes you think you're good enough for my sister?"

Viper shrugged. "I know I'm not good enough, but I'll spend my life working to be close to good enough. I will do everything in my power to take care of her, love her, and give her anything and everything she needs and wants."

Reaper gave him a scrutinizing look and then nodded. I guess he had given his consent for Viper to pursue his sister. It would be interesting to see how things went.

We called it a night and went back to the common room. I took Wren back to the house. It had been a long day for all of us. I could tell she was exhausted. I got her to sleep rubbing her back before I fell asleep. Peters was becoming more of a nuisance. He needed to be taught a lesson, but not yet. If anything happened to him now, the police would come looking for us. We had to bide our time.

It had been two weeks since the three-gun competition and the run in with Peters. It was only two days until Christmas. We planned to make a run tonight on the gun storage facility. Smoke's surveillance had shown Bastards and Savages going in and out of the building more than once. They had a schedule of hitting it every five days, always between the hours of nine and midnight. The last visit had been last night. The video feed showed trucks coming in and dropping off boxes, which meant the place should be full of guns. We planned to hit them at two in the morning. They had five guys guarding it at any given time. Reaper and three of his guys would join us tonight along with half my brothers. We couldn't afford to take too many and leave our compounds unprotected, especially ours with the women and children there. Tonight, I was going with Savage, Devil Dog, Viper, Menace, Torch, Steel, and Hammer.

We met at eleven that evening a mile from the storage facility on a hill overlooking the complex below. Devil would be our sniper tonight. He'd been a sniper in the Marines with Harlow and Finn. The rest of us would go in, take out the guards and then we'd set the charges to blow the warehouse and the weapons to high heaven. This would make a huge dent in the pockets of the Savages and Bastards as well as take out more of their members. They couldn't replace them as fast as we'd been killing them. By our calculations, they couldn't have more than twenty to twenty-five fully patched members left between the two chapters. Now, most people would wonder why we didn't turn the information over to the police and let them put them away? The problem with that is the system had a lot of holes and people could be bought. They would just come back again or send others after us. This way, there was no coming back for any of them.

There were two entrances to the warehouse. Guards stood outside on each side of the warehouse where they walked a back-and-forth patrol, guarding their side. The two guards would overlap each other on their passes. Inside was the fifth guard. We had to assume he walked the inside perimeter of the warehouse. Two of us would take each side leaving the remaining four to be on point to breach the doors and get into the warehouse to start the search for the fifth guard. The eight outside the warehouse would then enter to help set the C-4 charges. We were all in infrared color-reflective body armor and infrared goggles, so you could tell who our guys were. No friendly fire accidents for us.

We kept watch and at two a.m., we headed in. I was on the south side with Payne. We slid up looking for the guards. Payne found his first followed by me a couple of seconds later. We quickly and silently dispatched them. Our side and the north side held the doors into the warehouse. We took up posts by the door with Menace and Reaper. We got the signal when all sides were cleared, and we breached the building. We went in low and split left and right. It didn't take long before we heard a gunshot and Savage said the fifth guard was down.

We made sure to clear the warehouse just in case we were wrong about how many were guarding the inside. Rigging the warehouse to blow took the most time. We were away and on our bikes on top of the hill when it was detonated. In a way, it had been anticlimactic with how easily they'd gone down. We rode off, headed back to Dublin Falls. Reaper and his guys would rest at our compound and then head back out in a couple of days. He planned to spend Christmas with his sister. Since he didn't want to risk her going back to Bristol, he was coming to us. Bull and Demon would be riding in tomorrow sometime.

It was eight in the morning when we rolled back into the compound. I crawled into bed after my shower to get a few hours of sleep. Wren snuggled with me when I came to bed. I woke up around one o'clock in the afternoon, got cleaned up, and headed to the clubhouse. I knew Wren would be there helping the others cook and prep for the Christmas meal tomorrow. I was excited to spend it with her this year. In the common room, the guys were mostly sitting around, helping watch the kids and either talking, watching television, or playing cards. I went to find Wren first. She was busy with prepping the dressing. I gave her a big kiss.

"Hi, baby, you doing okay?" she asked me with a smile.

"I'm good, baby. Are you?"

She nodded.

We kissed again until the other ladies ran me off. I left laughing. Back out in the common room, I sat down with Ranger and took Gabriel out of his arms. He was awake. Reaper plopped down with us.

"I can't believe all these babies and shit, and you guys all playing nanny. What has happened to this club?" he teased us.

Ranger laughed. "We got smart and found us the perfect women. You wait until you do. You'll want to settle down and have kids too. I can't wait to see the one who captures you, Reaper. I'll give her a medal."

Reaper burst out laughing. I walked over and told him to hold out his arms. He got nervous. Ranger and I finally got him to hold Gabriel. He was stiff and looked scared to death. Harper came out and saw her brother.

"Oh my God, I need to take a picture of this." Before he could give up the baby, she snapped a photo and ran back in the kitchen.

He groaned. "There goes my man and biker cards. Assholes!"

We just laughed. Gabriel began to fuss, so Brielle came out to take him and feed him. I was amazed how the women could hear a baby and know whether it was theirs or not.

Various ones of us tried to help in the kitchen but were sent out. By evening, they had everything they could pre-cooked, or prepped. We spent time watching Christmas cartoons with Rowan. We'd each do our individual couples' gift exchanges in the morning at home, then we'd all meet in the clubhouse by ten for the group one with Rowan. The girls always seemed to find something special to do for the guys without women or families. Ranger and Brielle took Rowan to the house around eight. She wanted to stay longer but they reminded her Santa wouldn't come until she was asleep. This got her moving. Wren and I headed home at ten-thirty. I was looking forward to tomorrow morning.

I was up at seven. We'd put our gifts for each other under the tree last night. Wren was still asleep, so I slipped out of bed to fix breakfast. She'd cooked enough yesterday and would be doing more today. She didn't need to make breakfast as well. I made waffles, bacon, and eggs. There was orange juice in the fridge, and I would make her coffee when she got up. She only ever drank a cup in the morning. I was almost done when she came into the kitchen yawning. She was all rumpled and looked delicious. I took her in my arms and gave her a good morning kiss. She moaned and stood on her tiptoes to deepen it. When we broke apart, we were both panting. "Let's go back to bed, babe," I growled.

She shook her head. "We can't. We need to eat, open our gifts then get ready and go to the clubhouse. I got a text from Brielle that Rowan was up and going crazy already. Just keep this in mind for tonight."

I groaned but let her go. She was right. We had to wait.

Once we had finished breakfast, we sat down to open our gifts. She opened my gifts first. I had gotten her leather riding pants and a leather jacket. I wanted her to be as safe as possible when riding with me. There was sexy lingerie. I teased her it was really for me not her. I knew she liked sexy underthings in lace, silk, and satin. She'd admitted she liked how it felt against her skin. There was a perfume I'd found that reminded me of her. Finally, there were several pairs of jeans and tops. She exclaimed over all of them. When I opened up my gifts, she'd gotten me new leather riding gloves, several vintage-style Harley tee shirts which I loved, and a leather and beaded cord to use on my hair when I braided it. I could tell it was made in the Apache style. I remembered my father wearing something very similar. I often would wear a necklace, and she got me one made of silver, leather and beads that would fit like a choker around my neck. It was beautiful. I was admiring it when she got up and went to the hall closet. She pulled out a large box. I got up to carry it for her.

"What is this, babe?"

She smiled. "It's another gift for you."

I sat down to open it, wondering what else she'd gotten me. Inside, I found custom-made saddlebags for my bike. They were beautiful. I looked at her.

"Baby, how did you…?"

She laughed. "I saw you struggling one day to latch your old ones, so I asked Ranger to help me find you new ones that would fit your bike. He showed me this site and I picked out the one I thought you would like. If you don't, they said we can return them for a different kind."

I shook my head. "No, Wren, they're perfect. Thank you." I gave her a deep kiss; then I broke away.

"Stay right there, I have something else to show you," I told her. I kneeled down on the floor at her feet and took her hands in mine. "Wren, I love you more than I can ever tell you. I love you more every day. I want to spend my life with you. I want to have a home and children with you. So, what I'm really asking is, will you do me the honor of becoming my wife?" I reached into my front pocket and took out the ring box I'd slid into my pocket when I got dressed. She gasped as I opened the box. Inside was the engagement ring I'd bought a couple of weeks ago. It was a white gold band with bright blue turquoise stones running down the middle of the band. In the white gold were etched the Apache symbols for love, fertility, and strength. The center was a 1.25 carat diamond. She nodded speechlessly and held out her hand. I slipped the ring on her finger. It was a perfect fit. I had done some sneaking around to figure out her ring size. She threw her arms around my neck and took me to the floor where she proceeded to kiss me and tell me she loved me for the next ten minutes. I was kissing her back and telling her how much I loved her.

It took us about twenty minutes to get ourselves together. We cleaned up the gift wrap and then went to get ready to go to the clubhouse. I put on one of the tee shirts she'd gotten me along with the hair tie and necklace. She had on her new jeans, one of the tops and of course her engagement ring. We decided to see how long it would take for someone to notice she was wearing it. We'd all had the gifts for the kids hidden over at the clubhouse. Devil and the guys had promised they'd put them out under the tree this morning. We made it to the clubhouse by nine-fifty. Looking around, it seemed the only ones missing were Regan, Hammer, Steel, and the twins. They came puffing in a couple minutes later. Tomorrow was Sierra and Sienna's first birthday. Regan and the guys decided to celebrate it with Christmas until they got older and realized what was happening, then they'd split the celebrations. Hunter was sixteen months and Kenna was fourteen months. Sam would turn one in January. Savannah was five months and of course Rowan was four years old. So only Rowan really knew what was happening.

Reaper and his guys watched in amazement as Rowan, Hunter, and Kenna opened gifts. The two younger ones mostly liked to tear paper. Sierra and Sienna crawled in the boxes. Rowan was the true queen. She got loads of clothes which she loved. She was a little diva and liked to dress nice. Grandpa Bull got her a gold bracelet. She thanked everyone and gave hugs and kisses. For all the guys and this included Bull, Demon, Reaper and the others with him, the ladies had custom Warriors' hoodies made for everyone. The guys loved them. The single guys all went together and got each of the ladies, Ms. Marie, and Harper gold necklaces with their first initial on them.

We were picking up the wrapping paper and boxes when I heard Brielle gasp. I turned around. She was staring at Wren. "What's that on your finger?"

Wren looked down and back at her grinning. "Oh, this, just something Ghost gave me this morning. Do you like it?" Brielle let out a squeal and suddenly Wren was surrounded by the women all exclaiming over her ring. The guys looked at them and then congratulated me. It took a while for everyone to settle back down.

Like a repeat of yesterday, we watched the kids while the women cooked. They were able to spend more time with us in between popping things into the ovens at different times. Rowan had Reaper sucked into her game of dolls. By five, we all sat down to another outstanding Christmas dinner. Reaper and his guys were in heaven.

They'd never been with us for a holiday meal. It was different than the others. I guess with Harper being the only woman, she couldn't do as much for their holiday dinners like Sherry hadn't been able to do when she was the only old lady.

We stayed until eight and then excused ourselves to go back to the house. As soon as I closed the door, I had her up against it devouring her mouth. "I've been waiting all day for this. Get down the hall and strip. Take a nice long soak in the tub and then lie down on the bed in one of your new pieces of lingerie. I'll give you thirty minutes to get ready."

She smiled as I let her go, and swayed her ass down the hall. I knew waiting would make me even hornier, but I wanted to prolong the pleasure tonight. I planned to play more.

I took a quick shower in the other bathroom. Back in our bedroom, I could hear her in the tub. I lit candles and spread them around the room. On my nightstand I laid out a velvet bag. I could hear her getting out of the tub. I went to get our champagne I had put in the fridge to chill while we were at the clubhouse. I grabbed the bottle, two flutes, and a glass of ice cubes. I took my time and when I returned, she was lying on the bed in a sexy black corset and panty set. It made her pale skin glow. Her red hair flowed across the bed. I sat down the items in my hand.

I crawled up the bed to hover over top of her. "You look so beautiful. Let's see how long those clothes stay on." I kissed her lips and then over to her ear. I licked my way down to her collarbone. There I kissed clear along it and across the other one. I kissed from there down to the top of her breasts which were pushed almost out of the top of her corset. I cupped my hands under her breasts and pushed so they popped out of the top. I lapped at her nipples with my tongue. I nipped them between my teeth and sucked. She moaned. I worked her breasts until she was writhing on the bed. I eased back. “Sit up.” She did so slowly. I reached behind her and unlaced her corset and threw it in the corner. “Lie back down and play with your breasts. I want you to keep those pretty nipples hard for me.” She glanced at me in surprise but did as I commanded. I worked my way down her body to her stomach. I kissed all across it and swirled my tongue in her belly button.

I grabbed the champagne bottle and poured a little into her belly button. I sipped it out and then repeated it. She was still playing with her nipples and watching me. “This is the only way to drink champagne—off the body of a beautiful woman. My beautiful woman.” I set the bottle down and ran my hands down to her hips to snag the sides of her panties. I proceeded to work them down her hips, thighs and legs kissing her soft skin the whole way. I threw them to the floor. “Spread your legs.” While she did so, I grabbed a champagne flute off the table. I kneeled beside her and lifted her head off the bed so she could take a drink of the champagne. Easing her back down, I slipped to my knees on the floor between her thighs and drank in the sight of her pink, wet folds.

I groaned and ran a finger down her slit, gathering her juices as I went. She was so wet, and her arousal was perfuming the air. I was hungry to taste her. I leaned in and swiped my tongue up and down her folds. I hungrily ate her. I licked, sucked, and nibbled all over her pussy lips. I pushed her legs so her feet were resting on the bed. While I was pleasuring her, I reached down to the glass on the floor. She was so enthralled with what I was doing, she had her eyes closed. I thrust my tongue in and out of her opening and then slipped my fingers up to slide the ice cube into her opening. She shrieked and sat up. "What...?" I pushed her back down.

"Shh, just feel it. Feel the contrast between how hot your pussy is and how cold the ice cube is." She laid back and I sucked on her entrance, sucking up her juices and the melted ice. I pinched her clit between my forefinger and thumb. She went to grab my hair and then stopped. Good. She knew not to do anything without permission. "You can grab my hair baby. You can touch me any way you want." She ran her hands through my hair and pulled me harder into her center. I attacked her with even more zeal. She tugged on my hair. I grabbed another ice cube and ran this one down and around her puckered asshole. She jumped. I played with her there for a little bit. I wanted her to get used to me touching her anywhere and everywhere. Her body was mine just like mine belonged to her.

I stood and pulled her up into my arms. I took her to lie on the floor on a fluffy blanket I'd placed there earlier when I prepped the room. When she stretched out, I told her, "Get up on your hands and knees and face the bedroom door." She did so without hesitation. This put it so we were sideways in front of a tall dressing mirror. I kneeled up and rubbed my cock up and down her folds then pressed the head of my cock into her opening. She whimpered. I eased inside and groaned as her tightness gripped me. I pumped in and out. “Baby, look in the mirror to your right. Watch us. See how we look together. Watch me make love to you.” She looked over and her eyes got wide.

I watched as I thrust in and out while she was pushing back on my cock. She was thrusting back hard and sobbing. “Talon, please, please. I need to come. Harder. Harder.”

I sped up giving her faster, harder, and deeper. She never took her eyes off mine in the mirror. I could see every expression on her face and watched her beautiful breasts sway with every thrust into her body. I slowly drew out my cock and then inched it back in. I watched in the mirror as I did it. She was watching as well.

“Look. Do you see how beautiful it is to see my cock sliding in and out of your pussy? Here, you have to see what I see.” I pulled out and turned her, so she was facing the mirror. “Lean back on your elbows and look.” I spread her legs wide so she could see her pussy glistening in the mirror. “This is the most beautiful pussy in the world. So pink, soft, and wet. I get to touch it, taste it, and fuck it. Touch that pretty pussy. I want to see you pleasure yourself.”

She hesitantly slid her hand down to slide her fingers through her wet folds. She sighed. Then she began to work her clit and started thrusting her fingers in and out of her pussy. She never looked away. She was panting. I kneeled beside her, stroking my cock so she could see me getting hot from watching her pleasure herself in the mirror. She was thrusting her fingers in and out, faster and faster until she stiffened and moaned out her release.

Her hips jerking up off the floor. I had to stop stroking my cock before I came. She slowly slid her fingers out and then sucked them clean while watching me in the mirror. I groaned.

She had a pink blush up her chest and in her cheeks. I grabbed her and flipped her back on her knees. She turned her head sideways so she could see us in the mirror. I slapped her ass. She yelped and more juices flooded out of her. I thrust in hard. Her playing with herself had me close. I ran my fingers up to rub her clit. She was starting to quiver inside. I knew this meant she was almost ready to break again. I grabbed her hair and pulled on it as I brought one leg up to put my heel down. This allowed me to thrust harder. I pulled her glorious hair enough to give her a bite of pain while I thrust in and out going deeper each time. She came again a minute later, screaming. I thrust four more times and came, grunting.

"Fuck, baby. So hot. So tight. God, I love you, my beauty." I didn't stop until she collapsed to the floor taking me with her. Even then I kept gently thrusting until my cock was totally soft. I wanted to live inside this perfect place. When we both recovered, I carried her to bed, and we drank our champagne before falling asleep.

Chapter 12: Wren

It was three weeks after Christmas already. Things were going so well I wanted to pinch myself. I was engaged to marry the man I loved. Our house was being built and I had a job and family I loved. My biggest stress was now planning a wedding. Ghost had informed me on New Year's Eve we weren't to be married any later than the end of March. I'd laughed thinking he was kidding until I saw his serious face. He claimed he couldn't wait any longer than that to marry me. He also wanted us to think about having a baby sooner rather than later. I couldn't say I didn't want one seeing all the ones around us, but it surprised me he wanted one so soon, even if he'd joked a while back about starting immediately. We agreed I'd go off my pills and see what happened. I knew some women took a long time to ovulate again after stopping birth control. We might not get pregnant for months.

I wasn't at the daycare today. Others were working. I had found a place in Knoxville where the shop had the wedding dress I was looking for. It wasn't a traditional one, rather one that had some Native American Indian styling to it. I planned to incorporate some of Ghost's Apache culture into the ceremony. He had wanted to take me, but I told him I didn't want him to see the dress. Instead, Brielle was coming with me. Ms.

Marie agreed to watch little Gabriel for her. Our escorts would be Nick, Finn, and Adam. We were going to leave around ten. I was excited to see if it looked as nice as it did online.

We made it to the shop around eleven and the owner was expecting me. She brought out the dress. It was gorgeous. I told her what I was looking for in regard to the groom and groomsmen. She said she could find something to go with my dress. I tried it on, and she took measurements. It would need to be taken in to fit me properly. It was after twelve by the time we left the store. I was happy about finding the dress. It was perfect. She'd told me about another place I might want to check out for jewelry. We had the guys take us there next. There were several lovely pieces, but they weren't exactly what I had envisioned. I knew I'd know it when I saw it. We decided to hit a place for lunch before we headed back. The guys suggested a place on the outskirts of Knoxville toward Oak Hill. We went there and had a really good lunch. Brielle and I talked about wedding ideas. I swore Nick, Finn, and Adam with death if they breathed a word to anyone let alone Ghost. They'd laughed but promised to keep anything they heard a secret.

It was almost two-thirty when we headed back. We were riding in one of the SUVs with Adam driving. Finn and Nick were riding escort on their bikes even if I thought it was too cold to ride in January. We'd left Knoxville heading toward Dublin Falls when several bikes came up fast as they were riding up on us. I saw the worry on Adam and Brielle's faces. They bikers were weaving in and out trying to catch us. Adam yelled at us to call the guys and tell them where we were and what was happening. I called Ghost while Brielle rang Ranger. He answered on the second ring.

"Hi, baby, how's it going?" he asked.

I swallowed. "Ghost, there's a bunch of bikers chasing us. We're on the 168 headed home before you get on the 441 into Seymour. There are six of them. Adam said I needed to call you."

He swore. "Listen, baby. No matter what happens, do not get out of the car. It's bulletproof. Stay inside until we get there. Love you." He hung up before I could tell him I loved him too. I told Adam what he said to do. He nodded and kept his eye on the rearview mirror as we tried to outrun them. The problem was, their bikes could go faster than our vehicle.

I heard shots ring out. I screamed and ducked. Nick and Finn were weaving to make themselves harder targets to hit. They tried to stay behind us to slow down the other bikes. I watched as Finn took a shot and one of the other bikes went down. Nick was shooting at one of the other bikers. He missed and took aim again. One of them hit his bike. The last I saw. Nick was fighting his bike to keep from going down. I cried out. The other five bikes kept chasing us. Now we only had Finn outside to protect the SUV. Suddenly, Finn darted off on a side road. What the hell? The bikes soon overtook us. They forced us to the side of the road by shooting out our tires. We drove on the rims until we couldn't go any farther. Adam brought the car to a stop.

The bikers, who we could now see were Savages and Bastards by their cuts, came up shouting for us to get out of the car. I didn't think they knew it was bulletproof.

Adam sat there and shook his head no. They fired at him through the windshield. The bullet was deflected. Seeing this, they became incensed and fired shot after shot at the windows, doors and even the sides of the car. I cringed every time they did.

Brielle was telling me a story about the time a sheriff had done a similar thing but had threatened to kill the guys outside. Alannah had gotten out of the car. I thanked God; Finn had decided to get clear. Now they couldn't force us to open up using him or Nick.

I saw them turn. Out of nowhere, came Finn on his bike. He'd somehow circled around and was coming up on them, firing his gun. Since they were stationary, it made it easier for him to hit them. Finn took two down before they realized what happened. The remaining three were now shooting back at him. He raced back onto the road leading into the woods. About this time, we heard the roar of more motorcycles. Coming from the way we'd been heading were six bikes and one of the trucks. Even from this distance I could tell they were Warriors. I saw Ghost's bike in the lead. It was red with a tribal headdress painted on the tank. It was a custom bike he'd built himself.

The three remaining Bastards and Savages scattered, running for their bikes. They never made it. The Warriors shot the rest of them down. They came to a screaming halt and jumped off their bikes. Finn came darting back out. He stopped for a minute and then headed back the way we'd come. I hoped it meant he was going to look for Nick. I was worried about what had happened to him. Did he ever get the bike safely stopped? The others checked the downed bikers while Ghost and

Ranger came to the car. Adam unlocked the doors so they could pull me and Brielle out. I could see Ranger running his hands all over Bri and talking to her. Ghost was doing the same to me.

"Wren, baby, are you okay? You didn't get hurt being thrown around, did you?" He had such a look of concern on his face.

I gave him a kiss. "No honey, I'm fine. I'm worried about Nick. They shot his bike and he was struggling to keep it under control. Did Finn go to find him?" He nodded yes. "Thank God. Talon, you should have seen Finn. He tricked them into thinking he ran and then he came out of nowhere and shot two of them before he had to dart off again. Are all of them dead?"

He shook his head. "No there's one who's still alive. Now listen, I want you to head back home. A couple of guys will go with you. The rest of us have to clean up this mess." I shook my head. "No, don't argue. I'll be there as soon as possible."

I gave him another kiss and got into the truck they brought. We drove off, watching them putting bodies in the truck. Others were pushing the bikes off the side of the road into the trees. The remainder of the ride was made in silence.

Back at the compound, we entered the clubhouse to find people in an uproar. They had recalled all the men and old ladies to the compound. They rushed over to check we were alright. Brielle and I told them what happened. The guys paced, waiting to hear something from the ones still out there. It was another hour before we heard the roar of their bikes. They came racing into the compound. The truck kept going and headed to the back. I knew from Harlow and the ones who'd been around the longest, the club had a building where they took people they needed to interrogate. We weren't supposed to know it, but Harlow had been in it. They must have been taking the surviving biker there. Two of the bikes followed the truck. Ghost and Ranger were not one of them.

When they came through the door, I threw myself in Ghost's arms while Brielle did the same to Ranger. Behind them came Finn and Nick. I untangled myself from Ghost and ran over to them. "Are you okay? God, I was so worried. You two need to come over here and sit." They protested but I led them to sit down on the couch. The others fetched them a drink and fussed over them. The guys were grinning and teasing them about how much of a pussy they were. Finn grinned back.

"If being a pussy gets me all this attention from a bunch of beautiful women, then you can call me a pussy every day." This had the guys laughing and the ladies pampering them even more. Soon the others came back. They spent a little bit of time reassuring us they were fine then went into an emergency church meeting. I sat with the ladies. We whispered among ourselves.

Regan brought up what all of us was thinking. "How did they even know where you were today? They shouldn't have been down in our area to accidently see you. Shit! This is going to send the guys apeshit crazy. I wonder if they have someone keeping tabs on us. It has happened in the past."

We spent time trying to figure out how they knew. I

racked my brain to see if I recalled seeing any bikers while we'd been in Knoxville. Other than single riders here and there, I didn't recall seeing any.

The men came out of their meeting over an hour later. They didn't look pleased. I hugged Ghost close. It was now five, and I decided to head home to cook dinner. Standing around trying to think how they found us was giving me a killer headache. I told Ghost I was going to cook dinner. He said he'd come with me, but I convinced him to stay for a bit. Back at the house, I put the lasagna I'd put together this morning in the oven and set the timer. I went to lie down on the bed hoping to get my head to stop hurting. I woke sometime later. I realized I'd fallen asleep and went to jump out of bed. *My lasagna!*

Ghost was beside me. "Shh, babe. I took the lasagna out. It's cooling. Are you okay? You never lie down in the middle of the day." He had a frown on his face.

I eased up on my elbows. "I just had a headache and wanted to rest to see if it would go away. I didn't plan to fall asleep."

He reached over and pulled me onto his chest. He began to rub my scalp. I moaned. That felt so good. My head was still hurting and I told him so.

"Did you take anything for it before you laid down?" I shook my head no. He got up and came back with a couple of pills and a glass of water. I took them. He insisted I lay there and rest. He went out to the kitchen, and I could hear him moving around. Next thing I knew, he brought in a bed tray. On it was a plate of food and a glass of tea. He left and returned with another one. We sat in bed and ate dinner. When I was done, he took everything to the kitchen and cleaned up. He slipped back on the bed with me.

I thanked him. We spent the remainder of the evening relaxing in bed watching television. I took a bath with him since he insisted on helping me. I snuggled into his arms. "Honey, you didn't need to do all this. I'm fine. It's just a headache."

He shook his head. "No, it isn't. You never get headaches. Are you positive you didn't hit your head?"

"I didn't hit my head, honey. It's just a regular old headache.

"Then it's stress. I want you to stay home tomorrow and rest." I told him I'd be fine. We ended the argument with him agreeing to wait until morning and we'd see how I felt.

The next morning, I woke up fine. Ghost insisted on checking me out before he'd agree to me going to the daycare. He dropped me off with instructions to call him if I started to feel bad again. The day was a busy and tiring one. The kids were all full of energy, but it made the day go by quickly. He was there at six on the dot to pick me up. Tonight was my night to stay until the last child was picked up. Luckily, Dan Peters hadn't come to drop off or pick up Hannah again. Her mom, Cassie, told me today she would be taking her out of the center by the end of the month. She looked upset about it. I was positive her asshole husband was insisting on it. He blamed me and the Warriors for his company tanking, not his shoddy work.

I climbed on Ghost's bike to make the couple of

mile ride to the compound. Back at the house, we had leftover lasagna for dinner. I tried to ask him if they'd found out anything from the one surviving Savage. He said little and left it at that. I knew he wouldn't tell me more. They would consider this club business. That's why I never asked what happened to the bodies of the five they'd shot. Harlow and the other women were teaching me about club life. I knew not to ask too many questions.

After dinner, we went to the clubhouse for an hour. By eight, I was ready to go to bed. Ghost must have seen me yawning because all of a sudden, he scooped me up and shouted our goodbyes as he carried me to the house.

"Talon, you don't need to carry me. I can walk. And I'm too heavy to carry."

He laughed. "You hardly weigh anything. Now let's get you in the house and soaking in the tub. Then, if you're feeling up to it, I want to make love to my fiancé." I told him I could get behind that idea. He helped me into the tub where he soaked with me. Afterward, he took me to bed. We made love for the next hour. God, I was so happy.

The next three weeks flew by. I was working and Ghost was busy building a custom bike with Blaze. Harper was still staying with us because after the first of the year, she'd actually been offered the job at Dublin Falls General. She was talking about getting an apartment as soon as it was safe to live outside the compound. I saw Viper's face. He wasn't going to go for that idea. They seemed to be getting along but I wasn't sure if they'd progressed the relationship all the way or not.

We were now into the beginning of February.

Samuel's first birthday had been celebrated and the club was progressing on our house. It was hard to believe it was two months since we'd picked out our house plans. They were building and expected it to be complete sometime in April. Ghost was trying to see if they could have it done by the end of March. He and the other guys were working on it in their spare time. I'd set our wedding for March twenty-fourth. The venue was the biggest decision for me. I didn't want a church. Most of the others had outdoor weddings, and I wanted to have something different. Brielle had come up with a unique idea. Since we were incorporating the Indian aspect, we should have the actual ceremony in a huge teepee. I loved the idea. We were going to go with this and then have the reception at the clubhouse. We had room to set up the teepee on the compound grounds.

The guys were doing a lot of meetings and had done a run or two. None of us were sure what they were doing but they always came back tired. I hoped it was nothing that would end up getting them hurt or killed. I'd ordered the decorations for the wedding. Alannah was doing the cake and had a great idea for how to decorate it. The daycare was doing well. Today, Brielle, Alannah, and I were going into town to get things to make the centerpieces. Janessa was very crafty, and she had given me an idea. We were having an escort of at least three going with us. Even in town, they didn't trust that we wouldn't have trouble.

It ended up Hawk, Devil Dog, and Finn who came to escort us. We hit a craft store and then a local party store. We found exactly what we were looking for and the place settings for the tables. We were headed back to the car, when I ran into Cassie and Hannah on the street. We stopped to chat. She was telling me about the new daycare she had Hannah in. It was nothing like ours. She expressed her wish she could bring her back to be with us. I pulled her to the side. "Cassie, its none of my business, however, you don't seem happy. Is it because of your husband? I know he blames the club for his business, but I promise you they're not doing anything to ruin it. Please, if you ever need anything, just let me know. We'd love to have Hannah back."

She got tears in her eyes. "Wren, thank you. Dan is out of control. All he does is rant and rave about you and the Warriors. He doesn't care about me or Hannah. I haven't told anyone else, but I plan to leave him. I know he's been unfaithful, and I can't do this anymore. I've arranged to leave while he's in Nashville on business next week. I have family I can go to and take Hannah with me."

I gave her a hug and Hannah as well. I hoped she stuck to her plan.

After she said goodbye, I filled the others in one what she told me. They were glad to hear she was getting out of the relationship. We got the car loaded with the help of the guys and headed back to the compound. When we got back, I had a little bit of time before Ghost was done at the garage. He was close to having the new build done. I had thawed pork chops for dinner tonight. I made a stuffed one with mashed potatoes, gravy and corn for dinner. Everything was done by six-thirty, but he still wasn't home. I checked my phone to be sure I hadn't missed a text. There was nothing. It was unusual for him not to call if he was going to be later than six. I called him. He didn't pick up, so I sent him a text. Still no answer. I didn't want to disturb him at work, but I was worried. I decided to walk over to the garage and see if he was doing alright or needed me to put everything on a plate for him to eat later.

As I walked toward the garage, I noticed all the bay doors were closed. I went to the side entrance and slipped inside. I could hear male voices and laughter. I was about to step around the corner to let them know I was there when I heard female voices. I eased around the corner. In the center stall was Blaze, Ghost, and Hawk. With them were two of the bunnies, Amber and Lori. They were hanging on Blaze and Hawk. I was about to say something when a woman I didn't know came out of the back. She glided up to Ghost and put her hand on his chest smiling up at him. I couldn't hear what she said. I waited for him to tell her to back off like he did any of the others acting like that, but he didn't. He was smiling down at her and laughing. Then he leaned down and kissed her. Admittedly it was on the cheek, but he was also whispering in her ear and she was laughing and had wrapped her arms around his neck. I felt sick. What the hell? Who was she? Why was he letting her touch him? I swung around and headed back to the house.

Inside, I threw the dinner in the trash and went to the bedroom. I threw a bunch of clothes in my suitcase. I was on autopilot. I needed to get away. My thoughts were jumping all over the place. I couldn't believe this was happening again. I kept finding Ghost with women. I didn't want to hear what his excuse would be this time. I'd get the rest of my shit later. I put my engagement ring on the dresser. I hoped she wore the same size as me. I wanted to go to Brielle and Ranger's house, but I hesitated to put them in the middle of our issues. I thought of leaving but knew one of the prospects would be at the gate and unlikely to open it for me. My last choice was to go stay in one of the empty rooms at the clubhouse. I headed there. When I walked in, there were only a few of the guys there. They all looked at me curiously when they saw me carrying my suitcase. Devil Dog made his way over to me.

"What's up Wren? Why're you here with your suitcase?" I looked at him trying to decide what to tell him. Devil was one of the easiest of the brothers to talk to. I felt tears well up in my eyes. His got wide. "I-I need somewhere to stay. I thought about a hotel, but I can't leave without an escort. So, I was wondering if I could use one of the empty bedrooms t-t-tonight." I was openly sobbing by this time.

He wrapped his arm around me and took me down the hall to his room so the others wouldn't see me crying. He sat me down on his bed and then he sat with me. "Wren, tell me what's wrong? Why are you looking for a place to stay? Did you and Ghost have a fight? Please, I want to help."

I sobbed more. I felt like my heart was breaking. Underneath that pain was anger. He was rubbing my back and hugging me. I spilled out the story to him. He was talking really low into my ear. "Sweetheart, you must have misunderstood. There's no way Ghost would ever cheat on you. I don't know who the woman was, but you need to ask him."

I shook my head. "I can't, Devil. Not tonight. I need to think and right now I'm too upset. I'm holding on to my temper by a hair. I don't want to lose it. Can I use a room?"

He sighed. "Okay, you can stay in my room tonight. But in the morning, you go find Ghost and talk this shit out. Why don't you lie down and rest? I'm gonna take a quick shower and then I'll head out to the common room. I can sack out on one of the couches. I think you should at least tell him where you are so he doesn't worry."

I didn't agree or disagree. He grabbed a set of clean clothes and went into the bathroom. I took off my shoes and got in the bed under the covers. I was tired. All I wanted to do was sleep. I was drifting off when the door came crashing in and Ghost stood in the doorway. He looked around and saw me in the bed. Then his gaze swung to the bathroom door where Devil was exiting dressed in his clean clothes.

I heard Ghost bellow as he rushed toward Devil.

"Ghost, Stop it!" I yelled. Devil had his hands up in a placating gesture.

"Ghost, you've got it all wrong, man."

Ghost swung at him and Devil ducked. I heard feet pounding down the hall. I jumped out of bed and smacked Ghost on the back to get his attention. He never even looked. He was pulling back to hit Devil again. I shoved Devil aside and stepped up to tell Ghost to stop. The last things I remembered were the punch, shooting pain, and the sensation of falling.

Chapter 13: Ghost

I hurried to the house. I was super late for dinner and I'd seen Wren had called and texted. Shit! I got caught up in talking with Blaze and Hawk when Amber and Lori showed up, bringing someone with them. It was Angie. She'd been one of the bunnies a few years back. She'd been a favorite of most of the guys. She'd moved on and left Dublin Falls. I was surprised to see her. She had stopped by to fill us in on what was happening in her life. I was happy for her. We'd fucked around back when she was with the club, and I'd always gotten along with her as a friend.

I left when the other two started to get amorous with Amber and Lori. Angie was headed back to town. She hoped to get to see the others before she left. When I got to the house, all the lights were off. That was strange. Had Wren gone over to see Brielle or maybe fallen asleep? Once in the house, I went down the hall to see if she was sleeping. The bedroom was empty, the bed was made. I saw the closet door was ajar, and I went to close it. That's when I noticed her suitcase was missing. My gut clenched. I went to the dresser and began opening her drawers. It was obvious she'd taken several items. I had slammed the last drawer closed when a sparkle caught my eye. On top of the dresser was her engagement ring.

My gut was churning now.

I raced out the front door and headed straight to Ranger and Brielle's house. I pounded on their door. Ranger answered. "Hey brother what's up...?" He stopped when he saw my frantic expression. "What's wrong?" he asked.

"Is Wren here?" He shook his head no. Brielle was now standing behind him.

She spoke up. "No, I haven't seen her tonight. What's wrong?"

I explained to them what I found at the house. Bri ran off to try and call her. I was busy texting her. Ranger suggested I go to the clubhouse and he'd meet me there after he got his boots on. I took off running. I busted inside, taking a quick look around the room. I didn't see her in the common room, but I did see Adam and went up to him. "Have you seen Wren?" He got a nervous look on his face and was looking everywhere but at me. I got in his face. "I asked if you've seen Wren. Where is she, prospect?"

He gulped. "I-I-I saw her about twenty minutes ago. She went with Devil... to his room and never came back." I jerked back. Surely, I hadn't heard him right. He was looking sick. I stalked down the hall to Devil Dog's room. I grabbed the doorknob and turned it. It was unlocked. I shoved it open to find my woman lying under the covers in Devil's bed. Her hair was mussed and she looked sleepy. I scanned the room for him when the bathroom door opened, and he came out fresh from a shower. I roared and rushed at him. I couldn't think of anything other than killing him. I could hear her yelling and Devil was saying something. All I could think was I was going to kill him. He fucking touched my woman. I threw a punch and he ducked. We were throwing more punches, when I felt a smack on my back. I ignored it. Next thing I knew, I was throwing an uppercut and Devil was moved out of the way. Wren stepped between us, and I tried to stop my punch, but I couldn't. The most I was able to do was slow it down and pull it a little. I watched in horror while another part of my brain was screaming at me to stop as my fist hit her along her jaw. She went down hard. Devil caught her as she fell.

I dropped down on my knees. She was out cold, cradled in his arms. I tore her away from him. I rocked her back and forth. "Shit! No, baby, Oh, fuck. I'm sorry. I'm sorry. I didn't mean to hit you. Open your eyes, Wren." I was desperate for her to wake up. I heard others in the room. Next thing I knew, Ranger was kneeling down on the floor beside me.

"Brother, we need to get her on the bed." He yelled at someone to go get Regan. I laid her gently down on the covers. Devil came toward her, and I swung around.

"You stay the hell away from her! You fucking don't touch her. What kind of brother sleeps with his brother's woman? I'm gonna kill you!"

He gave me a pissed look. "I didn't sleep with Wren. She came here all upset. She asked for a room. We talked, and I told her she could have this one and I'd sleep on one of the couches. I just wanted to take a shower first. I came out and you went all crazy on me before I could explain. Maybe instead of kicking my ass, you should kick your own. You're the reason she came here in fucking tears.

Her other suggestion was to leave the compound and find a hotel. I thought this was safer. I was going to text you and tell you where to find her after I got out of the shower. Though why should you care? You fuck around on her and then think she should just take it. Why would you want a skank when you have her?"

I stared at him stunned. *What the fuck was he talking about?* Before I could ask, Regan came rushing in. She darted over to the bed. "What happened?"

I swallowed. "Devil and I were fighting, and she got between us. I hit her. It was an accident. I couldn't pull the punch in time. I hit her in the jaw, and she went out. Shit, Regan, she has to be alright." She motioned for the others to leave. I stayed along with Ranger and Devil. I wanted to order him out, but it was his room. Terror and Savage came in next. I had to tell them what happened. They were both giving me and Devil hard looks. I sat on the bed and rubbed her face.

"Babe, please open your eyes. I don't know what's going on, but you need to wake up and tell me." Her eyes remained closed. I helped Regan assess her vitals and her pupils. She hadn't hit the floor so nothing should be broken. I didn't think I'd hit her hard enough to break her jaw. I could see her skin already turning purple, though, where I'd hit her. I wanted to scream. I'd hurt my woman. Regan said she couldn't find anything wrong, so we'd wait for a bit to see if she regained consciousness on her own.

"Ghost and Devil Dog, to my office, now! Terror ordered.

"Terror I need to stay with Wren. Can't this wait?"

"Regan can send for you if she wakes up before you get back. It shouldn't take long." Terror answered. I reluctantly followed them down the hall.

Inside the office, I took a seat and Devil took one across the room. We were both glaring at each other. Terror ordered us to talk. I told them about coming home, finding her gone, suitcase and all and her ring on the dresser. Then I mentioned going to Ranger and finally coming to the clubhouse where Adam told me she'd went to Devil's room with him. Terror turned to Devil. Devil told him everything Wren told him. I groaned as I realized she'd seen Angie at the garage and got the wrong idea. I could see how that might happen. Angie had always been a very touchy-feely person and she had put a hand on my chest, and I had kissed her cheek. Devil was glaring at me. He thought I'd cheated on Wren! Savage turned back to me.

"Ghost, mind telling us what happened at the garage?"

"Ange, you remember her, she was here for a few years as a bunny? She came by the garage with Lori and Amber. She was telling me, Blaze, and Hawk she was in town visiting and wanted to stop by. She was sharing the news that she's getting married. We were all congratulating her." I sighed. "When I congratulated her, I did kiss her cheek. It was an innocent kiss."

Devil jumped in, "Innocent? So, if Wren had an old fuck buddy show up and you saw her kissing his cheek, you'd be okay with that, would you?"

I glared at him. He was pissing me off because what

he said was true. I wouldn't like it. I was about to blast him when there was a knock on the door. I jumped up and opened it. Ranger was standing there.

"She's awake, but we think she needs to go to the hospital."

My heart dropped. I pushed past him and headed down the hall with him on my heels.

"What's wrong with her?"

He sighed. "She's vomiting. Regan is worried she might have a head injury." I went to shove the door open. He caught my shoulder. "She doesn't want to see you, brother. She doesn't even know I went to tell you she was awake. She's really upset. Regan doesn't want to upset her more if she has a head injury. Let us get her to the hospital and then once we know more, you can see her."

I was shaking my head no. I had to see her. I went to shake him off, but Terror and Savage grabbed me.

"Think of her. You don't want to aggravate whatever is going on. We'll get her there. You follow." Savage told me.

I sagged against the wall. I stood in the hallway while Ranger carried her out of the room and down the hall toward the parking lot. Regan didn't think they needed to call an ambulance. It killed me to stay out of sight while they got her in the car. I could see she seemed to be drooping over and weak.

As soon as they pulled out, I got on my bike and headed out. Several of the guys were following us. They pulled into the ER entrance and took her inside. By the time I got in the door, they'd already taken her back. I paced the waiting room. Regan came out and came over to me.

"They're going to check her out and do some tests just to be safe. She's alert and oriented. She just vomited a couple of times and I was worried since the hit was to her face, she might have a head injury. Now tell me why you and Devil were fighting and why she was in his room?"

I groaned then told her.

She was shaking her head. "Dumbasses," she muttered. She went to sit down. I couldn't sit. I paced around the waiting room. The doors opened and in came Brielle and Devil. I shot him a glare. He just glared back.

The next three hours crawled by. I was about to scream and storm the back of the ER. Regan had been back a couple of times and said she was doing okay, just getting tests done. It was going on eleven o'clock at night when the doctor came out. He spoke to Regan. I saw Regan's look of surprise. She came over to me. "She's okay. The vomiting wasn't due to any type of head injury. They'll keep her for observation for a few hours. She's been moved to a room on the second floor. She's going to be tired and likely going to sleep. I'll sit with her and you can go home."

I shook my head. "No, I'm not going anywhere. I want to see her. She doesn't have a head injury. I'm going." She tried to talk me out of it, but I refused to budge. Finally, she broke down and told me she was in room two forty-five. Up on the second floor, I found two forty-five and slipped inside. She was sleeping. Her poor face was bruised, and she looked pale against the white sheets. I sat down and watched her sleep. I'd wait for her to wake up and then we'd talk. I was sitting there a couple of hours later when her eyelids fluttered open. She looked confused and looked around the room. She froze when she saw me, and her face went blank.

"What are you doing here, Ghost? I told them I didn't want to see you."

I eased up closer to the bed. "Baby, we need to talk. There's been a misunderstanding. Let me explain."

She shook her head. "I don't want to talk. I want you to leave. Send someone else to sit with me if you want. Where's Devil?" Her asking for him sent anger shooting through me.

"I don't care where Devil is as long as he's far away from you," I snarled.

She blinked at me in surprise. "Why should he? He has as much right to be around me as anyone," she said.

I got up and paced. "Oh, you think? Why did you go running to him when you got upset? What's going on between the two of you? You think something was going on between Angie and me, right? Maybe I should be worried about what has been happening between the two of you when I'm not around," I growled. As soon as I said it, I knew I'd let my anger get the better of me. She shrank away from me. "Shit, baby, I didn't mean that. Please, I don't want to fight. I want to explain what you saw."

She rolled over and placed her back toward me. She hit the call button for the nurse. I rounded the bed. "Wren, talk to me. It wasn't what you thought when you saw Angie. She's—" she held up her hand.

"I don't want to hear about your dear Angie. Go back to the compound. Go see Angie. I want nothing to do with you. I don't care what you did or didn't do with her. I have other things to worry about. Now leave!" She was half sitting up in bed and shouting now. Just then, a nurse came rushing in. Wren suddenly moaned and then threw herself sideways to hang over the side rail. She vomited all over the floor. I ran to help her. She cried out to the nurse, telling her she wanted me to leave. I finally left only because I could see she was getting more upset and this was making her vomit more. I walked wearily down the hall. I'd stay in the waiting room. I found Brielle and Ranger sitting there along with Devil.

"What the fuck is he doing here? He needs to stay away. I swear he goes near her and I'll kill him," I raged to Ranger. Devil stood up and came to stand toe to toe with me.

"I'm here to be sure she's okay. I'm here in case she needs something. I'm here because she asked me for help earlier. I'm going to go see her now." He walked off.

Ranger grabbed me to keep me from going after him. "Settle down. He hasn't done anything other than try and help your upset fiancé. She is obviously pissed about Angie and is in no frame of mind to talk to you. I know it hurts, but she'll come around. Let him talk to her."

I shrugged him off. "Fuck, how did this go so damn tits up? One minute I'm telling Angie about Wren and our wedding, and the next thing I know my woman has run off to one of my brothers. She thinks I'm fucking around on her. And let's face it, when she found Becki in my bed, she gave me the benefit of the doubt that I hadn't slept with her. What if she doesn't this time? Shit!"

I ended up spending the night in the waiting room. By the next morning, I was ready to storm her room. Regan had come to sit with her a couple of hours ago. She came to the waiting room. "The doctor is going to release her in just a little bit. She's still refusing to see you Ghost. She wants to be taken to either Brielle's house or a hotel. She said she's not going back to the guest house with you. I suggest you let us get her home and then talk to her."

I reluctantly agreed and headed back to the compound to wait for her to get home. She was fucking going nowhere but our house. She could go to Ranger's long enough to have our talk and that was it.

Two hours later, they pulled into the compound and went straight to their house. Ranger helped her out of the car and then inside. I waited ten minutes then headed over. Ranger opened the door before I could knock.

"Get in here. I'm amazed you took this long. Brielle got her settled in the last room at the end of the hall on the right. Try not to upset her too much. She vomited again before we left the hospital."

I promised him I'd try to be calm before I headed upstairs. At the end of the hall, I paused and then opened the door. She was lying on the bed facing away from the door. She didn't turn over. She just spoke tiredly. "Brielle, I told you, I can't keep anything down. Please don't fuss. I need to think what I'm going to do. I can't stay with you guys indefinitely and I'm not staying on the compound. Maybe Harper and I should be roommates."

I walked around the bed. Her gaze jumped to mine, her mouth dropping open. She rolled over and sat up.

"What are you doing here?"

I leaned down. "I came to see my woman and talk to her. She's been shutting me out long enough. We're going to talk." She opened her mouth, but I cut her off. "No, listen. I know what you saw. However, it wasn't what you thought. The woman you saw me talking to was Angie. She was a bunny several years ago." She rolled and put her legs over the side of the bed. I jumped to help her. "Where are you going, Wren?"

She glared at me. "Somewhere else. I don't need to hear about you and your friend, Angie, or should I say your former fuck buddy. Leave."

"No, you will listen. Yes, she and I had sex in the past. She was a bunny. That's what she did. But she was also a really nice person. We were friends. She left the club and moved away a few years ago. She showed up last night out of the blue. She was visiting Dublin Falls and wanted to see the club. She ended up walking into the garage. We were all talking."

She sniffed. "Yeah, I saw how you talk. Kissing is the new talking. I'll have to remember that. I'll use that the next time I talk to a man."

I leaned over her making her have to lean back on the bed. "You do and I'll fucking kill the man. Yes, I gave her a kiss on the cheek. It was innocent. She'd just told me she was getting married. I told her about us and the wedding. That was all it was. You got pissed and went off in a tizzy over nothing."

She looked at me. "I don't believe you."

I reared back.

She sat up. "You always seem to have women in your arms or bed but it's supposedly innocent. I think I've been an idiot. I don't think you can be faithful. I don't want a man like that. The engagement is off. I'll be out of here as soon as I can find a place to go. We won't need to see each other again."

My heart stopped. She didn't believe me. She thought I was cheating on her and lying about it. I could see the indecision, pain, and sadness in her eyes. I dropped to my knees beside the bed.

"I swear on my club, I'm not lying. I've never touched another woman since the day I met you. I realize my comfortable behavior with Angie could be seen in the wrong light. One of the guys asked me if I'd like it if your former lover showed up and you kissed him even if it was just on the cheek. I realized I wouldn't like it. I'm sorry, baby. I didn't mean to hurt you or make you doubt me. Jesus, do you know what it did to me to find you gone and your ring on the dresser? You tore my fucking guts out. Now you refuse to see me or talk to me! You can't do this."

She was looking more and more upset. I reached out to take her in my arms. I needed to kiss her so she could feel my love. She shoved, struggling to get away, and I let go. She jumped up and then went pale. I thought she might faint, but she rushed to the bathroom. I was right behind her. She dropped to her knees and vomited over and over until all she could do was dry heave. She moaned. I grabbed a washcloth and wet it, then placed it on her forehead.

"Baby, what's wrong? I thought they figured this out and you were okay. You need to go back to the hospital." She shook her head. Her eyes were closed in weariness. I helped her stand and rinse out her mouth with mouthwash then I scooped her up and carried her to the bed. She rolled over and curled into a ball. I ran out of the room to the living room. Ranger jumped up when he saw me.

"What's wrong?"

"Something's wrong. She got upset and she's vomiting again. She can barely move or keep her eyes open. We need to take her back to the hospital."

Ranger looked at Brielle. She was staring at me with indecision in her eyes. She stepped up. "Ghost, think. Why would a woman be sick out of the blue and have no energy and be overly emotional? So emotional that when she sees her man kissing another woman she leaves and won't speak or see him."

I was about to tell her I had no idea what she was getting at when it struck me. "Is she pregnant, Bri? Did they find out she was pregnant?" She didn't confirm it, but she also didn't deny it. I spun around and headed back to her room. She was still curled up on her side. I crawled onto the bed. She barely moved. I leaned over and whispered in her ear, "Are you pregnant with my baby, Wren? Is that why you're vomiting?" She remained silent. I took that as confirmation I was right. I felt joy rushing through my body. She was having my baby! I kissed her cheek and down to her mouth. She jerked away and rolled over to glare at me.

"It doesn't matter if I'm pregnant or not. I won't be raising a baby with a cheating bastard. Now for the last time, leave me alone."

I gently pinned her to the bed. My patience had run out.

"If you believe nothing else, believe this. You will be raising this baby with its father. Its father who loves its mother more than his own life and will for the rest of his time on this earth and beyond. I swear I'll never give you reason to doubt me again. I know this seems like a second strike, but it isn't. Ask Blaze and Hawk. They were there."

She huffed. "As if they'd betray a brother. They'd lie for you."

I growled and then laid my head down on the mattress beside her head. I could feel the tears burning in my eyes. I shuddered and looked at her. She was watching me and jumped in surprise when she saw my face. She reached out and caught a tear on her finger. She was looking at it and then me like she had no idea what to think. I let my tears run down my face. Time to act all macho was past. If she didn't believe me and I lost her and our baby, I'd cease to exist.

"Wren, I want nothing more in this life than you and this baby. I've fucked up with the way I behaved, and I have no one to blame but myself. I didn't think how it would appear to someone if they saw me with Angie. All I saw was an old friend who had come to share her good news. Yes, we'd had sex in the past but that was secondary to the friendship. If I could go back, I'd have gone to get you so I could introduce you to her. You would have seen there is nothing between us. None of this would have happened and you would have no reason to doubt my love or faithfulness again. What can I do to make you believe and trust me? You can't leave and take our baby away from me. You can't. If you do, then you need to kill me." I pulled out my gun and laid it on the bed. She looked down at it and back to me with wide eyes.

"If you believe without a doubt I cheated with Angie or even Becki then take this gun and shoot me. Kill me now. Because if you leave, I'll eat one of these bullets as soon as you walk out the gate. This I swear to you. Now I'll leave you alone for a while to think. Just know I love you, Wren." I gave her a kiss and then left my gun on the bed as I walked out. I couldn't take it. Her doubt was gutting me. I walked out of the house without saying a word. I could hear Ranger asking me what happened. I went to the guest house, grabbed another gun, and my jacket. I needed to ride. I got on my bike and took off. It didn't matter I was alone. If someone wanted to take me out, I'd welcome it. I had nothing to live for anyway. She was going to leave me. I'd never get to hold her or make love to her again. I'd never get to see my child grow up. A part of me wished I had never met her then I wouldn't be hurting so much.

I drove around for a couple of hours. I stopped to gas up and ended up going to the property owned by Terror. It was so peaceful and beautiful out here. Two of my brothers got married here. I sat on a log for a long time. It was almost dark when I heard bikes coming. I looked around and in pulled five of my brothers. Terror, Ranger, Blaze, Viper, and Storm all swung off their bikes. I gave them a dull look. I'd started a fire earlier, and I went back to staring at it. They came and sat down.

Terror spoke up. "We've been worried about you, brother. You took off alone and have been gone for hours. You've had your phone off and no one could get a hold of you. You need to come back to the compound."

I shrugged. "What for? There's nothing there for me. Wren's going to leave. I just want to be alone."

Ranger cleared his throat. "Brother, we've been trying to get a hold of you. She wanted to talk to you, but you were gone. We told her we didn't know where you went. After you didn't come back for several hours, she got too upset. We had to take her back to the hospital, Ghost. She's there now."

I jumped up. "She's back in the hospital! Why didn't you fucking say so as soon as you rode up? I have to go see her." I ran to my bike. One of them put out the fire. I fired up my bike and we were soon headed back to Dublin Falls. All I could think about was what if something was really wrong and she lost the baby, or she died. Crazy shit was going through my mind. I wasn't in medic mode. I was in fiancé mode. I swallowed to keep the vomit down. In less than an hour, we were pulling into Dublin Falls General Hospital again. I raced into the main entrance. None of the crew was in the waiting room. I looked around for the information desk. Ranger caught up to me.

"She's been admitted to room three-twelve." I ran for the elevator with my brothers behind me. Up on the third floor the first room we came upon was the waiting room. I saw almost the whole club there. I went straight to Regan.

"What's wrong? What did the doctor say?"

She shook her head. "He can't find anything wrong other than the almost constant nausea and vomiting. He thinks she has hyperemesis gravidarum."

I groaned. Shit, that was fucking just our luck. I knew it was a pregnancy complication only about one percent of women got. It was manifested as severe nausea, vomiting, weight loss, and possible dehydration and even fainting. I looked at Regan.

"Tell me what the worst-case scenario is with this. I know about the dehydration and weight loss. What else?" Even though I had medical knowledge, I didn't know everything about every subject.

She sighed. "The worst cases are where the mother becomes malnourished. They can develop Wernicke's Encephalopathy. This is a neurological condition caused by lesions in the central nervous system after the person exhausts their vitamin B reserves, especially B1. It leads to eye movement issues, uncoordinated gait, and confusion. There are other symptoms. The good news is it can usually be treated and have complete reversal of the symptoms. The key is if she keeps it, we keep her hydrated and if needed give her tube feedings to prevent malnutrition though that is rarely needed."

I sank down on in a chair. "Could this endanger her or the baby?"

Regan shook her head. "This alone is unlikely to cause permanent harm as long as we treat it. There is a slight increased chance of miscarriage if she becomes too malnourished."

Jesus Christ! Could nothing go right? She hated me and now I'd put a child in her belly that could severely affect her health and the child's as well. Brielle came over and put a hand on my shoulder.

"She's been asking for you, Ghost. I think you should go see her."

I swore and stood up. "How can I, Bri? Every time I tried talking to her before made her more upset and the vomiting worse. Maybe I should stay away so they both have a chance to be okay." It tore at me to say it. I wanted to see her, hold her and talk to her.

She smiled. "But this time, not being able to see and talk to you made it much worse. I think she needs you and she's ready to talk."

I swallowed the lump in my throat and headed down to her room. I knocked softly then opened the door. I came to a dead stop. Devil was sitting by her bedside. He saw me and came over, pushed me outside and closed the door. I went to blast him for being with my woman again, but he stopped me.

"Listen, I know this looks bad and you want to tear my head off but let me explain. When no one could find you, she asked for me. She's torn up, man. She was apologizing for dragging me into this and causing us to fight. She wanted to talk about what you told her, and she asked for my opinion. Man, listen, I know you really didn't cheat on her. I was just pissed you were such a bonehead and caused her to think it especially a second time and after all she has gone through. Nothing is between Wren and I other than I feel a kinship to her and friendship."

He paced away and then back to me, running his hand down his face. "Shit, no one knows this but Harlow." He paced away and then back again. "Okay. I had an older sister who was raped like Brielle and Wren." His words jolted me. He was looking pale. He went on. "She was grabbed and raped by a couple of men. They let her go after they were done with her. She never saw their faces. Only she couldn't cope like Bri and Wren have. She let it eat her alive until one day she couldn't take it anymore and she took her own life. I was sixteen and she was twenty. I've never forgotten that. I want Wren to be strong and stay strong, so she never ends up doing what my sister did. I really like Wren and think you two are perfect for each other."

I grabbed him and gave him a man hug slapping him on the back. "Shit, I had no idea. I'm sorry for your sister and for being a bonehead like you said. Thank you for staying with her. Do you think she's okay with me coming in and talking?"

He nodded. "Yeah. She's asleep right now but why don't you go sit with her so when she wakes up, you're there. Call me if you need anything. I'm going to head back to the compound." I thanked him and he nodded. I took a deep breath and then went in the room. She was still asleep, so I sat in the chair beside her bed. She was in a private room, thankfully. I sat back to wait for her to open her eyes.

Chapter 14: Wren

My first thought when I began to resurface from sleep was, I wanted to talk to Ghost. I needed to see him and apologize. I'd so overreacted when I saw him with that Angie. Yes, I was still upset he felt it was okay to kiss a former bunny he'd slept with; however, I shouldn't have jumped to the automatic conclusion he was cheating on me. I felt like my emotions were all over the place. Now that we knew I was pregnant, Regan explained that was normal. I'd thought about what he'd said back at Ranger and Brielle's house, and about how he had looked when he said it. When he pulled out his gun and told me to kill him, my heart had stopped. Then he left. I'd kept thinking for another hour before I knew I needed to talk to him, but he was gone, and no one knew where he went or could reach him. I'd begun to worry he'd done something stupid then the vomiting came back, and I couldn't stop. They'd rushed me back here.

I opened my eyes. It was very dark in the room. The only light on was a small one in the corner. I looked over at it and saw Ghost sleeping in the chair. He looked so tired. I wanted to hold him. I had no idea what time it was or how long I'd been asleep. When I fell asleep. Devil had been sitting with me. I scooted around in the bed to get comfortable. He jerked awake. When he saw me staring at him, he jumped out of his chair to come over to my bedside. He caressed my face.

"Baby, how are you feeling? Do you need anything? I can get the nurse if you need her."

I shook my head no. "No, I feel okay. Thank you. When did you get here? I've been wanting to talk to you, but no one knew where you went. Damn, Talon, that was reckless for you to leave the compound without someone with you."

He smiled. "I know. I'm sorry I made you worry. The guys found me. They said you wanted to talk to me. Do you want to talk now or later? I could have someone else sit with you if you prefer. I don't want to upset you. Tell me what you want."

I could see he was trying to give me whatever I wanted. He really didn't want to upset me.

"I think we need to talk. I want to apologize. I overreacted when I saw you with Angie. I should have said something. Asked you about her. Hell, even made my presence known and watched how you reacted. All I could think about was you were with her and did I really believe you'd want to be with me forever. I don't know if that will ever go totally away, Talon. The rapes have done something to my esteem, I think. I have days when this little voice tells me there is no way someone like you could ever want me. I fight it and usually I win. But never when I see you in any kind of situation where you're touching another woman or she's touching you."

"Does that happen if you see me with the other old ladies?" he asked.

"No, it doesn't, which I think is because I know they're in committed relationships with your brothers and would never come between you guys like that. I guess I trust them. I think it's more about not trusting the other woman to not have something more than I do which you could come to realize you want and need. Does that make any sense? I don't want to be this way. I hate to jump to conclusions and make accusations without merit. However, I'm not sure I can prevent it from ever happening again. Especially when my hormones are so crazy." I paused and took a deep breath.

"As you've already guessed, the doctor told me I was pregnant when I came in here last night. I had no idea. I never paid attention to not having a period after going off the pills. I thought they were still messing with my ovulation. We just stopped them five weeks ago. No one usually ovulates so soon after stopping birth control. I thought we'd probably go months before this would happen. The doctor estimates based on the first day of my last period which was December twenty-sixth that I'm six weeks along. That's how they calculate it. Anyway, if this is correct, I should be due September thirtieth."

I stopped and looked at him with apprehension. I was nervous about how he was taking the news I was pregnant even after all he'd said. He put down the bedrail and crawled in beside me to take me in his arms. "Babe, I'm ecstatic we're having a baby. It happened sooner than I'd even hoped. The only thing is, will I be allowed to have anything to do with it or be part of this baby's life and its mother's life? Please tell me you forgive me for being a dumbass. Please tell me you still love me and want to marry me and spend the rest of our lives together.

Because if you don't, I don't think I can live."

I slid my hand up his cheek and drew him down to my lips. I kissed him and he responded. I got lost in our kiss until I heard a throat being cleared. I pulled back to find a nurse standing there smiling. She was in her late thirties and her name tag said her name was April.

"Now I'm supposed to tell you no one is allowed on the bed except the patient. Germs you know, but I say carry on. I never get to see anything that hot at work. I need the entertainment," she said with a wink.

We both burst out laughing. I eased back.

Ghost laughed and told her, "Good because I don't plan to stop. What can we do for you? Do you need to assess her? Her vitals have been stable and her IV has been infusing well though it looks like she'll need another bag hung soon." She looked at him in surprise. He shrugged. "I was a Navy corpsman. It never goes away."

She smiled. "Yes, I'm here to check her over. I'm April and her nurse for the rest of the night. It's midnight. She'll get another bag of fluids in another hour or so. The doctor wants to make sure she's well hydrated. I wanted to see if you think you can eat anything. You didn't eat dinner. You have to keep up your nutrition with this baby. I can get you some yogurt, fruit, milk, ginger ale. You tell me. We're giving her an antiemetic with the fluids, so she hopefully doesn't vomit."

I decided to try some fruit and yogurt. When April came back, she'd brought me a ginger ale too and Ghost a Coke. I thanked her. She left telling us to call if we needed anything. He sat with me encouraging me until I had eaten all the fruit and half the yogurt. I sighed. "Talon, there is nothing to forgive. I need to ask you to forgive me for being such a bitch."

He kissed me to silence me. "No, baby, you don't. I swear. All I want is you in my life. If you say you are then I'm happy."

I smiled and nodded. He gave me another kiss. We laid there holding each other until April came in to hang a new bag of fluids. April told us the doctor was due to make rounds sometime between six and seven. When she left, we settled down to sleep after he helped me to the bathroom. The fluids were starting to make me have to go. It was after two when we drifted off asleep.

I came awake to find the sun was starting to shine through the blinds. Ghost was sitting beside me and a man with gray hair was standing at the bedside grinning at us. "Well, hello, Wren. I'm Dr. Hunter. I see I'm getting another Warrior baby." I knew him. He was the OB that took care of all the other old ladies when they were pregnant. I nodded. He laughed. "Good. I was starting to worry. Everyone else has delivered. I can't run a practice without at least one Warrior as a patient. I might not survive. Now I know the resident saw you last night. I see here they think you're six weeks along making you due September thirtieth according to the first day of your last period. I'd like to have an ultrasound done before you leave today to be sure. I'm also going to give you a prescription for nausea pills. Has anyone explained about the hyperemesis gravidarum diagnosis?" I nodded. "Great. We'll want to see you every two weeks rather than monthly because of this. I want to be sure you stay hydrated and well nourished. We'll be starting you on folic acid, an additional B1 supplement plus a prenatal vitamin. Any questions?"

Ghost broke in, "If the oral meds don't work, can she get a script for an intramuscular maybe for Zofran. Only to be used if she can't keep down the pills or they don't control the vomiting."

Dr. Hunter got a considering expression on his face. "Are you medical?" Ghost told him he'd been a Navy corpsman and was a trained paramedic. Dr Hunter nodded. "I could write her a script but if she has to use it more than a couple of times in the same day, I want you to call so we can check her out. I'll write out the directions for how I want it administered. Also, if she should need to have fluids, we could administer it at home with you, Regan, and Janessa being there, since all of you are medical. I'll get everything together and the tech in here. You'll be out of here before noon. Make your next appointment for two weeks from now with my office. Congratulations on the little one."

We both thanked him.

I looked at Ghost. "I really like him. I know all the other ladies do, too. He's easy to talk to and to get along with. I hate the idea I might have to inconvenience you guys with shots and IVs."

He shushed me. "It won't be an inconvenience. If it's what's needed to keep you and our baby healthy, we'll do it. It's not a big deal. I worry more about you having to go through all this."

We talked for a little longer. There was a knock on the door and a woman came in pushing a machine. It was the tech to do the ultrasound. She got me in position with the gel smeared around. She inserted the internal ultrasound wand and slightly moved it around until we could hear the whooshing of a heartbeat. Ghost had such a smile on his face. She was talking and telling us she was taking measurements. When she was done, she showed us a tiny blob on the screen. She left us to look at it while she got Dr. Hunter. He came in and did his own checking and measurements. He nodded. "Everything looks good. The measurements correspond to you being six weeks like we thought. Again, congratulations and I'll see you in two weeks. Call if anything changes before then."

We agreed.

While we waited for my discharge paperwork, Ghost made the call to set up my appointment with Dr. Hunter's office. Brielle showed up with Ranger around nine. They'd brought the car to bring me home. By ten o'clock, I was being wheeled out to it. Ghost was hovering making sure I wasn't exerting myself. He rode his bike back while I rode in the car with Ranger and Brielle. She was sitting in the back with me. "I take it you two made up."

I nodded. "Yes. We talked. And we got to see Dr. Hunter this morning. He did an ultrasound. I'm six weeks along. I'll have to see him every two weeks due to this hyperemesis thing. Ghost got him to give me a prescription for nausea shots as well as pills. They were rambling about a bunch of things, so I let them decide. If I need the shots or an IV for fluids, most likely we can do those at the compound and not have me go into the hospital." She agreed that was a good thing. In no time we were pulling into the compound. Ranger drove me straight to the guest house.

Ghost drove up to park outside the door. He was off his bike and over to the passenger door before I even got my seatbelt unhooked. He swung me out of the car and into his arms. "Ghost, I can walk." He grunted and kept going. I sighed. He was going to be unbelievably protective with this pregnancy. I made him take me to the couch and not to bed. I was tired of lying down in a bed. He put pillows behind me and went to get all of us drinks. We spent time talking to Brielle and Ranger. Ms. Marie had Gabriel today. I told them I wanted to see him. Ranger headed out to get him. While he was gone, I told Brielle what Dr. Hunter had said about having another Warrior baby. She was laughing with me when Ranger brought little Gabriel back to the house. He was now two months old and a bruiser. She'd finally healed completely from the C-section.

He was a quiet boy and liked to watch people. I had him on my lap cuddling him. Ghost was sitting on the couch beside me. He was caressing Gabriel's head.

Ranger started to tease him. "Well enjoy it, brother. You need to get all the sleep you can while you have time. Once your baby comes, those days will be over. Gabriel is up every three hours through the night."

Brielle interrupted him. "I tell him to go back to sleep, but he refuses to do it. He stays up with me while I feed him and then get him back to sleep. In fact, he takes him as soon as he's done breastfeeding and rocks him back to sleep."

Ranger agreed. "I can't help it. I hear him and then want to stay up while he's awake. Truthfully, I can't wait to have another one."

Brielle gaped at him. "Are you nuts? I'm waiting a little bit before I get knocked up again. This C-section was a bit much. I know when we have more, I'll be doing it again since they're all going to be big as a moose like their father." He got up and had her pinned in the chair tickling and kissing her, asking who she was calling a moose.

Gabriel began to fuss. I felt his diaper. "Oh, little man seems to need a change. Where's his bag?" Bri said she could change him, but I wanted to do it. I loved babies and kids. That was one of the reasons I'd became a teacher. Ranger brought me his diaper bag and I stretched him out to change him. Ghost was sitting there watching intently. I got his sleeper off and then undid his diaper. "Honey, hand me that spit cloth right there." He looked at me funny and asked why I needed that. We all laughed. "Because little boys tend to be naughty and like to pee everywhere when the cool air hits their little willies. That includes in the face if you're not careful." I showed him how to shield from it while I cleaned him and put on the new diaper. Ghost was taking it all in. I knew he was making notes in his head, so he'd be prepared for our baby.

Not long afterward, they all headed home to let me rest. Ghost insisted on cooking me lunch. I didn't have an appetite, but I ate anyway. Thankfully, the medicine was still working. After lunch, he laid down with me and we took a nap. The rest of the day passed with me resting and various people dropping in to check to see how I was doing. One of those was Devil. I was nervous when he dropped in because of the fight he and Ghost had gotten into the other day. They seemed to be getting along fine now. I blew out a breath of relief. Before I knew it, it was time for bed. I was helped in the shower and then tucked into bed with Ghost hugging me close. Before I fell to sleep, he kissed me one more time. We said *I love you* then I was out. It had been an exhausting couple of days.

The next several days passed much the same. I rested and Ghost hovered. I'd taken the rest of the week off from the daycare. Today was Saturday and the guys were all in their weekly church meeting. I'd gone to the clubhouse so I could hang with the other women. All of them had been over to check on me several times separately, but I wanted to see them and get out of the house. I felt like I was on house arrest. I hadn't said anything to Ghost, or he'd have made me stay at home, but I was feeling nauseous again this morning. I'd been taking the pills like Dr. Hunter had said. Overall, they helped but I had no appetite. I ate to stay healthy and to keep Ghost from worrying too much.

We were all talking, and I was fighting to keep my breakfast down. The nausea was getting worse the longer I sat there. Nick came in. He was at the gate this morning. He wasn't alone. He was accompanied by a woman. The woman I'd seen Ghost kiss on the cheek in the garage earlier this week. It was Angie, the former bunny. She was chatting with Nick and smiling. The others looked at her with curiosity. I must have made a noise because they looked at me and then back to her.

Harlow exclaimed, "Shit, is that Angie? Fuck, what is she doing here? I'll go get rid of her."

I put a hand on her thigh to stop her from rising. "It's okay, Harlow. She's probably here to see the guys.

Ghost said she was going to stop back by and say hello to the others she hadn't seen before she left town again. She's getting married and came back to Dublin Falls to see family. Please don't make a big deal out of it."

She nodded but kept an eye on her. Nick led her over to our group.

"Ladies this is Angie. She said she was here to see the guys. I didn't know what to do so I brought her here. Do you think I should interrupt their meeting?"

Harlow shook her head. "No, Nick, don't interrupt. You never interrupt church unless it's life or death. They should be out soon. She can sit with us and wait."

He nodded and went back out to the gate. Angie gave us all a tentative smile. Harlow made the introductions. She pointed to me last. "This is Wren."

Angie's smile got wider.

"Oh, your Ghost's old lady. I'm so glad to meet you. He told me about you the other day when I stopped by with Amber. You're so beautiful. I was so happy to hear he'd found a lady of his own."

I was taken back by how nice and warm she was. I greeted her. She must not have been told how her appearance that day had lit off a big fight between Ghost and me.

We were all chatting with her. She was telling us about how she met her fiancé. She also was very candid with us. "I hope this isn't too weird for all of you. I was a bunny with the club for two years until about three years ago. I know old ladies don't generally like bunnies. I can't say I blame you. But I assure you, if I was with your men, it was just sex for them and me. I'm not proud of it; however, at that point in my life, it was all I thought I deserved."

I was smiling at her but wrestling to keep the vomit down. I was about to puke, I knew it. I was just about to excuse myself to go to the bathroom when the guys came out of church. They were talking and laughing as they did. When they looked over at us, they froze. I saw Ghost go pale and look sick. I wanted to reassure him everything was fine but at that moment, my stomach gave up the fight. I jumped up and raced down the hall to the bathroom. Slamming the door shut, I dropped to my knees, barely in time as I lost my breakfast. I was heaving over and over. A hand pulled back my hair and a mouth grazed my ear.

"Fuck, baby, I'm sorry. I didn't know she was coming here today. I swear. I would've told her not to come. I don't want you to have to see her. I know she upsets you. Jesus Christ! My stupidity made you sick again. Please, baby, calm down. She means nothing to me. I swear to God."

I could hear the panic and remorse in his voice. I wanted to reassure him, but I vomited again. This time all I brought up was bile. This vomiting made me feel weak. I rested my head down on my arm. I heard the water running and then a cool cloth was on the back of my neck. I tried to tell him again it was okay, but I went into a fit of dry heaves. When I was finished, I collapsed on the floor. I heard Ghost yelling for Regan.

"Regan, go to our house. Get the Zofran out of

the cabinet in our bathroom. I need to give her a shot. She can't stop. She's dry heaving now and exhausted. I'm gonna take her to my room here." She told him she would be right back. I hung in his arms with my eyes closed as he carried me to what I assumed was his room. He laid me gently on the bed. "Baby, can you hear me? I have you in my room. There's a waste basket here if you need to vomit. I want you to rest. Don't move."

I gave him a weary nod without opening my eyes. Others were in the room and asking if I was okay. Not long afterward, I heard Regan talking.

"Here's the Zofran. I already drew up the dose. Let's get it into her. Do you think we need to give her some fluids, Ghost? Has she been vomiting like this?"

He rolled me onto my side. "Wren, you're gonna feel a stick in your hip. And no, Regan, she hasn't been vomiting. The pills seemed to be working until today. I think seeing Angie sent her over the edge. She needs to get the hell out of here. I don't want Wren to have to see her. As for fluids, wait to see if this works or not. She's been drinking well the last several days."

I felt the prick in my hip and opened my eyes. "Honey, it isn't because of Angie. I admit I was surprised to see her here, but I've been feeling nauseous all morning and was about to excuse myself to vomit when you came out of church. I don't know why I'm suddenly so sick. I've been taking the pills, you know that." He ran his hand through my hair.

"Rest, babe. Don't talk. Let the medicine work. It may make you drowsy. If it does, just sleep."

I sighed and closed my eyes. I was already tired from vomiting. There was an ongoing low murmuring around me. I drifted while Ghost held me and caressed my hair. I must have fallen asleep because I jerked awake and noticed by the clock on the wall it was now noon. Ghost was the only one with me. He sat up.

"Wren, how do you feel, baby? Can I get you anything?"

I grimaced. "I need to get this horrible taste out of my mouth and use the bathroom. Then maybe something to drink." He helped me up and carried me to the bathroom even though I told him I could walk. I relieved my bladder then brushed my teeth and rinsed with mouthwash. I felt better just doing that much. He carried me back to the bed.

"Ghost, I can walk. I feel better. My stomach seems to have settled down. Can we go out and sit in the common room at least?"

He looked conflicted. "I don't want you to stress yourself. It will only make the nausea worse. We'll try it but if you start to feel sick or tired, you tell me immediately. Do you understand?" I nodded. He insisted he carry me out to the common room. Most people were still hanging around and came over once I was seated to ask how I was feeling. Ghost went and got me a drink. I'd found water flavored with fruit seemed to be more palatable to me and I could drink more fluids. He brought me water with slices of strawberry in it. He sat down and pulled my feet up on his lap. I relaxed as we chatted. He kept an eye on me the whole time. I finally called him out.

"Honey, I'm fine. Stop worrying. If I start to feel sick again or tired, I'll tell you." He kissed me.

"I hate to see you sick. It takes so much out of you. This one was the worst. You literally threw up and heaved until you collapsed. If it happens again, I want to go see Dr. Hunter. You have at least six weeks maybe more of this if it runs its usual course. I can tell you already lost a couple of pounds this week."

"I know. Hopefully this works. I'd hate to be at the daycare and have to puke like that. It would scare the kids," I joked. He gave me a stern look.

"You probably will have to take a break from the daycare. It'll be too much of a strain on you being sick like this."

I sat up straighter. "I can't not work, Ghost."

He cut me off. "Yes, you can. We'll hire another person if we have to. And you don't need to worry about money. You're marrying me and I have plenty of it. Plus, we're going to get married in less than two months. I need you and our baby healthy more than you need to work."

I could see he was serious, and I didn't want to do anything to put the baby at risk.

"You're right. I'll do what is best for the baby. Now settle. Go talk to your brothers."

He shook his head. "My brothers know where I'm at. They can come over here if they want to talk to me." And he was right. All of them spent time sitting with him and us. He excused himself a little later to go to the kitchen and came back with fruit, dry toast, and milk.

"Here, you need to try and eat something. The little bit you ate this morning came up."

I was able to get three quarters of it down. I looked over to see Steel and Hammer handing him a book. "What is that Ghost?" I asked curiously. Hammer and Steel laughed.

"It's the pregnancy handbook. Just don't read the *what-if* sections because that shit will give you fucking nightmares," Steel said. I saw Terror, Savage, Menace, Viking, Tiny, Ranger, and Hammer all nodding in agreement. I looked at them in amazement.

"All of you read this?" Again, all of them nodded. The title of the book was *What to Expect When You're Expecting*. I looked at the other moms. They were smiling and nodding. Well, I guess I knew what the next book on my reading list was.

Around four o'clock Ghost insisted I had to go home and take a nap. The nausea was coming back. Regan told me if it got worse to take another dose of Zofran but no more than one. Back at the house, Ghost was in the kitchen. "Talon, honey, what are you doing?" He came out and gave me a cup of hot tea.

"Try this. It's ginger tea. It can help with nausea. I also need to research some other herbal remedies to see if they're safe to use when you're pregnant. Native Americans used a lot of herbal remedies. I'm just not sure if their safe. In the meantime, try this. If it works, we can get you ginger lollipops or capsules."

After I finished the tea, I took a nap and when I woke up, he had a simple dinner fixed. Anything with strong smells or spice made it worse so he made sure to make things bland for me. We rested for the remainder of the evening and watched a movie. I fell asleep by ten. I hoped this nausea and tiredness passed quickly because it was for the birds.

Chapter 15: Ghost

It was now just over a week since Wren had seen me with Angie and we'd found out she was pregnant. I thanked God every day she'd forgiven me and allowed me to stay with her and our unborn child. It was just over six weeks until the wedding. She was battling the nausea and working on the wedding. The other ladies were making sure to take on the bulk of the work. She'd decided to take a break from the daycare. They had enough people to cover for her and still make their minimum required staffing ratio for licensure purposes. She'd stop in and see them but not stay to work. I knew she missed the kids, but her health and the health of our baby came first.

Today she needed to go to Knoxville to try on her wedding dress after the first round of alterations. She'd do it one final time right before the wedding. She'd also said the shop had found the outfit she wanted me to wear. I was going to go with her and try it on. Then I'd leave the store so she could try on her dress. A couple of the other guys would guard her on the inside during that time. There was no way she was going without me, a large escort, or to be in the shop without guards. Brielle was to go with her again.

Our group headed out around ten. She was in the SUV with Brielle. Ranger was driving this time. I rode my bike along with Steel, Hammer, Blaze, Torch, and Hawk. When we got there, Ranger and I went in with her and Brielle while the others sat out front and behind the store. The owner greeted Wren. She told her our plan. She smiled and went to get my clothing. She came out and unzipped the garment bag she was carrying. Inside was a modern but beautiful tunic made in the Apache style of old. It was long and hung above my knees. It had fringe, beads and was made of soft white hide with mostly red accents. There was a matching pair of breeches. I stood gazing at it.

"Honey, don't you like it? We can do something different if you want. It was just an idea," she told me nervously. I shook my head.

"Babe, this is beautiful. I knew you said you were going to have Indian influences as part of the ceremony, but I never imagined this. Are you sure you want to go this far? I love it but it should make both of us happy."

She was now smiling in relief. "No, I love the whole idea. If you're okay with this, I'd like you to wear something like this and your groomsmen in one similar just less ornate. My bridesmaids are wearing something more traditional too. I have them coming to be fitted at the end of the week. The dresses came in." I knew she'd asked Brielle to be her matron of honor and then Alannah and Regan to be bridesmaids. Blaze was my best man and Ranger and Hawk were my groomsmen.

I tried it on, and it felt wonderful. The material was actually made of the softest hide, bleached to be white. Very little needed to be done to tailor it to fit me. Since Ranger and Blaze were with me, the owner showed me the groomsmen outfits and they did their fittings while we were there. Once this was all accomplished, I went outside while she and Brielle did their fittings. Ranger and Hawk stayed inside to guard them. In total, it took us almost three hours at the dress shop. I knew she'd be tired and in need of food when we were done.

When they finally came out, we went to a small café. She ate sparingly but at least she ate. They had good, country comfort food. We left and were on our way home by three. She needed to rest and take a nap. We'd just pulled into the compound, when Terror came out of the clubhouse. He waved at us. I helped Wren out of the SUV, and she went to the house to lie down with Brielle accompanying her. The guys and I headed inside the clubhouse with Terror.

"Sorry to flag you down as soon as you rolled through the gate but we need to meet. We got news on the Bastards and Savages. I've called in everyone else and we were just waiting on you guys to get back. How did the appointment go by the way?" I told him it had been really good.

In church, everyone else was seated. Once we took our seats, Terror called the meeting to order.

"Sorry for the urgent summons and on a non-church day. I spoke to Reaper earlier today. He's had more news about the Savages and Bastards. Apparently, he has someone else who has some kind of contact or ability to spy on them. They were heard talking about revenge." We all nodded. This was no surprise. "They're planning to get revenge..." He paused and looked around at all of us. "On Harper. She has had a hit put out on her." He looked at

Viper when he said the last part. Viper was up and out of his chair.

"What do you mean, they put a hit out on her? How? Why?"

Terror stood and paced as well. "They've put it out to their own people as well as any other clubs who might be willing to do it. If one of them or their own guys bring her to them alive, they get twenty-k and if they kill her, it goes up to twenty-five-k. They want to hurt us and the Punishers. Of course, they want to see all of us dead as well as our women and children it seems, but Harper has gained their hatred because of the intel she fed us."

Viper yelled and slammed his fist down on the table. "If they fucking touch her then their all dead and their fucking families too. I swear, Terror, they hurt her, and I'll kill them all. She's mine and no one harms her and lives," he hissed. I knew he meant it. And he could do it too. He'd been a Seal with Savage.

"I know, brother. We'll protect her. Reaper has alerted the other chapters of the Iron Punishers. Most of them are much farther away but still willing to help. He's also going to talk to Sean, Gabe, and Griffin, our friends from the Dark Patriots. With them being ex-military and having so many contacts they still use for their business, they can find out more on their possible drug and weapon businesses and holding places. As for the prostitution, so far, we left that business alone. No more. We'll be searching out those and helping to liberate the women who want out. We can't and won't kill them. However, it's likely some of them are doing it against their wills, and those we'll help. We need to be prepared for them to make a bigger strike against us directly. I want us keeping a guard with the vehicles when we leave the compound so they don't plant bombs like they did with Harper. Smoke, I need you to get us detection equipment. We keep up the guards on the women and go back to minimal trips from the compound. No one rides with less than two people though I prefer if everyone travels in groups of four. I want us to tag Harper and Wren with trackers like the other women, by the end of this week at the latest. I know this is a lot. I've asked each of our chapters to send two men to help. Reaper needs his men in Bristol, but the other Punisher chapters are sending a few men to his compound to help and two here. Finally, I updated Wrath and Agony, from the Pagan Souls so they'd be aware. They vowed to send us two guys each as well. This means we'll have twelve extra men to help with guard duty and runs. Any questions, ideas, or concerns?"

I spoke up. "When should we expect the first ones to get here?" He told us by Friday. That was three days away. We discussed getting the clubhouse cleaned and ready. Brielle and her crew could help if needed so Ranger said he would talk to her. More food and household supplies would be needed. Alannah and Ms. Marie could spearhead that. Menace volunteered to talk to them. More guns and ammunition would be Ranger's job. Savage and Viper would get us more C-4. Smoke would work on the bomb detection equipment and getting even more cameras around the various businesses and the compound. He would need help monitoring them, so we decided to use Nick and Adam to help with that.

The final thing was the daycare. All of our children went there or would go there. They would have no less than four guards at all times. We'd been working to enclose the actual daycare building in a high wall similar to the one around the compound. Mostly it had been for keeping the kids from wandering. Now we would make sure it was to make it a fortress as well. The wall had been completed at the end of January. We'd used outside masons to do the work from town. The same ones who had helped with our other walls. We'd make sure weapons were securely stored at the daycare. Not only were we responsible for our children, but others. The children would be met at the gate of the enclosed walls rather than inside like they were now to ensure no one got inside that way.

We ended the meeting with each of us knowing our assignments. I headed straight to the house. I wanted to be sure Wren had laid down to rest. We'd been in church for an hour and a half. I found her lying down on the couch watching television. I sat down and put her feet on my lap. I looked at her. "Babe, we need to talk." She sat up and caressed my face.

"What's wrong, Talon? You look worried."

"I can't and won't tell you everything. Just know the Bastards and Savages made some threats. We'll be increasing security. One of those is to have you and Harper get the tracker like the rest of us and the old ladies have and to get it by the end of this week. It's harmless even if you're pregnant. I need you to please get it. I'd really prefer it if you'd get it by tomorrow. I can administer it. It takes a second and doesn't hurt much more than a regular shot does. Secondly, we'll be having a dozen guests from other clubs coming to stay with us. They're from the other Warrior chapters, the Iron

Punisher's sister chapter, and the Pagan Souls. They will be helping us with guard duty. We'll be taking fewer trips off the compound and have more guards when we do. Finally, we'll post guards at the daycare and all drop-offs and pick-ups need to occur outside the walls not inside. We're doing this to ensure the safety of not only our children but those who pay us to care for theirs. Will you please help me to communicate it to the staff and parents there and to enforce it with them?"

She'd gone pale. Shit! I didn't want to stress her, but she needed to know so she could be prepared and help. I pulled her toward me until she was sitting on my lap. "Baby, please don't look like that. It's all precautions. We want to keep everyone safe. We're going overboard, I know. I don't want you to stress about this. Please." She gave me a little nod and I kissed her. God, she tasted so sweet. I'd missed making love to her for the last week. She'd been tired and I didn't want to stress her. But God, did I want her. I could feel my erection growing. She squirmed and rubbed her bottom across it through our pants. I moaned.

She wiggled more. "I feel something. Is that all for me? Hmm, it feels good. I wonder if I could have some of this tonight. I've been missing it and find I'm in desperate need. I need my man to make love to me until I can't move. Do you think I could convince him to give me that?" she teased. I flipped her to lie on the couch on her back with me hovering over top of her.

"Oh, I think it's a definite possibility. How about we eat dinner, we get our bath and then we see what might crop up." She giggled and latched onto my mouth. We spent the next fifteen minutes kissing each other senseless. I broke away and told her to rest while I made dinner. She needed her strength for later. She behaved and rested. After dinner and the dishes were done. I took her to our bedroom. She stripped to get in the tub. She preferred baths to showers. Except now she had to be careful not to make the water too hot or stay in it too long. I'd found this out from the dreaded book the guys got me. The damn thing was full of great information but also scary shit.

I slipped in the water with her. She sat between my legs and leaned back against my chest. I was able to wash her soft skin. I was doing my fair share of caressing while I bathed her. Her breasts were peeking out above water all rosy and her nipples hard. The areolas were darker already from her pregnancy and her breasts bigger. They'd always been a good handful and were even bigger now. I massaged them and tweaked her nipple as I kissed her neck. She moaned.

"God, that feels so good Talon. Don't stop. I've been craving you so much this past week. I know I fall asleep almost as soon as we go to bed, but never doubt I want you every day and would gladly stay awake to have you deep inside of me." Her admission had me growing harder and bigger. I rubbed my cock against her back and buttocks.

"Wren, I want you every day and every way I can have you. I hunger for you as well. I've been letting you get your rest. I never want you to tire yourself out too much. Tonight, I'll feast on this lush body. Prepare yourself. I plan to make love and fuck you until we both can't breathe." I bit down on her shoulder and thrust my hard cock into her back. She moaned louder. I slid my hand down her chest, past her belly to her pussy where I pushed my fingers into her folds. I could feel her slickness. She was wet and it wasn't from the water. I massaged her folds from top to bottom and back. She bucked her hips up. It was time to move things to the bed.

I stood, pulling her out of the tub. After I dried her and myself off, I carried her to the bed. She laid there spread out before me like a dream. I crawled up her body to kiss her lips. I fucked her mouth with my tongue like I wanted to fuck her pussy. I worked down her chest to her breasts where I played for a long time. She was so sensitive and sucking on those hard beads had her thrashing around on the bed. I knew I could probably make her come just by playing with her nipples. I wanted to see. I licked, sucked, and bit while tweaking them with my fingers. She came moaning her release rather quickly. Orgasm number one. I planned for her to get off at least three times before I did. Maybe more.

I kissed down her still flat tummy to her pussy. She was glistening with her juices. I yanked her legs farther apart. "Put your legs on my shoulders," I ordered. She did so instantly. I got down to eating her sweet pussy. I sucked on her clit making her hips jump. I licked up and down her folds over and over, lapping up her juices. Then I slid two fingers deep into her pussy thrusting in and out repeatedly. She was getting wetter. I knew she'd come again soon. I wanted to try something. I looked up at her. She was watching me. "Wren, do you want to try something new?" She nodded yes. "Are you willing to trust me no matter what?" Again, she nodded. I went back to licking her.

I coated a third finger in her juices and slid it down

to her puckered asshole. She'd let me play with ice around it before. This time I wanted to breech that opening. It would give her more pleasure once she got past the burn. She tensed. I waited to see if she'd tell me no. She didn't. I felt her trying to relax. I eased the tip inside and only the tip. She gave a small hiss. "It helps if you bear down when I'm doing this. At least until I get past your sphincter muscles. I assume you've never done this."

"No, I haven't," she told me.

"It'll burn and hurt but if you're patient, it'll pass and I promise, it'll make you feel wonderful." She didn't object and I felt her bear down. I eased my finger in a bit more. I kept my attention on her clit and thrusting in and out of her tight pussy. This helped to distract her a little. I eased the finger back and then pushed more. I kept this up. Twice I had to stop and wait for her to let the burning subside. I wanted her to enjoy this. I enjoyed anal sex and wanted her to enjoy it so we could experience it together. If she didn't, I could live without it. I knew from prior discussions and seeing what went on in the clubhouse, that all my brothers seemed to like anal as well. Though we didn't talk about what we did with our women, I assumed the other old ladies were probably engaging in it. None of my brothers looked to be deprived in the sex department.

I had finally gotten all of my finger worked into her ass. I proceeded to thrust in and out of her ass at the same time I did her pussy. She was tight in both holes. So tight I could so imagine my cock in either of them. It made me want to explode. She was whimpering now. Her hips thrusting to meet my fingers. I continued to pay attention to her clit and folds with my tongue as my fingers did their job. When she finally went off a few minutes later, she squeezed the hell out of my fingers. After she'd relaxed and stopped her spasming, I eased my fingers out of both holes.

I crawled up to take her mouth so she could taste how good she was. "Taste that. Taste how sweet your pussy is? I could feast on you for hours. But I can't right now. I want you too much." I sat back on my heels and pulled her upright, so she was straddling my thighs. I slid her forward until my cock was nudging her entrance. I guided it inside and impaled her in one continuous stroke. We both moaned. "Shit. You feel so good, my beauty. So, fucking good. Now ride my cock."

She slid back and forth with me helping her so she wouldn't tire herself out. The feeling was indescribable. She was panting and a fine sweat coated both our bodies. She was caressing my chest and kissing my muscles. She traced my tattoos as well as my scars with her tongue. The scars I'd gotten from various battles not only in the Navy but in the club did not turn her off. She'd once told me they were sexy.

I could feel the need quivering through her body again. I could come too but I wanted to hold out. She was sliding faster and harder on my cock. I helped her to do so even more. It wasn't long before she gave a cry and her body clamped down on my aching cock. I gritted my teeth to keep from spilling my load. She glided back and forth throughout her orgasm. As she slowed down and began to relax her grip on my cock, I slid out. She gave me a surprised and worried look. I kissed her.

"Get down on your knees beside the bed. I want you

to suck my cock and clean me off." She sank to her knees as I sat on the side of the bed. The carpet in here was plush so she wouldn't hurt her knees. She took my cock in her hand and lowered her head. Her mouth was hot, and I was a tight fit. She licked and sucked up and down my entire cock. Her hands were stroking the base and my balls. She licked down to my balls and sucked gently on each of them. I groaned. I loved to have my cock sucked and especially my balls. She worried them around in her mouth and then engulfed me again. She was bobbing her head up and down. I wrapped her hair around my fist and used it to guide her at the speed I wanted. I could feel my cum beginning to boil. I didn't want to come in her mouth as good as it was. I thrust in and out of her mouth a few more times and then lifted her off me. Her eyes were half closed and full of heat.

"That's good. Now go to the chaise and lean over the arm. Make sure you don't lean on your stomach, babe." I helped her to her feet, and she went to lean over the arm of the chaise that sat in the corner of the bedroom. She often sat in it to read. I pressed up against her. "Do you know how beautiful this ass is? I want to sink my cock in it one of these days. One day real soon. When you're ready." I slid into her as I said the last part. She groaned and I growled. Shit, she was so wet, hot and tight. I pulled back and slid back in again. I wouldn't be able to last long with her feeling like this. I leaned forward and kissed up her back to her ear. "I want to fuck you hard and deep. I know it won't necessarily hurt the baby, but I want you to tell me if you feel any discomfort or pain. Pregnancy hormones can make you very sensitive. Promise me you'll tell me if it's too much." She nodded.

"I promise. Please, I want you to do it."

I slid back and then powered into her. She immediately began to thrust back harder to meet every stroke. I was thrusting into her harder and harder and so much deeper. I slapped her ass and she cried out while flooding my cock with even more of her juices. She was heaven. I could hear my balls hitting her pussy with every thrust. I spanked her ass cheeks a few more times. She was now begging me.

"Please, Talon. Babe. Make me come. Make me come all over that glorious cock."

I started to slam into her over and over like a machine. I couldn't control it. I had to come, and I wanted her to come with me. She was panting and moaning. I slid my hand up to cup her throat. I didn't choke her. I wasn't into breath play. I just wanted to feel her pounding heartbeat, her swallowing, and the moans vibrating under my hand.

She whimpered. "I'm gonna come." She didn't need to tell me. I could feel her pussy clamping down harder and harder on my cock. She was almost there. I thrust a few more times and she came wailing my name. "Talon!" I was able to thrust two more times after she began to orgasm before I spilled my seed. I grunted and growled with every thrust. I kept stroking in and out until she was done coming and I'd released my last bit of cum and even then, I kept thrusting. I didn't want it to end. She felt too good. I had to finally stop when my cock went soft.

She was hanging limply over the arm of the chaise. I rested my head on her back. "My beauty, that was amazing. You're amazing. Thank you. Now let's get you cleaned up and in bed. You need to rest, baby." I slid out of her body and helped her to stand. She was a little wobbly as we walked to the bathroom, so I carried her.

"That was amazing for me too. I feel like you took the life out of my whole body," she whispered. We took a quick rinse off in the shower and then I got her tucked under the covers in my arms.

"I love you, Wren," I whispered as she was drifting off. She smiled and opened her eyes.

"I love you too, Talon. Good night, honey." She was asleep almost as soon as she said those words. I knew I went to sleep with a smile on my face.

Chapter 16: Wren

It was Saturday. The extra guards we were expecting would be here today by two. The club was having a little party to welcome them. I was under strict orders from Ghost to rest. He wanted me to attend the party but not to exhaust myself. Tiredness and nausea were almost my constant companions. I would see Dr. Hunter next week. I was now nearly eight weeks along and praying it would go away once I passed twelve weeks like most women did. The guys were going to barbeque and had ordered the side items from the Fallen Angel. They didn't want the ladies to tire themselves out. Sometimes they did this.

The party would officially start at three. I planned to go to the clubhouse then with Brielle. Ms. Marie would be with the kids as usual. We all tried to tell her we would help so she could enjoy the party. However, she always said she enjoyed the babies and Rowan more. Cindy and one of the workers from the daycare, Monica, were going to help her. They'd earn extra money. I would get ready for the party with Brielle at her house.

At two I headed over. Ghost was at the clubhouse already helping to greet our guests. All the rooms had been cleaned and prepared for them. Inside Rowan was playing dolls and keeping an eye on her little brother,

Gabriel. She loved to help with him. She gave me a hug and kiss. "Auntie Wren, look at my dolls." I spent a few minutes admiring them until Bri told her we needed to get ready.

In their master bathroom she had it set up to rival a beauty parlor. She was working on her hair while I did my makeup. I was applying violet red and plum shadows in varying tint to make my greenish blue eyes pop. I lined and smudged them lightly with black liner and a couple of coats of mascara. I was lucky to have naturally long lashes. My complexion was thankfully smooth and unblemished so I could skip foundation or concealer. On my cheeks I had a hint of peach blush and my lips were lined and filled in with dark plum lipstick. I finished it off with a slick of gloss. My eyebrows were a dark red so all I did was smooth them.

When I was done with my makeup we switched off. I went to work on my hair. Now my auburn hair was dark and hung long to my waist. I wore it a lot of the times in a bun or ponytail. Today I wanted to be sure to make a good impression. I let it hang down like Ghost liked it best. I put curls in just the ends and sprayed them so they would hold. As for my clothes, I had on the leather pants Ghost got me for Christmas. I'd paired them with a black corset top with tight lace long-sleeves. The neckline was low but not indecent. My breasts normally would look really good in this top. My bigger pregnancy breasts looked great. I had on a gold cuff bracelet with a matching choker necklace and dangling earrings. On all of them were grape-colored garnets. Everything was finished off by my property cut Ghost' had given me a week ago and my four-inch heeled black boots. They made me five foot eleven which I loved.

Brielle was a petite pixie. Even in three-inch heels she only hit five foot five. Ranger was so much taller than her. She was in tight jeans and a sexy blue top which set off her strawberry blond hair and green eyes. Her jewelry was silver. She had on her property cut. Her hair was up in a high ponytail with the ends curled like mine. She didn't look like she'd just had her second baby two and a half months ago. I nudged her. "Looking like that, you'd better look out. Ranger will knock you up again." She laughed.

"If he does, I may have to kill him. And you're lucky Ghost has already knocked you up. Because looking like that, he'd be doing it tonight too." We left the house telling Rowan and Cindy goodbye and still laughing about the guys' response when they saw us. Ghost always told me how beautiful and sexy I was. It was just nice to amp up the looks once in a while.

We strolled into the compound arm in arm. It was full of men. Our twenty-one men, which included the four prospects plus the twelve newcomers, made it a feast for the eyes. They were all good-looking and sexy. But Ghost was the one I was drawn to— ever since the first day I met him when the club rescued Brielle and me. The other ladies all seemed to be here except Harper. She said she was going to join when we talked earlier. I looked around for Ghost while Brielle was busy looking for Ranger. We both spotted them together over by the bar. They were in deep discussion with Terror, Viper, and Savage and what looked like all twelve of the guests. We headed in their direction. We greeted everyone with a hello and kissed our men. I could feel the newcomers staring at us.

They had all their cuts on so I could remember their names and which club they came from. From the sister Iron Punisher chapter was Mayhem and Lash. The Pagan Souls from Lake Oconee, Georgia sent Ryder and Crusher. Pope and Knight were from the Cherokee, North Carolina chapter of the Souls. Tiger and Falcon came from the Gastonia, North Carolina chapter of the Archangel's Warriors. Saber and Ice from the Louisville, Kentucky Warriors. Rounding out the dozen were Rebel and Ace from the Hunter's Creek chapter of the Warriors. Ranger introduced Brielle and then Ghost introduced me. Mayhem and Lash were looking around and then at us.

Mayhem whistled. "Man, no offense guys, but you have the sexiest and most beautiful women I've ever seen in this club. Every damn one of them. Jesus Christ! I'm pissed none of them are available. Lucky bastards." Lash agreed with him. I just blushed.

From what I gathered it looked like all the other guys had been to the club before, so they'd meet most of the other ladies. Only Mayhem and Lash were totally new. We talked for a bit and then they broke into smaller groups and floated away to mingle with the other brothers and their wives. Ghost pulled me into the corner and kissed me. I moaned.

"Wren, you look so hot. Babe, I'm so damn lucky. Mayhem is right. We do have the sexiest and most beautiful women. I want to take you home right now and fuck you until we drop." I laughed.

"Didn't we do that just here the other night? Are you calling for a repeat?" He nodded and gave me another kiss. I pushed him away. "Behave. We need to mingle. You can ravish me later."

"You can count on it, babe," he told me.

I saw most of the guys starting to head outside. It was an unusually warm day for February. The high was sixty-five degrees. Usually, it was anywhere from thirty to fifty degrees. No need for a jacket yet. Once the sun went down, I'd have to get one if we stayed outside. The guys were grabbing more beers from coolers set up near the barbeques. Terror and Savage were firing up the big grill so it would get hot. The food from the Fallen Angel had come right at three thirty. I saw Adam and Tyler bringing it into the kitchen when we're talking to the group. Ghost had fetched me a flavored water. He'd made sure they included those just for me. God, I loved that man. He was so caring and loving.

Pope, Knight, Tiger, and Falcon was standing with us as well as Hammer, Steel, and Regan. Falcon nodded to my water. "Why aren't you drinking, darlin'? Don't you drink alcohol or something? Let me go get you one instead of that water." I went to explain when Ghost answered.

"No, brother, she doesn't have anything against drinking though she rarely does it. She can't have any alcohol. She's pregnant." All four of them looked at me surprised.

"Shit, you guys really do catch and knock them up ASAP. When is your little Ghost due to arrive? I'd have never guessed you were pregnant, Wren. Congratulations to you two," Pope said. The rest gave us their congratulations.

"I'm due at the end of September. I'm only two months along so I'm not showing yet," I told him.

"Yeah, she's been so damn sick, she's actually lost weight. We're hoping it goes away soon," Ghost told them. They were asking when we'd know what we were having when we heard a commotion. I looked around and saw Viper had Mayhem by the collar and shoved against the side of the clubhouse. Ghost took off and I followed. I could see others racing to get to them. This wasn't a good thing if one of our guards had pissed off a patched member already. When I got close, I could see Harper and Lash standing not too far away. She was trying to get Viper to let Mayhem go. Viper wasn't having any of it.

He was yelling at Mayhem. "Don't you ever touch her again. She's fucking off-limits. I should rip your fucking head off."

Mayhem sputtered, "She didn't have a property cut on. She's the only unattached one I've seen and she's hot. I was looking for a little company. What's it to you? Is she your sister or something?"

Viper tightened his grip. Savage was trying to get him to let Mayhem go.

"She doesn't have a property cut on because it's not here yet. She's something alright but not my sister. She's mine. And you, dumb fuck, she's one of the reasons you're all here. This is Harper. Her brother is Reaper. You know, the president of your sister chapter in Bristol. The guy who had you sent here to protect her and the others. So, keep your hands off her or you'll lose them." He stepped back and released him. Harper was staring at Viper with her mouth hanging open. He turned and wrapped his arm around her. "Come with me, babe," he said to her. She went with him in what looked like a stunned silence.

Mayhem was apologizing to Terror and Savage. "I'm sorry. I didn't know she was claimed, or she was Reaper's sister. He's gonna kill me when he finds out. Even if we've never met her, everyone in the Punishers knows Reaper loves his little sister and would kill anyone who touches her. How in the hell did Viper get her and not die?"

Savage shrugged. "He and Reaper came to an understanding. So, keep clear. He wasn't kidding. He will kill you."

Mayhem nodded and threw up his hands. "Hands-off, I promise. Now I need another drink. Fuck!" He headed toward the coolers with Lash in tow. I looked at Ghost.

"Viper was ready to kill him for touching Harper. Wow."

Ghost stared at me. "Baby, I did the same thing, remember? You're mine and I protect what is mine. That is the two of you, you and the baby. Now come sit for a while. You've been on your feet long enough. And when the food is ready, I want you to be sure to eat. Do you think you'll need a dose of Zofran?" I shook my head.

"No, I feel okay. A little queasy but not enough to take medicine for it. I think the ginger tea helps."

We went and sat down. He insisted on staying with me. I leaned over to him. "I didn't think of it until Pope asked. Do you have a preference on what the baby is?"

"No. I just want a healthy baby. No matter what we have is perfect. And besides, I plan to knock you up a few times. We'll eventually have at least one of each. If not, we'll keep going until we do." I smacked him.

"I'm not having a basketball team so you can have both. You'd better hope we get them within no more than four tries. I don't want more than four kids. I may want less. Four sounds like a lot." He kissed me.

"Four sounds perfect. No basketball team I promise. I'll just have to be sure to get that vasectomy once we're done. Because as much as we practice, you'd be having that team and more." I gasped at him.

"You'd have a vasectomy when we're done having kids?"

"Of course, I would. It's a helluva lot easier to 'fix' a man than a woman. Less complications. I have no problem with it." We talked a little more about it. I was amazed. Most men felt like a vasectomy made them less of a man. Which was utter nonsense. We stopped discussing it when Harlow and Terror joined us. They asked how I was feeling. I reassured them. Everyone was so concerned about me. They would check in on me and offer to help with anything I needed or wanted. They were constantly refilling my water when they saw it was low or empty. Ghost had them well trained.

Tiny and Hawk were the ones to do the actual barbequing of the meat. Within an hour we were all sitting down to eat. They'd cooked a bunch of ribs last night and were warming them on the grill. In addition to the ribs, they had brisket, smoked sausage, and pulled pork. The Angel had prepared the standard side dishes to go along with a barbeque: baked beans, corn on the cob, potato salad, coleslaw and a variety of desserts. The ribs and pulled pork had sauces and the sausage spices so even though I loved those, I stuck to the brisket. The corn I could eat and rolls. Ice saw my meager plate.

"You're not eating much. You don't like this kind of food?"

"I love this kind of food, but spices and rich sauces don't agree with me. It makes my morning sickness flare big time. I don't want to lose my meal and have to take a shot. If it gets too bad, I'll have to get IV fluids and God forbid, a feeding tube." I probably told him more than he wanted to know. He sat frozen with his fork almost to his mouth. Several of the other newcomers had sat with us. They were staring at me too.

"Shit! That sounds terrible. Do all pregnant women go through this shit?" Lash asked.

"She has a condition called hyperemesis gravidarum. Its vomiting that can get out of control and cause her to get dehydrated and malnourished. She takes medicine for the nausea, but it doesn't always work so I give her shots when it's really bad. She's working really hard to keep her and our baby healthy," Ghost told them. Ice was nodding.

"Damn, women are so much tougher than we are. I'd be in a ball in the corner crying if I had to put up with that shit. Let me know if you need anything special while I'm here, darlin'. You're growing a little Warrior in there. We want all of them we can get, male or female." I gave him a smile and thanked him. They were all very sweet guys.

I finished over half my meal under not only Ghost's watchful eye, but the eyes of the newcomers. I was sitting there thinking about maybe trying to eat dessert. Maybe something simple. Saber came back to the table from the kitchen with a bowl of mixed fruit. That's what I'd get. He plopped the bowl down in front of me.

"Here, little momma, you should be able to keep the fruit down." I gave him a stunned smile and thank you. The fruit did taste good and for now wasn't causing any nausea. We stayed until I started to get tired. It wasn't that late, but my body said it was time to go. At nine we said our goodbyes and headed to the house. I groaned when I took off my high-heeled boots. Ghost frowned. "

"Why did you wear them if they hurt your feet?" I shrugged.

"Because they look sexy and I like the added height. All women wear shoes that hurt their feet because they know it turns guys on," I teased, and he growled.

"You don't have to do that to get me turned on, baby. All you have to do is breath. I've been fighting myself all night not to take you off somewhere and ravish you. How tired are you? Do you feel like you could stand to have me ravish that sexy body?" I moaned.

"Oh yes. Ravish away."

He toed off his boots and swung me up in his arms. He didn't head for the bedroom like I thought he would. He headed for the kitchen. As he passed the couch, he grabbed the throw I had over the back of it.

In the kitchen he sat me down by the table to spread the throw on the table. When he had it on there to his satisfaction, he turned to me. "Strip and get up on the table on your back with your legs spread." I began to strip off my clothes. He never looked away as I did. I secretly loved it when he got all commanding during sex. He was stripping his clothes off too. I went slow in order to tease him. He growled a time or two. Ghost was naked before I was. I saw him reach down and stroke his big, hard cock. He had pre-cum glistening on the head of it. God, did I want to taste him. I caught his eyes.

"Baby, please. Can I taste you first before I get on the table?"

He seemed to consider it then he nodded. He pushed his discarded clothes together, so I had something between my knees and the hard tile floor. I kneeled down and put my hand on his cock. It jerked. I licked the head swiping up all that salty, delicious cum. "Mm, you taste so good babe. I want more." I lowered my head and sucked him into my mouth. He threw back his head, moaned and grabbed my head. I let him control how fast he stroked me up and down his cock. It was like he was masturbating using my mouth. I sucked and licked. I could taste more of his cum. I hummed. He pumped in and out of my mouth several more times before pulling out.

"Now get on the table." He gave me his hand to help me stand. I sat on the edge of the table and laid back spreading my legs. He pulled up a chair. "Now it's time for my feast." Ghost went straight for my pussy without warning. He was sucking, licking and nibbling on my folds and clit like he was desperate. I moaned and raised my hips off the table. He slapped my hip and raised his head. "No, don't move your hips. Stay still." He went back to working me toward my first orgasm. I knew I'd have at least two tonight.

Then he thrust his fingers into my entrance. I screamed. God, that felt so good. I needed to come. He licked and sucked while he thrust in and out repeatedly. I could feel the tingling amassing in my belly. I came hard yelling. "Jesus, Talon, that feels so good. Don't stop." He kept it up until I was a wrung-out mess. He pulled out his fingers and stood licking them clean. He grabbed my hips and pulled me, so my ass was right at the edge of the table then he thrust his cock into my still sensitive pussy. I whimpered.

"Is this too much? Am I hurting you?" he growled.

"No, it's not too much or painful. I'm just sensitive. Please, don't stop, Talon. You feel so good inside of me." He kissed me and kept thrusting in and out. Each time it seemed like he went deeper. He was definitely going faster and harder. He was hitting my clit with his pubic bone. It only took me five minutes or so to come again. And I came hard and screaming. I'd barely finished catching my breath when he pulled out and picked me up off the table. He took me to our bedroom and laid me down on the bed. I watched as he got in his drawer and pulled out what looked a dildo with a smaller second protrusion.

"What is that?" He grinned.

"Let me show you, my beauty." He got on the bed and spread my legs. I felt him slide it down my folds and then it was slipped inside of my pussy. It felt fine but nothing like his cock. It was pushing a little on my asshole. Suddenly it began to vibrate. I cried out. That vibrating sent jolts of tingling through my core. He thrust it in and out a few times. Damn, it was making me ready to come again. I was lost in the feeling when on his next thrust he pushed the vibrating smaller protrusion inside my asshole. It wasn't as long as his finger had been, but it was a surprise. I moaned louder and longer.

"God, that feels amazing." He kept working it in and out of both of my holes. Then he lowered his head and started to lick and suck on my clit and folds. It was too much sensations all filling my body at once. I soon came yelling and quivering. He stopped his licking and sucking and slowly withdrew that magical toy. I wanted to be sure we kept that. "Baby, make sure you keep that toy. I'll want you to use that again," I rasped. Ghost laughed.

"Ah, so I guess my woman liked that a little bit. Well guess what? I liked it too. Stay on your back and put your hands above your head." I hurried to comply. He pulled a blindfold out of his drawer and slid it down over my eyes. It was pitch dark. I was anticipating what he would do next as he rummaged in his drawer again. Then I felt him touching my raised hands. Cloth wrapped around my wrists and they were pulled higher toward the headboard. I went to pull them down and found I couldn't move them. I was tied down!

I felt a bit of panic start in my gut. He was kissing me and sucking on my nipples. Usually that would have me panting and loving it. But I wasn't this time. All I could think about was being unable to get lose. I was defenseless. Anything could be done to me and I couldn't fight back. The panic was growing. I breathed through my nose trying to quell it. This was Ghost. He wouldn't hurt me. He'd slid down and then I felt the head of his cock at my entrance pushing inside of me and he began to thrust in and out. That was it! I couldn't fight it. The panic took over. I could hear myself screaming and fighting to get lose. I was sobbing and he was trying to calm me down and get the restraint off my wrists. When they were finally loose, he yanked off the blindfold. I curled up in a ball and cried. He hovered over me with an anguished look on his face.

"God, Wren, baby, I'm sorry. I didn't think. Fuck! I didn't mean to do this to you. Please, baby, stop crying. You're okay. It's me, Talon. Shit! Wren, please." I could hear the regret and panic in his voice. I knew he hadn't intentionally done it. He couldn't know it would trigger a flashback to the kidnapping and rapes. I knew this but couldn't get the words out past my sobs. I heard him in the distance talking. "Fuck, Ranger, I need Brielle. Wren and I were making love and I tied her hands. She fucking lost it. I think she had a flashback to the kidnapping and rapes. I can't get her to stop crying or talk to me. I need Bri. Thanks, man. Just come in, the door is unlocked."

He pulled on his pants and then got in bed to curl around me. He was whispering to me that I was safe, and he was sorry. He'd pulled the blanket up over us. A couple of minutes later, I heard Brielle's voice. "Ghost, why don't you go out and talk to Ranger. Let me talk to her. Please. I promise to come to get you soon." He must have agreed because I felt him move then heard the door click.

Her hand was stroking my hair. "Wren, honey I need you to stop crying. You're gonna make yourself sick, and this isn't good for the baby. You had a flashback, I assume. Honey, I've had them. Especially in those first few years. They come with no warning. Please, you need to talk about it. If not with me, then with Ghost. He's freaked out, Wren. You should have seen his face. He looked like he was about to die. He loves you so much. It's killing him that he caused it. He said it happened when he tied your hands. Why?" I sniffed. I'd stopped crying for a minute.

"I was fine when he put the blindfold on. But once he tied my hands and I realized they were tied to the headboard; I could feel the panic start. It just kept growing and then when he entered me, I lost it. They did that to me when they raped me, Bri. I knew on some level it wasn't them. It was him. He was giving me so much pleasure and all I could do was think about them. He must hate me and think I'm crazy. Ghost deserves someone better than me. One that won't freak out when he's making love to her." I was back to crying. It wouldn't stop again. She stayed with me and rocked me, but I couldn't make it stop. The images of those two men were flashing across my mind. I wanted to scream so the images would stop. It was then that I realized I was screaming out loud.

Ghost burst into the room. He ran to the bed and laid down beside me. "Baby, please you have to stop. I called Regan. She's coming. You need to calm down. You've been crying too long." I jerked away from him. The next thing I knew was I was sitting naked in the corner of the room with my knees drawn up and my arms wrapped around them. Ghost was standing there with tears welling up in his eyes. I couldn't see Brielle. My eyes darted to the door when Regan hurried in. She stopped to stare seeing me in the corner. She pulled her gaze away to look at Ghost.

"I called Dr. Hunter. He told me what was safe to give her. I need to give her this shot. She has to calm down or she could end up in the hospital." He nodded and crouched down in front of me.

"Beauty, I need to pick you up and put you on the bed. Please, don't fight. It's me, Talon. I won't hurt you, baby." He slowly slid his arm underneath me and picked me up. I could feel him cradling me to his chest and then I felt the soft sheets. I closed my eyes and I could feel when Regan jabbed the shot into my hip. I laid there with my eyes shut. I just wanted to disappear. I was mortified. I'd acted like a lunatic and Regan, Ranger, and Brielle and God knows who else, knew I'd freaked out while having sex with Ghost. I sobbed again. I could hear Regan speaking softly to Ghost.

"If she doesn't snap out of it soon, we'll need to call an ambulance. She may need professional help and drugs. If it doesn't cause her to panic, stay with her and talk to her. Let's give it a half hour and then we'll see. I'll be in the living room if you need me."

He slipped into bed and took me in his arms cautiously.

"Wren, baby, It's Talon. You're okay. You're safe. I won't let anything happen to you. Please don't cry. I need you to talk to me. Tell me what I did that triggered this. I never wanted to cause something like this."

I cleared my throat and took several shuddering breathes. I began to tell him in a whisper. I couldn't look at him as I told him about the rapes. Even though he already knew some of it. "You know about the kidnapping and then the rapes by two of the men you guys killed last year. What I didn't tell you was when I was kidnapped, they put a hood over my head and they tied my hands." He moaned.

"Shit!"

"After they put me in the cell, more than one guy tried to rape me. I told you that. I was always able to fight them off. So, when those two came for me, I fought like usual. I told you about them overpowering me and holding me down to rape me. But they didn't just hold me down, Talon. They tied my hands together and then tied me to the bars of the cell. I couldn't fight them then. They had a hard time getting me in that position, but they eventually did. Both times. They took their turns raping me and laughing about how helpless I was and how good I felt." He was shaking and muttering over and over.

"Fuck what did I do, what did I do? Sweet Jesus, I fucked up."

I rolled over and caressed his face. He looked at me. He had tears in his eyes again. I gave him a quick kiss.

"It's not your fault. I didn't tell you and you didn't know. I didn't know it would trigger me. I was fine with the blindfold. It was when you tied my hands and I couldn't get them loose or undone from the headboard that I panicked. I knew on some level it was you and I was alright, but I couldn't stop the panic from taking over. I'm so sorry. I never meant to hurt you. You deserve so much better than a woman you have to be careful of how you make love to her, so she doesn't freak out." I could feel myself fading. It must have been the shot.

The last thing I heard was Ghost saying, "I have the woman I deserve and want. I don't want anyone else."

Chapter 17: Ghost

Wren fell asleep in my arms. I held her and thought of the last hour. When she'd freaked out on me, my heart had almost stopped. I couldn't get the tie around her wrists undone fast enough. She'd been deathly pale and her eyes wild as she fought me. I was afraid she'd hurt herself. Then the crying started and she wouldn't stop. I'd called Ranger in a panic then Regan. When Bri came to talk to her and I was in the living room, I'd paced while I told Ranger what happened. I felt I could tell him since he was with Brielle and she'd been raped as well.

He was empathetic and said Brielle could be leery of some things they did in bed, but so far hadn't had a flashback or a panic attack. I hated to give her a shot, but she had to calm down before she hurt herself or the baby. She'd cried so much I knew she had to be dehydrated. I was thinking about getting her hooked up to an IV just for some hydration when Regan popped back in. She gave a sigh of relief. "Thank God she's asleep. Did she tell you what happened?" I nodded. "Good, that should help. Let her sleep and when she wakes up if she's still upset call me."

"Hey, Regan, will you get in my kit? It's in the bedroom next door. I want to hook her up to some fluids. She's cried so much I'm worried about her being dehydrated." She nodded and went to the next room. She was back quickly with an IV pole I had, a bag of 5% Dextrose in water, D5W, and an IV starter kit. She needed the glucose in it for the calories. Regan prepped her vein for me and inserted the cannula in the back of her left hand. She hooked her up and got the IV rolling at 40cc/hr. As soon as she woke up and could drink, I'd stop it. She never even moved while we did it. Regan told me goodbye and headed back home. I stayed there with her wrapped in my arms. I was thinking of what she told me. God, what a thing to have to live with and then I triggered it with our lovemaking.

I drifted off with her. It was at least a couple hours later when I felt her get restless and start crying out in her sleep. I whispered in her ear. "Shh you're safe. You're here with me, Talon. God, baby I love you and I'm so fucking sorry. Shh!" She seemed to settle back down. That was how the rest of the night went. She'd get restless and cry out and I'd talk to her and she'd settle down. By seven the next morning, I was tired. I'd napped on and off, but my mind never totally shut down. I was thinking of getting up to go to the bathroom when she jerked awake. She looked around confused and a little alarmed until she saw me then she relaxed.

"Good morning, baby. How do you feel?" She shrugged.

"Tired and I have a headache. Plus, I need to go to the bathroom," she croaked. I slid out of bed.

"Let me unhook you first." I undid her IV. For now, I'd leave in her hep-lock until I knew we didn't need to give her more fluids. She looked down at her hand in surprise.

“When did you put that in?” I helped her to the edge of the bed to dangle for a minute.

“Regan put it in after you fell asleep. I was busy holding you. You needed fluids after how much you were crying. I was afraid you’d become dehydrated. I’ll pull it as soon as you start drinking. Let’s get you to the bathroom. Would you like to take a shower?”

She groaned. “That would be great.”

I helped her to the bathroom, and she did her business. While she was doing that, I got the shower started. She’d slept nude so she jumped in the shower as soon as the water was warm. I remained outside. She looked out at me. “Aren’t you going to join me?”

“I didn’t know if you would want me to or not. If you’re sure, then yes, I’d love to join you.” She nodded so I got in and started to help her wash her hair and then wash her beautiful body. I made sure to keep my touch impersonal. She was quiet. When we got out, she headed to the bedroom with her head hanging down. She was avoiding looking at me now. “What’s wrong, babe?” She looked up and I saw tears in her eyes.

“You can’t even touch me now. I ruined it. I ruined us by freaking out like a cry baby.” I pulled her to me.

“You didn’t ruin anything. I don’t want to do anything to make you feel threatened. Of course, I want to touch you. I always want to touch you.” She was hugging me. I rocked her in my arms. “I know I’ve already said it, but I’m so sorry, Wren. I didn’t think. Shit, I promise never to blindfold or tie you up again.”

She pulled back shaking her head. "No, don't say that. The blindfolding was fine. It was the two together. If you tied me so I could see you, then I think I'd be fine." I shook my head.

"There's no need to tie you. Yeah, I find it fun but not something I need. We'll find lots of other ways to play," I reassured her. She kept frowning but didn't argue. We got dressed then we went to the kitchen so I could make breakfast. She ate but not as much as I'd like. She seemed to be drinking fine, so I took out the hep-lock after breakfast.

My phone rang. It was Regan asking how Wren was doing. I told her fine. I'd barely hung up and Brielle called to ask the same. When I got off the phone with her, Wren was shaking her head frowning. "What baby?" She sighed.

"Now the whole compound probably knows I freaked out when we were having sex. How can I show my face again?" I protested.

"No, the only ones who know outside of you and me are Ranger, Bri, and Regan and maybe Steel and Hammer. They won't tell anyone. And I promise you none of them will think any differently about you. Shit, Wren. You were raped. Of course, you had to have a flashback sometime. I'm just sorry I caused it." She came over and hugged me.

"You didn't cause it. You triggered it accidently. You didn't do it on purpose. If I have to go see everyone and not worry their talking about me, then you have to stop blaming yourself. Deal?" I gave her a kiss.

"Deal." We decided to take a walk around the compound first before heading to the clubhouse. She'd been taking walks to be sure she stayed fit. Sometimes she did light weights in our gym at the clubhouse. She used to run but not since she got pregnant. It made the nausea worse. Today was another unusually warm February day. We walked around for about a half hour then headed inside. In the common room, it was still a little light on people.

Several of our guests and single brothers must have partied into the night. Regan, Hammer, Steel, Bri, and Ranger were there along with most of the other married couples. The five of them greeted her like they normally would which I could see made her relax. She'd been afraid they'd treat her differently. We were all sitting drinking coffee or in Wren's case, tea, when Viper and Harper came in. I could tell something had changed. He was holding onto her and she wasn't pulling away. Before he would stick close but never really get handsy with her. Hmm, I guess last night had been a turning point for the both of them. Wren looked at me and raised her eyebrows. I shrugged.

The rest of the day was spent relaxing, getting to know our newcomers and just talking. We had our appointment tomorrow with Dr. Hunter. I wanted him to check her labs to see how she was doing. She ended up vomiting a couple times throughout the day but not anything so severe she needed a shot. I had her go take a nap in the middle of the day. She protested but ended up sleeping for two hours. That evening after dinner, we watched a little television and then went to bed. I was glad the aftermath hadn't been a big lingering one.

I hoped to never trigger her again though I knew it was likely she would have them at some point.

The next morning, we were on our way to see Dr. Hunter. Me, Devil, Rebel, and Ace were the guards. When we pulled into the parking lot, Rebel and Ace went inside first to check it out. They came back out a few minutes later and nodded. Devil and I took her inside. I knew Rebel and Ace would station themselves at the front and back door of the doctor's office. For it being early in the day, the waiting room was full. The women waiting inside kept throwing glances at me and Devil Dog. Some of them were looking a little frightened, but most were throwing us curious or even interested looks. I ignored them. Devil seemed to be doing the same.

We weren't there long before a nurse called us in the back. She looked flustered when Devil came with us. He'd stand outside the door of the exam room with his arms crossed across his chest. She got Wren's weight, vitals and took some blood and then set us up in the exam room. She took her seat on the exam table while I took the extra chair. About fifteen minutes later Dr. Hunter came breezing in the room. "How are you doing Wren? It looks like you're better than when Regan called the other night. Tell me, what happened?" She hesitantly told him she had a flashback and had gone into a panic attack and couldn't stop crying. He was nodding. "I assume it's because of the kidnapping and rape last year." She nodded. "Alright, I'd like to not give you anything for that unless we find you having more attacks and on a semi-regular basis. The fewer medications you take the better for the baby, even if their considered safe. How many times have you had to give her Zofran IM?" he asked me.

"One day I had to give it to her twice. The rest of the time the pills and ginger tea seem to be helping." He seemed to approve.

"I want to add more vitamin B6. It can help sometimes as well."

He examined her and used a doppler to listen to the baby's heartbeat. "Everything sounds good. You've gained a couple of pounds but those were ones you had already lost. You need to try and gain the other three you lost and a couple more on top of it. A healthy pregnancy should gain around twenty-five pounds. You need to gain thirty to make up for the five you lost. None of this worrying about gaining weight. You need it for the baby. I should have your labs results in a day or two. I'll have my nurse call with the results even if they're all normal. I know your man here will be anxiously waiting to know every single value. Unless you have questions, I think we're good. Keep up the good work." We told him we had no questions and bid him goodbye.

Outside Devil stood against the wall. I found it curious Dr. Hunter never mentioned our guard. Maybe he was used to the Warriors being overprotective of our women. We stopped at the desk to get her prescription for the B6 and to make sure our next few appointments were still on the books. Outside Rebel was waiting. He sent a text when he saw us, and Ace came around the building a minute later. We headed out. Since we'd wanted to be able to have fasting bloodwork, we stopped at the Fallen Angel to eat breakfast before heading back home. Rebel and Ace were looking around in interest. Our waitress came to take our order. I saw Rebel eyeing her and her eyeing him.

I saw a hook up in the future. Hopefully he told her up front it was just that and he was here for a short time only.

Wren ordered fruit, dry toast, an egg, and bacon. We all ordered the huge ultimate breakfasts. She sat eating hers and shaking her head. “Why are you shaking your head, babe?” She smiled.

“It’s like watching a swarm of locust seeing you all eat. I don’t know where you put it all and how you don’t weigh five hundred pounds.” Rebel grinned.

“I work mine off with plenty of sex. And what about you, woman, how can you survive on that puny amount of food?” He spent the next five minutes teasing her about how little she was and that she needed to eat more because she was growing a Warrior. Ace, Devil, and I just laughed watching them argue.

When we were done, we headed back to the compound. I was going to work on the bike we were building. Wren was going to rest and then work some more on the wedding. I got her settled in before I headed to the garage. Several of the new guys were there checking out the bike. Mayhem, Lash, Tiger, Falcon, Saber, and Ice were expressing their appreciation. This bike was for a guy out in California. Our reputation as custom bike builder company was growing. We had to turn shit away. We were telling them about it when Tiger and Falcon spoke up.

“Well, if you need any help, let us know. We’ve got experience in building our own bikes and some others.” Hearing this, we went outside to check out their rides. They were beautiful and well done. Blaze looked at them appraisingly. He was our main builder.

"You did all this yourselves?" They nodded. "Well, we just might be able to use you. Fucking nice work."

Back in the garage, we kept talking while we worked.

Mayhem spoke up. "We saw you ride out this morning with some of the others and your old lady. She okay?" I nodded.

"Yeah, she had to see the doctor. Since she has this vomiting condition, she has to see him every two weeks not monthly. Her appointment was this morning." He nodded.

"Yeah, one of our brothers' old ladies had some vomiting when she was pregnant. Not like yours but still it sucked. Honestly, I was surprised to see how many of you were married and had kids around here. Shit, you've been busy the last couple of years it seems." Blaze laughed.

"You could say that. Once Terror met Harlow, it all snowballed from there. You have to be careful drinking the water around here otherwise you'll find yourself committed and your woman pregnant. The only ones not to knock up their old ladies right away were Tiny and Viking. Tiny had been our sole committed brother for ten years before they had Sam. They were high school sweethearts. Viking had to work for a while on his old lady and they're young, so they were together a year or more before Saxon came along."

They chatted for a while longer before they headed out a little while later. A couple of them were going to go pick up Janessa, Regan, Harper, and Alannah from work at the hospital. Harlow and Sherry were at the spa so I knew some of the guys would be there today. Brielle was at the daycare. The four guards had started today. On Sunday, Wren had sent notices out to the parents of the six other children we had at the daycare informing them of the new drop off and pick up procedure and to let them know we were adding security as well. She couched it as something we'd been planning all along so as not to alarm them. I was waiting to hear how it went today.

I took a break around two o'clock and went to check on Wren. She was up working on her laptop. She smiled when she saw me come through the door. She got up to give me a hug and kiss. "How are you feeling, babe? Did you eat any lunch?" She gave me a look.

"I feel fine and I ate a little, but I know not enough to satisfy you. Can I get you anything?" I shook my head.

"I'm just going to grab a sandwich. How's the wedding planning coming along?" We spent the next fifteen minutes while I ate talking about the wedding. It was now just over a month away. I gave her a kiss to head back to the garage. I told her I'd be home at six. I knew she'd want to have dinner ready even though I always told her I'd do it or help. She would tell me she had to do something all day besides sit on her ass.

The rest of the day went by quickly. Before I knew it, it was six and time to go home. Blaze and I had just finished off the main work we'd planned for the day. Even though we could work all the time, we made sure to balance work and our own down time. Even if he didn't have an old lady, he liked to relax. At home, I walked into the house smelling wonderful. She had a beef roast in the oven and twice baked potatoes. A salad stood on the counter and she was stirring green beans with bacon in them on the stove. I hugged her and kissed her neck. "Everything smells great, babe. Let me get cleaned up." She nodded

"Everything will be done in about ten minutes, honey."

That gave me time to take a quick shower. Ten minutes later I was freshly showered, sitting at the table dishing up dinner. We settled into eating. Everything tasted as good as it had smelled. "Sweetheart, this tastes great. Damn, I sure found me the best woman." She laughed. I kept an eye on what she was eating without being too obvious about it. She did eat a slice of the roast, most of her potato and a small amount of salad and green beans. She drank milk with her meal. I had to be satisfied with that. I insisted on cleaning up the dishes and put away the leftovers for lunch tomorrow.

We settled down on the couch and went over some of the websites she had been looking at for furniture. In addition to the wedding, I'd told her to find what she liked to get to furnish the house. It would be done hopefully in a month and a half. She was showing me living room furniture. Who would have thought a year ago I'd be so domesticated? Around ten o'clock we headed to the bedroom. She took her shower while I watched a bike show on television. She came out all fresh and naked from her bath fifteen minutes later. I wanted to groan. God, she was so sexy. I wanted to consume her. But I was hesitant to do anything since she'd just had such a trauma two nights ago. So, I pulled her into my arms and gave her a kiss but nothing else. She laid there for a little while and then sat up.

"Why won't you make love to me, Talon? Is it because of the other night? Have I turned you off because of that?" I gave her a shocked look.

"No, baby, I'm not turned off. I just don't want to push you before you've had time to recover." She leaned over me and began to kiss me.

"I'm fine. I want to make love with my man. Now." She didn't have to tell me twice. I had her under me and was caressing, licking, sucking, and nipping all over her body. We played with each other for a good half hour. By the time we were done, I'd gotten her off twice and couldn't wait any longer. I laid on my back.

"Climb on top and ride me, Wren. Ride me hard," I growled. She didn't hesitate. She climbed on top of me taking my cock deep in one long stroke. Then she proceeded to ride me slow until I was begging her to let me come. "God, a baby, I need to come. Harder. Make me come, beauty." Only then did she speed up and slam down on me harder. I soon came roaring out my release as she cried out with hers. When we both came down from the high, she collapsed on top of me.

"I can't move, Talon. I'm nothing but jelly now. We'll have to sleep like this," she teased. I laughed. After I softened and pulled out, I got up to get a washcloth to clean her up. We fell asleep soon after wrapped together.

Chapter 18: Wren

Things were moving along with planning the wedding and getting things ordered for furnishing our house. I couldn't believe how things were going in my life. I had a man who loved, me, was marrying me soon, building us a house, and expecting a baby. Things were crazy but in a good way.

I was at the daycare today. It was Thursday and three days after my visit to the doctor. All my labs had come back good and my nausea seemed to be okay. Ghost didn't want me to work, but I wanted to see how things were going and spend some time with the kids. I went after lunch and planned to stay until the end of the day. He hadn't liked it, but he'd grudgingly agreed. Him and Blaze had taken me there. Today, Tyler, Finn, Pope, and Knight were on guard duty at the daycare. They saluted us when we rolled through the gate. Ghost gave me a hard kiss before telling me to be ready to go at six on the dot.

Inside everyone was working. Bri was here again as well as Trish. The other three workers were busy. Monica, Ashley, and Paige were great choices. I was happy we'd hired them. The afternoon flew by. I had fun playing with the kids. And I got some paperwork that I needed to do done. Two of the guys stood outside the gate and the other two roamed the perimeter inside the walls. The kids were fascinated with them. I had to say, the guys were all good with the kids. They'd push them on the swings or help them build things in the sand. But they always stayed alert and constantly were looking around. The last kid was picked up at five forty-five. I was about to text Ghost I was done, and the guys would bring me back with Bri and Trish, when I heard Tyler swear. He yelled for us to get back inside the daycare.

We ran back inside with the babies and stood huddled together looking out the window toward the front gate. Through the gate I could see several bikes. They weren't ours. They were swarming around, and I heard shots fired. Trish screamed. Bri was texting like mad on her phone. I knew she had to be texting the compound telling them what had happened. I did the same sending it to Ghost though they might have heard the shots. Luckily, the guys had made it inside the gate and had it shut before the other bikers had gotten to them. The gate was set up like the one at the compound. The open sections had bulletproof glass. So, you could look out but be safe. I heard Finn I think yell and the guys all scattered. Then the building was rocked by an explosion. We were all thrown down on the floor. The explosion had caused all of us to scream. Trish and Bri were holding Saxon and Gabriel who were crying from the noise and our screams. We were trying to get them to settle down.

Then I heard the roar of more motorcycles. I got up and peeked out the window. The ones outside the gate took off with a pack of Warriors in pursuit. From what I could see, there appeared to be six of the bad guys with eight Warriors chasing them. More gun shots were heard. Five more Warriors pulled through the gate once Pope opened it. I saw Ghost, Viking, and Ranger running toward the building. I'd turned to tell the others they were here when they came crashing through the door. When Viking reached Trish, he ran his hands all over Trish and Saxon while Ranger did the same to Bri and Gabriel. Ghost had me in his arms and he was shaking.

"Fuck, baby, are you alright?" I nodded. I was shaking myself. He was rubbing my back. I pulled back.

"What was that explosion?"

Tyler answered from the doorway. "It was a grenade. They threw one over the wall!"

I flinched. Suddenly, my gut clinched. I tore out of Ghost's arms and ran to the bathroom. I threw up my lunch and then some. He was holding my hair back and rubbing my back. I spit and stood up. He handed me a glass with water and mouthwash in it. I'd taken to keeping it there as well since I never knew where I might vomit. I rinsed out my mouth. He helped me back to the front.

"We're gonna take you home. Let's get in the car." Luckily the SUV had seating for seven because with Finn driving, three women and two car seats we made for a full load. The guys on their bikes surrounded us as we left. Within five minutes, we were at the compound and being hustled inside. Terror was pacing when we came inside. He raced over.

"What in the fuck happened?" Pope, Finn, Tyler, and Knight explained. Him and all the guys were swearing. Looking around it appeared the eight to chase after the group had been Mayhem, Lash, Savage, Menace, Viper, Tiny, Razor, and Hawk. I could see Janessa, Sherry, and Alannah pacing with worried looks on their faces. Who could blame them? Their husbands had gone after a bunch of guys with guns and it seemed grenades. A half an hour later, Terror got a call. He pulled the guys aside and a few more headed out. He reassured the women everyone was okay but said nothing else. I watched as the others left with the van.

Ghost was trying to get me to go to the house and rest. I refused. Not until all the guys were back safe. My stomach continued to churn but I didn't tell him that. He was already worried enough after the explosion and me vomiting at the daycare. It was maybe an hour or so later when bikes pulled back into the compound. The van, Hawk, Mayhem and Lash were not with them. I felt panic. It must have shown on my face because Ghost hugged me. "Wren, they're okay. They just had to do some cleanup. I promise." The others came inside. They were looking pissed. It was going on eight=fifteen before the rest pulled into the compound. The other ladies had made a quick dinner for everyone. I couldn't eat.

When they got inside, Terror called for church. I stayed in the common room with the ladies. Regan came over. "Now that they're all back safe, you need to eat."

"Regan, I'm so nauseated, I don't think it'll stay down."

She frowned. "Try." I gave her a nod. She fixed me dry toast, tea, applesauce, and an egg. It would more likely settle on my stomach than the pasta they'd made. She was explaining the BRAT diet to me. It consisted of bananas, rice, applesauce, and toast. It was bland and recommended for someone like me. I was happy to find the food seemed to be staying down after I ate it.

An hour later the guys came out of church looking weary. The ones who hadn't eaten wolfed down dinner. Ghost hustled me to the house. He was frowning. Once we were inside, I asked him.

"Was it the Bastards and Savages?"

He hesitated then nodded. "Yeah, a couple of them and some others they must have recruited to help." I hugged him.

"Did they get them?" He just nodded. I knew he wouldn't tell me more. I read between the lines. They'd killed them. I didn't feel a bit of remorse. What if all the kids had still been there and out in the yard? I shuddered to think what could have happened. He felt my shudder and pulled me down the hall. He had me take a bath and then when I got in bed, he massaged my back and shoulders. I fell asleep with him rubbing me. It was a very restless night. I woke up several times thinking about what could have happened.

The next couple of days were tense. Everyone was on high alert. They'd increased security at the farm. Smoke added cameras to be watched by one of the guys on guard duty at the daycare. They were placed two miles before the entrance to the drive into the farm. One in each direction. Any strange bikes or vehicles would be treated as suspect and the daycare locked down. Everyone was stopped from going to the restaurant or spa to help out. The only ones allowed to go to work were Regan, Janessa, Harper, and Alannah. They couldn't just call off indefinitely. They had four guys posted outside the hospital at all times. The tension had made my nausea flare and I was vomiting more. Ghost was worried but I convinced him I didn't need to see Dr. Hunter or need any shots. When he wasn't hovering protectively over me, he was making love to me almost desperately. He acted like I was going to disappear or something.

Today was Sunday. Everyone was off of work and trying to relax at the compound. Rowan was reading to Mayhem and Lash. They had such stunned expressions on their faces. She was pretty amazing and super smart for her age. At four she could read at a second-grade level. I'd helped Bri to develop some activities that would keep her active mind busy. Ghost was playing a game of pool with Ranger. Finn, Hawk, Ice, and Saber were playing darts. Some of the others were playing cards. I was sitting with the old ladies taking care of the babies and going over wedding plans. They'd had their fittings before everything went crazy. The guys had done theirs as well. The food would be done by the Fallen Angel with help from the ladies. Alannah was making the cake. All the decorations were bought. We were making the centerpieces together. The teepee was on order. I think everything was on point to come together.

Ghost had called Bull to ask him to give me away. It was the tradition now for those without a father to have Bull, Harlow's dad, be the father of the bride. He had happily agreed. My dad had died when I was eight and my mom had evaporated as soon as I turned eighteen. No loss. She hadn't been much of a mother anyway. My dad had been the one to really raise me, not her. Both of my parents had been only children. Ghost had some cousins back in Arizona, but he wasn't close to any of them. I was showing the girls how I was going to do my hair for the ceremony. Ghost came over to check on us. I hid the picture.

"What are you hiding, babe?" He teased.

"None of your business. You go back to playing and leave me to my secrets." He just laughed. After kissing me and making sure I wasn't tired or needing anything, he went back to his game. Brielle was laughing.

"I swear I thought Ranger was protective. Ghost beats him. Do you ever piss without him knowing about it and making sure you're alright?" I grinned.

"No. He's determined, me and this baby will be healthy. I guess his mom had a couple miscarriages before him and a few after. He worries about it." They nodded their understanding. It had come up one night when I'd called him out on being so protective. That's when he told me about his mom.

That evening we made homemade pizza for the crew and watched movies. The newbies got introduced to cartoon movies with Rowan. She insisted they had to watch *Brave*. They'd all moaned but I noticed every one of them remained totally focused on the movie until the end. When it was over Ranger and Bri took her and Gabriel home. Then the guys put in an action movie, *13 Hours: The Secret Soldiers of Benghazi*. It was based on a book about true events when militants attacked an American diplomatic compound in Benghazi, Libya on September 11, 2012. Six security team members had held them off. I had to admit I even enjoyed it. Of course, the guys like Terror, Menace, Savage, Viper, Ghost, Devil Dog,

Pope, Knight, Mayhem, and Lash who'd served had added lots of commentary. Harlow had added to it as well since she'd been a Marine sniper.

When the new guys heard she'd been a sniper, they were floored. They looked at her in awe. She seemed not to pay attention. Saber looked at Terror. "Man, you'd better never fuck up. She can take you out from a mile away and you'd never know it was coming." Terror laughed and agreed. He didn't look scared. From what I'd heard he'd been a Delta guy along with Ranger and Menace. They were bad-asses. It wasn't long after the movie ended that Ghost and I headed home and to bed.

It was the following Tuesday and I had convinced Ghost to let me go to the daycare again. He'd been reluctant but gave in only when I agreed to let him come with me. It was going on three o'clock when he got a call. He told us to lock down the building. Luckily no one was outside playing since it was a colder day. We got the kids and the staff all in the central room. I watched from the front lobby as he went outside. I wanted to see what was going on. He headed over to the front gate where a car was pulling up. Dan Peters got out of it. He seemed to be yelling and waving his hand around. I could see something in his hand but from this distance I couldn't make out what it was. Out of nowhere one of the guys tackled him to the ground. They scuffled around on the ground for a minute, then I saw Finn sit upright on top of Dan. Ghost, Finn, and Torch got him up and in his car. They drove off with Dan. Ace came inside to tell me everything was okay, and that Ghost would be back. He wouldn't say anything else. I fretted as I waited.

Chapter 19: Ghost

Torch and Finn sat in the backseat with Peters while I drove his car to the compound. I was fighting to contain my rage. How dare he come to a fucking daycare waving a gun and ranting? He'd been screaming about killing that red-haired whore who'd ruined him. He went on to say his usual shit about the Warriors blackballing him, so his business was ruined. Though he had added a new offense this time. He was blaming Wren for his wife leaving him and taking his daughter. The whole time he was yelling all this, he was waving around his handgun. He never took his eyes off me and that was his mistake. He didn't see Finn sneaking up on him until he tackled him to the ground.

Dan was still ranting in the backseat. He'd been disheveled even before he was taken down to the ground. When he'd gotten out of the car, his shirt was wrinkled and stained. His hair looked like it hadn't been washed or combed for days. A scruffy beard was coming in on his face. His eyes had been wild. Nick was at the gate and didn't open it until Finn hung out the car window and told him it was us. Once inside, I drove straight back to the Hole. The Hole was a building we kept at the very back of the compound. We used it to hold people and conduct interrogations when needed. It also had been the last place some people ever saw. We did and would always rid ourselves and the world of dangerous people. Sometimes the law wasn't the way to go. Finn and Torch wrestled him out of the backseat and into the building where they locked him in one of the cells. We'd let him stew for a bit while we decided what to do with him. He was screaming as we left. Torch would remain outside on guard duty. I needed to tell Terror what happened then get back to the daycare to Wren. I knew she had to be worried to death.

Back at the clubhouse I sent Rebel and Saber to the daycare. I didn't want them to be down on guards for long. After that was taken care of, I filled Terror and Savage in on what had just happened. They were shaking their heads and muttering. Terror came to a decision.

"We'll wait until everyone is done with their workday and back here. Then we'll have church to decide what we do. I know what you'd like to do, Ghost. Can't say I blame you. My damn kid was there as well as all the other Warrior kids. On top of it for those others to be there and in danger is unacceptable. I'm glad our new measures worked. Go back and bring them home soon."

I slapped him on the shoulder and headed out. I'd ridden in the SUV this morning and it was still at the daycare, so I took my bike. The guys motioned me through the gate. I had barely parked when Wren came running out to me. She wrapped her arms around me and was crying. I hugged her and whispered in her ear, "Baby, I'm fine. No one got hurt. Our new safety measures worked. Please calm down before you get sick." She nodded and sniffed. After a minute or two she stepped back so I could get off my bike.

"What did Dan want? I could see him yelling and waving his hand holding something. Why did he come here? Hannah doesn't go here anymore." I led her to the playground. They still had all the kids inside. I sat her down on one of the benches.

"He came here ranting about you, Wren. He had a gun and was threatening to kill you." She gasped and went pale. I didn't want to tell her this, but she needed to know for her own safety. "He still thinks his business failed because we were blackballing it after he touched you at the party. And he said his wife and daughter had left him." She got a satisfied look on her face.

"So, Cassie did leave him. She told me a couple weeks ago when I ran into her that she was going to do it when he was in Nashville on business. Apparently, he has been insufferable, and she mentioned he had cheated on her. I guess she finally got fed up."

"Well, I can see how that might push him over the edge. Now let's get the day finished and the other kids off with their parents so we can go home. When everyone gets back to the compound tonight, we'll be having church. You can stay and rest at the house if you want. If you don't, then at least rest on the couch at the clubhouse. You've been up on your feet a lot today." She shook her head.

"You worry too much. And why would you need to have church tonight?" I hesitated.

"We need to decide what to do with Peters. I couldn't just let him loose after he came here waving a gun. That's all I can say. Don't worry about him." I could tell she wanted to ask more but she didn't.

The last couple of hours passed quickly. By five-thirty all the kids had been picked up. The other old ladies and the Warrior kids were bundled into the SUVs and cars so they could be taken back to the compound. A thought flittered through my mind. With the way we were growing in women and kids, we'd need a minibus soon. I'd have to mention that to the others. We were back and unloaded in no time. As I expected, Wren wanted to stay at the clubhouse. I got her seated on one of the couches with her feet up and her flavored water refilled. I sat with her rubbing her feet until it was time for church. Some of the single guys were razzing me about being pussy whipped. I grinned. If taking care of my woman and baby was pussy whipped, then I guess I was. The married guys just smiled and never said a word. They knew what was going on.

Finally, everyone was back from work, and we went into church. Terror called the meeting to order. "Okay, settle down. I know we don't usually have church on Tuesday, but there was an incident at the daycare today." This got all of their attention. "Ghost, how about you tell the guys what happened."

I stood up and filled them in on Peters. All the married guys were sitting there with pissed expressions on their faces. Their kids had been there as well as some of their wives. "We need to decide what we're going to do with him. He's gone around the bend. I don't think he can be trusted to leave Wren or us alone even if we beat him within an inch of his life," I told them.

Hammer cleared his throat. "I agree. We just heard

today that his business has gone completely under. He's bankrupt and clients are clamoring to get advances back from him. He doesn't have the money. Apparently, he's been charging for premium building supplies but using substandard, cheap shit and pocketing the difference. Someone's whole bathroom floor on the second story gave way because the flooring had been made with cheap materials and without all the necessary supports. We don't even know how he was passing inspections."

Savage groaned. "No wonder he went over the edge. This and his wife. I agree with Ghost. I don't think he'll stop. So, the question is, what do we do with him? Do we beat him almost to death and hope he stops? Get the police involved and hopefully he gets some jail time. Or do we kill him and bury him deep?" None of us ever wanted to jump automatically to killing someone. But there had been several times we had done it in self-defense and to protect our families. We spent the next half hour debating. Finally, Terror called us for a vote.

"Let's vote on this. Who is in favor of us beating the hell out of him and then seeing how he acts? If he's still ranting and making threats when we're done, we know he's not going to stop, and we'll end him. All in favor say aye." Terror went around the table. I could tell a few wanted to just end his ass like me, but we all voted to try this avenue. Once the motion passed, Terror said we should go eat dinner and then meet at nine at the Hole to dispense justice. It was agreed the men with kids at the daycare would be the ones to dole out the beating. Some of the single guys groaned because they wanted to get their hands on his ass too.

Back in the common room, you could tell all the

women had been brought up to speed on Peters coming to the daycare. There was a lot of pissed off women. Harlow marched over to Terror.

"You don't have to confirm or deny you have him in the Hole. Just make sure if you don't kill his fucking ass, you beat him as close to death as you can get. I personally say plant his ass. Let me know if you need me to shoot him between the eyes or not." She turned around and went back to the women who were all nodding in agreement, even Wren. None of us were surprised Harlow would say something like that. The newcomers were. They stood there staring at her in shock and awe.

Mayhem spoke up, "Where can I get one like that?" Terror laughed.

"You'd have to patch over to the Warriors in Dublin Falls, man. They only seem to be here." Mayhem nodded.

"I may just have to think about that. Damn."

The women hadn't been sitting around while we were in church. They'd been cooking dinner for all of us. Well, I guess Ms. Marie had started it earlier in the day and they helped to finish it. There was a huge vat of chili on the stove, toppings were set out for it including onions, cheese, sour cream, cilantro, tortilla strips, and avocado. A huge pan of corn bread sat beside it. And there was even dessert. A several layered chocolate cakes covered in chocolate icing and fruit plus a couple of peach pies. We all sat down to eat. The newbies were groaning.

"Man do they cook like this all the time?"

"Not every night but at least once or twice a week, usually," Savage told them with a grin.

"That's it, I'm patching over for sure." The rest of us laughed.

Wren sat down beside me with a small bowl of the chili and a piece of the corn bread. "Baby, is that gonna settle on your stomach. It's spicy," I warned her. I'd taken a bite already. She smiled.

"Ms. Marie made me some without the cayenne and onions so hopefully that will keep me from getting sick. It smells so good and I'm tired of eating bland shit." I laughed. We both dug in. She ended up eating at least three quarters of it, a piece of corn bread and a small slice of the chocolate cake. For right now it looked like it was going to stay down. Amen. She was nine weeks along and we were praying after week twelve she'd be over the nausea and vomiting. She still usually vomited once a day and it was typically first thing in the morning.

After dinner was over and the mess cleared, I took her to the house. We sat and watched part of a television show and then she went to take her bath. As she was in the tub, I told her I had to go out for a bit but would be back. She stopped washing and looked at me.

"You're going to take care of Dan, aren't you?" I didn't say anything. She sighed. "Fine. I know you are. Just make sure whatever you do, he doesn't ever do this again to me or anyone else. You understand?" Shit, she was telling me to kill him. I nodded. She seemed to relax. I helped her wash and then got her into bed. I hated to leave her sexy body. I kissed her.

"Take a nap because when I get back, I intend to ravish that sexy body of yours." She laughed and promised to rest up.

Out at the Hole we all gathered outside. We wanted to enter as a huge force to scare his ass even more. When everyone was there, we stomped inside with glares and hard looks on our faces. Dan was slumped down on the floor in the corner of his cell. He looked up when we started to file in. His eyes got bigger and bigger as more guys came in to stand silent outside his cell. They all stared at him with grim expressions on their faces. Savage and I opened his cell door and dragged him out. We tied him to the chair in the center of the main room. The chair sat on heavy duty plastic. I saw him eyeing it. Terror walked up to him first.

"Do you remember who I am?" Dan shrugged like he didn't care. He was scared, I could tell, but he was trying to act all bad ass. Terror got closer. "I'm Terror and I'm the president of this chapter of the Warriors and father to one of the children in the daycare you decided to wave a fucking gun outside of today! See this group over there?" He pointed to those of us who had children and wives at the daycare. We'd separated ourselves from the others. He looked at the eight of us plus Terror. "All of them had their children and some of their wives in that building." Terror stepped back and I stepped forward. Dan threw me a look of hate.

"You fucking threatened to kill my woman. My woman who is pregnant. So, you threatened not only her but my kid! Over what? Your damn stupid conviction we're blackballing your company. We didn't do or say a thing about your fucking company. You sank that all on your own. And your wife left because she was fed up with your shit. You've been in the wrong since the day you grabbed my old lady at Rowan's birthday party, yet you persist in getting in our faces and now making threats. What do you have to say about that?" I asked him, since I could see the rage bubbling up in his face getting ready to blow. I wanted him to rant and rave. The more he did the more likely we'd be planting his ass not just kicking it. His face was beet red.

"I know you ruined me on purpose! All because I touched that red-haired whore. She was asking for it. She shook her ass at me and flirted. But as soon as she thought she was caught, she acted like I'd touched her against her will. She's a no-good whore. Everyone knows you guys share women, so what difference would it have made if I got a little of what she was offering?"

I punched him in the mouth. Blood flew. "We don't fucking share our old ladies, you dumbfuck. She didn't offer you shit. You just thought you'd take what wasn't yours. Maybe that's worked in the past for you but not anymore." He laughed.

"Oh yeah, what're you gonna do about it? Beat the hell out of me and tell me to stay away. Well, you can try. But if I ever catch her out alone, I'll teach that bitch a lesson. Women are here to serve men. I'll have her down on her knees sucking my cock like she should be. I bet she's got a tight little pussy and ass. Have you tried that ass yet?"

I lost it. He was threatening to rape Wren. She'd already lived through that hell once. I roared and started to beat the hell out of him. The guys let me go at him for a few minutes and then they pulled me back. It took more than a few to get me off him. The fucker was bleeding and still laughing. He was crazy. Terror grabbed my shoulder.

"Take a break, brother, and let the others beat on him some. I promise, you'll get the satisfaction of ending his ass. He needs to be put down like a rabid dog."

I nodded and watched as the other systematically beat him almost to death. Every one of them got in their punches. When they were done, he had his head hanging down, moaning, his eyes almost completely swollen shut, his face unrecognizable, with cuts and blood all over his body. They'd ended up cutting off his clothes, so all he was wearing were his shoes. I walked over and lifted his head back by his hair, so he'd have to look at me. He glared at me through the slits of his eyes.

"Do you have anything else to say, fucker?"

He spit at me and laughed saying, "She'll feel so good."

I dropped his head and went over to the guys. Terror waved for us all to come outside. We followed him.

"Okay, I don't think I need to ask but to be sure, who is for us killing this psycho and getting this shit over with?" Every one of them raised their hands. Peters would never stop going after Wren or us. Terror nodded. "It's official. Ghost, you get to end him since it's your old lady he's threatening. You decide how he goes out."

I gave him a grim look and nod. Back inside I headed over to Peters. I crouched down so he could see me.

"Guess what, psycho? You've earned a one-way ticket to hell. Now, I get to decide how we send you there.

There are so many options. For pieces of shit like you, the options are even better. You know, we once had a human trafficking bastard in here. We shoved a hot branding iron up his ass. Another one was a raping asshole we cut the cock off of. Some we've cut their throats or shot them between the eyes. But for you, since you seem so intent on being a rapist, I think you should go out in a way that highlights that."

He was looking afraid now and all the bravado was gone. I walked over to our table and picked up one of the sharp knives we kept there. I walked back and nodded to Menace and Ranger. "Stand him up and hook his hands to the hook above him." They quickly got him undone. He tried to fight but was too weak. They had him strung up in no time. I walked around him caressing the knife. He tried to twist so he could keep me in sight. I came to a stop in front of him. I stared at him saying nothing while he stared back at me. Suddenly, I grabbed his cock and sliced it off. He screamed as the blood ran down to the floor. Then I proceeded to remove his balls and cut him from there to his ass. I stood back and we all impassively watched him bleed to death. It didn't take long. When he was finally dead, Hawk, Torch, Finn, and Tyler got him down and wrapped up. They would dispose of the body. Storm and Nick would clean up the knife and any other blood that might have spilled. They'd also make sure the cell he'd been in was bleached and any DNA was gone. Dan Peters would disappear never to be heard of again. Most people would assume he fled because of all the money he owed customers that he couldn't pay back.

The rest of us went back to the clubhouse. I wanted to shower there before I went home to Wren. The guys were expressing their relief he was gone. He'd been totally insane. He would have never stopped. It was almost midnight when I got home. I knew Wren had to be asleep by now. I tiptoed down the hall to our room after taking off my boots. I quietly opened the door and found her sitting in bed reading. She looked up and smiled. Fuck, she was beautiful. I stripped off my clothes and slid under the covers with her and gave her a kiss.

She moaned and pushed the cover down. She was naked and she crawled over onto my chest pressing me back into the pillows. She was devouring my mouth. Her tongue was dueling with mine. She sucked on it and bit my bottom lip only to lick it afterward. She was almost panting when she pulled back.

"Shit, babe. I think you might be a little horny," I teased.

She bit my earlobe and whispered, "I'm so fucking horny, I can't stand it. I've been lying here thinking about you and I even masturbated but nothing worked. I need you inside of me. Now. I want it hard and fast."

I rolled her off me and onto her back. I was hard as hell. I pushed her legs back, so they were now bent and almost touching her shoulders. Wren was very flexible. She grasped her thighs and spread her legs even wider. Her pussy was glistening with her juices and her folds were swollen and dusky pink. She hadn't lied. She was ready. I aimed my cock at her entrance and thrust inside her in one stroke. She moaned. I had to groan. She was so wet, scorching hot and tight. She instantly clamped down on me.

"God, baby, you feel so good. You're so hot and wet

and tight. So tight." I thrust in and out rocking her body. She kept moaning and trying to thrust back. I shoved her thighs back more and grasped them as I started to slam my cock in and out of her pussy. She was lifting her hips and begging me.

"Please, harder. I need harder and deeper. Fuck me, Talon!" She screamed. I sped up and thrust even deeper and harder. She lasted a few more minutes before she came screaming my name. Her pussy clamped down on my cock so hard I saw stars. I gritted my teeth and hung on. I didn't want to come yet. I had plans. Something I'd been thinking about for days or to be honest months. Once she relaxed, I slid out. She frowned.

"Honey, you didn't get off. Why'd you stop?" I smiled.

"I have something else I want to try. Relax your legs. Roll over onto your stomach." She rolled over. I tucked a pillow under her hips to raise her up off the bed. She watched as I got in my drawer and pulled out the toy we'd used before. The one she liked that had a second protrusion on it. She smiled. I grabbed the lube. I crawled back up on the bed and straddled her legs. She was watching me over her shoulder. I lubed up the longer protrusion. Last time I'd fucked her in the pussy with the long one and in the ass with the nub. This time I was gonna put the long one in her ass and let the nub tease her pussy. I needed to see if she could take this bigger object in her ass. She had done well with my finger.

I bent down and rubbed the long piece against her asshole. She jumped. As she watched me. I began to work it into her ass. She moaned and lifted her bottom up in the air. I worked it in and out until I had it all the way in. The small protrusion was barely inside the entrance to her pussy. Then I began to fuck her ass with it. I started slow, and then sped up as she began to moan louder and push back. She was loving it and taking it without a problem. I kept it up for almost ten minutes before she came a second time yelling.

"God, I love you, Talon." I kept working it in and out of her ass until she collapsed down on the pillow. I slowly pulled it out and sat the dildo on the nightstand. She was laying there looking at me. "Talon, honey, you haven't gotten off. I want you to. What can I do to get you there?" I leaned down and kissed her.

"Let me fuck that ass. That's what I want. Are you willing to try? I've been dreaming about it. How tight you'll be. How much you'll enjoy it. Baby, you think my finger and this toy were great, wait until you feel my cock," I growled. She looked hesitant. "We don't have to if you don't want to. I never want you to do something you don't want." She shook her head.

"It isn't that. Your cock is so much bigger than your finger or that toy. It's gonna hurt." I smiled.

"Yes, it'll burn and hurt until you get used to it and stretch enough but we'll take our time. Just like I did the first time with my finger. But then it'll subside, and the pleasure will begin. So much pleasure," I promised her. I waited to let her decide. I wouldn't push her to do it if she didn't want to do it. She finally smiled and lifted her ass up.

"Show me how good it can be."

Her words made me crazy. I wanted to pound in and out of her ass, but I knew I had to take it easy. At least at first. I had the feeling once she was past the burning and pain, she'd be begging me to do her harder. My woman liked it hard and deep. Just the way I liked it best. I slid another pillow under her belly to push her ass higher. I slid my lubed finger in and out of her ass a couple of times then I went to put some on my cock.

She stopped me. "Let me." She reached back and I put some lube on her hand. She stroked up and down my cock coating it in the lube. I groaned. Shit it felt good to feel her hand on my cock. I grabbed her hand.

"Stop or you'll have me blowing my load. I want to do that in your sweet ass." I leaned over and teased her puckered hole with the head of my cock a few times. Then I started to push inside. I worked the head in and stopped to let her adjust. I pulled back and inched in more before I stopped again. I kept this in and out motion going for several minutes. She was relaxing and I was now almost completely in her ass. She was no longer hissing like it hurt or burned. She wasn't asking me to stop either. She was starting to moan. I slid the last inch in. Fuck I'd made it! She was as tight as I'd imagined. She was gripping my cock like a fist. She looked at me.

"I'm so full. God, your cock is so much bigger but once the pain and burning eased, it's starting to feel good." I grinned.

"That's what I hoped you'd say. Now relax and let me fuck this ass until we both come. I want you to milk me for every drop of my cum."

She whimpered. I pulled back and then slid back in one complete stroke. She bucked her ass up off the pillow. I thrust in and out slowly at first and then with more speed and depth. Soon her moans and whimpers made me lose control. I began to power in and out, powering as deep as I could reach. She was pushing back to meet my thrusts. Our skin was slapping together and both of us had a fine sheen of sweat on our bodies. I growled.

"Wren, you feel like heaven, baby. Like a fucking glove. Are you close?" She nodded. I went faster and harder. It took maybe eight more strokes and she came keening out her pleasure while I grunted and groaned as my cum bathed the inside of her ass. She was clamping down and releasing my cock milking me dry like I'd asked. When we both stopped coming, I laid down across her back and kissed her neck.

"You're perfect. So, fucking perfect. I love you. Thank you for this." She twisted so she could see me and kissed my lips.

"Talon, you're perfect and I love you. As for thanking me, I should be thanking you. You were right. Once you were in, it turned to nothing but pleasure. I loved it. You can have my ass anytime you want." I groaned and kissed her. I finally had to pull back and slid my softening cock out of her ass. She moaned as I did. I rolled her over and scooped her up. She grabbed my shoulders.

"Where are we going?" I headed to the bathroom.

"We need a shower after that. Then you need to sleep." I helped her wash and she helped me clean myself before we went to bed. God, I loved her. She was my perfect match.

Chapter 20: Wren

Today was my every other week appointment with Dr. Hunter. I was now nine weeks and six days along. I was hoping he was happy with my weight. I knew I'd gained some. I'd read if you're within your normal weight range when you get pregnant, you should gain two to four pounds in the first trimester then a pound a week thereafter. In my case since I'd lost five pounds, I'd need to gain seven to nine pounds in the first trimester and I had only two weeks to go before I was at twelve weeks. I was fidgeting in the waiting room. Ghost clasped him hands.

"What's wrong? You're worried I can tell." I sighed.

"I'm worried he'll be disappointed at how much I've gained. I know it isn't enough. I'm really trying, honey." He hugged me.

"You're doing your best. As long as you're both healthy who cares. Let's see what he has to say."

We were called back five minutes later. The nurse weighed me. I'd gained in total to date three pounds. I weighed a hundred and twenty-three. After she took my vitals and blood, she left us in the exam room. We sat waiting. I couldn't talk. I was nervous. It wasn't long until Dr. Hunter came sailing in with a smile.

"Well, hello, Wren and Ghost. How is that baby Warrior doing today?" I told him about how the nausea and vomiting was. He seemed to be okay with it. He used the doppler to listen to the baby. He explained once I began to show, he'd start measuring my stomach. I guess that told him how the baby was growing in relationship to how far along I was. Right now, I barely had a tiny bump. Honestly no one would guess I was pregnant.

Ghost spoke up "Shouldn't she be showing more by now. She hardly has a baby bump. She eats but only small amounts at a time and mainly bland food since anything else makes her sick. Her fluid intake has been good." I laughed.

"Yeah, he monitors that every day and makes sure I drink every single ounce. He fills a container every morning with my quota," I teased. Ghost looked satisfied with himself. Dr Hunter was nodding.

"Good. He'll make sure you and this baby stay healthy. Now as for your weight. I'd wished you had gained a little more. So, for your next appointment your goal is three pounds. You'll be at twelve weeks and right in the middle of what you should have gained. Then if you can gain a pound a week until you deliver, you'll have gained thirty-four pounds and put you at one hundred and fifty-four. At a minimum, you need to get to at least one hundred and forty-five. And make sure it's a lot of vegetables, fruits, lean protein, and good carbs. Watch the caffeine. No more than one caffeinated drink a day. Hopefully you're on the tail end of the hyperemesis. Let me know if you have to use the Zofran again even if it is only once. Any more questions?" Ghost asked a couple about the caffeine. I saw my iced tea becoming a thing of the past. We left the office with handouts on the foods I should be eating.

He took me back to the compound before he went to the garage to work. I spent time with Harlow and Sherry finishing off the centerpieces Janessa had shown us how to make them. All I had to do was go do my final fitting and we'd be ready. I planned to do it next week. The bridesmaids and groomsmen outfits along with Ghost's were ready. I wanted to be sure I didn't suddenly gain and have my stomach make it not fit. Though it wasn't skin-tight in the middle, it was a tighter fit gown. I'd found the jewelry to go with my dress and the shoes. It was only nineteen days until the wedding. We invited all the Warrior clubs, the Souls and Punishers. Not everyone would be at the actual wedding just those from Bull's club. Everyone else would be at the reception. Ms. Marie had taken command of the wedding making sure everything was on task and arranged. She said she had the time and loved doing this kind of thing. She was a god send. She'd adopted all of us as her children and the kids as her grandchildren. Rowan calls her grandma like Alannah.

I was hoping Ghost really liked it. I'd really relied on the Native American and desert aspect for the theme. His culture was beautiful, and I didn't want him or our children to lose it. I was borrowing the round grapevine arch Brielle and Ranger used for their wedding, but I was wrapping it in the desert flowers I would use in my bouquet. Janessa had helped me with the hairstyle I wanted. I was a bit nervous but mostly excited. I couldn't wait to marry Ghost.

We were now talking about the honeymoon. Ghost

insisted we were going to have a couple of nights away from the compound. Even with the threat of the Bastards and Savages, he said it would happen. Only he wouldn't tell me where. Our house wouldn't be done until a few weeks after the wedding. Though, anywhere alone with him would be perfect.

I was in the kitchen getting more to drink when a pain cramped my stomach. I doubled over. What the hell? It went away as I breathed through it. That was weird. I hadn't felt anything like that before. I refilled my water and headed back to the common room. I was almost back to the couch when another cramping pain hit me in the lower abdomen. I dropped my water and cried out. Harlow and Sherry ran over as well as Adam. He swung me up in his arms and carried me to the couch. Harlow hunkered down beside it.

"What's wrong, Wren?" I grimaced.

"I'm having cramping pains in my lower stomach. I don't know what's wrong. I've never had this," I told her in fear. She looked at Adam.

"Go get Ghost, he's at the garage. Hurry." He raced out of the building. I sat there afraid for my baby. What if I was miscarrying our baby? I had tears in my eyes just thinking about it. Ghost came running in the door with Adam, Blaze, and Viper with him. He ran over to me with concern written all over his face.

"What's wrong, Beauty? Adam said you were in pain." I nodded.

"I'm having cramping pains that come and go in my lower stomach. I don't know what it is." I was half crying. I flinched as I felt another one. He scooped me up and told Adam to get the SUV.

"Baby, I'm taking you to the ER. They need to check you out." Harlow said she'd come with us. He raced me out to the car and jumped into the backseat. Viper, Blaze, and Adam all got on their bikes. Rebel and Ace came outside. They must have been in their rooms. They asked what was happening and Ghost told them. They got on their bikes as well.

Harlow held my hand all the way to the hospital. I had a few more cramps. She was texting I assume Terror. Ghost kept looking back in the mirror and asking if I was okay. He pulled into the ER and had me inside within a minute. He went to the desk and was telling them I needed seen right away. No one argued and they took us in the back. Ghost insisted they call Dr. Hunter. They were saying they'd have the resident check me out. Ghost grunted and pulled out his phone. Next thing I heard was him talking.

"Dr. Hunter, this is Ghost, Wren's man. She's in the ER with cramping. They wouldn't call you. Can you come check her out?" He paused to listen. "Great. We'll see you soon." He hung up and glanced at the nurse. "Dr. Hunter said he'd be here in five minutes. Just so you know, the Warriors all use Dr. H. If our women are pregnant and come in, we expect him to be called." She scurried off. I grabbed his hand.

"Don't be scaring the nurses. They have their protocols." He frowned.

"I don't give a shit. Not when it comes to my woman or baby. You know he's always said to call if we have questions or problems. This is a problem. Now try and relax." He stood pacing. Dr. Hunter came strolling in.

"What happened, Wren? You were fine this morning." I told him about the pain, what it felt like and also how many I'd had. He pulled in the resident and ordered a urinalysis and an ultrasound. He also had them take more blood to test for things he hadn't on my regular bloodwork at the office this morning. The next couple of hours were filled with test after test. Finally, Dr. Hunter came to talk to us. By then I was a wreck and Ghost was looking like an avenging angel.

"Good news. You're not having contractions or dilating or bleeding so you don't appear to be miscarrying. No bladder infection. The ultrasound and dopplers studies show the baby is fine and no indication of an ectopic pregnancy we missed, ovarian cysts or uterine fibroids. I believe you're having uterine pains from the muscles and ligaments stretching. Usually, you feel that more in second and third trimester, but you're close to the second trimester. You shouldn't be surprised to feel them along the sides as you get bigger. However, if they become severe, you have bleeding or a fever, you need to come in and call me. We're going to send you home to rest. Everything looks fine. Try not to stress," he told us. Ghost asked about me being on bedrest. Dr. H didn't think it was necessary. If I found the cramps too much, I could lie down.

After I was discharged, Ghost took me straight to the house and had me lie down on the bed. Harlow said she'd let everyone know I was okay. For the rest of the evening, Ghost waited on me hand and foot. He would barely let me go to the bathroom. I pulled him down on the bed.

"Honey, stop. I'm fine. I'm sorry I scared you. I didn't know what was happening. But you heard Dr. H., I'm fine and so is the baby. Now come to bed and hold me. Let's watch a movie and veg out." He finally settled down and we spent the rest of the night watching our favorite shows on Netflix. I knew that the remainder of this pregnancy would have him worried and he wouldn't be allowing me to work even a day at the daycare. God, I loved this man, but he could be a little too overprotective.

Chapter 21: Ghost

It had been a week since Wren had stomach cramps and had scared me to death. All I could think was we were losing our baby and what if something was wrong with Wren? Dr. Hunter had reassured us everything was fine, but I was still worried. I tried to get Wren to rest more but she said, she couldn't sit all day. She did take things easy and not overstress herself. The cramps had happened here and there but nothing as intense as the first time.

I was finishing work on the bike Blaze and I had been building. It was five-thirty. I planned to head home at six. My cell went off with a text message. It was a group text to all of us telling us to come to the clubhouse for church at six-thirty. It was mandatory. This got my curiosity going. Why would Terror be calling church in the middle of the week? It had to be something about the Savages and Bastards. We hadn't heard or seen anything since they'd tried to attack the daycare. We knew for actual members they couldn't have more than a dozen guys and or even less. Reaper had told Terror a week ago that prospects were abandoning them scared they'd be killed. I decided to stop and go to the house so I could tell Wren I was needed at the clubhouse. When I came in, she was finishing off dinner.

"Hey, babe, I need to go to the clubhouse at six-thirty. Terror called church. Do you want to come and hangout there or stay here at the house?" She was ladling up the food.

"I'll stay here, I think. I'll relax and read or something." I pulled her into my arms.

"Are you feeling okay? Do you want someone to come over and sit with you?" I hated to leave her alone. She shook her head.

"I'm fine. Just not up to chatting with people tonight. Why don't we eat and then you can go?" I sat down to her excellent dinner. We had an herbed pork roast, Au gratin potatoes, fresh peas, and spiced apples. I was glad to see she ate more than she had been. I insisted she leave the dishes for me and I'd do them when I got back. I left her with a kiss. I was at the clubhouse by six twenty-five. Everyone else was gathered and we headed straight into church as soon as I arrived.

Terror and Savage were already in there and Smoke was set up with his laptop. Terror called us to order. "I heard back from Sean, Gabe, and Griffin. They have found more of the gun and drug storage areas for the Savages and Bastards. They said they can help us out by blowing them up. Also, they have done recon on their two clubhouses. They got a guy into both their chapters as new prospects since they lost all their other ones. They have church every Thursday night at seven. They don't allow anyone else in the clubhouse when they're having it. That means no bunnies, old ladies, or family members." He paused and looked at us. "I think it's time to take care of them once and for all. They've been a pain in our ass long enough. They keep picking at us and we keep knocking out parts of their business here and there. I spoke to Bull and he's in agreement. We're gonna go in with Sean, Gabe, and Griffin and blow their clubhouses up while they're in church." Everyone looked at each other and began to murmur. He called us back to order.

"I didn't come to this decision lightly, but we know they won't give up until they kill us. This way, we don't have to worry about taking out any innocent people. If they're in church, then they are the enemy. I'd like to do this on Thursday. We need to have them out of the way before your wedding, Ghost. I don't want to chance them deciding to hit us during that. What I need is for us to vote on this as a club. It has to be unanimous."

His revelation sure sparked off the conversation. We talked about all the possible things that could go wrong. As well as what the positive outcomes could be from getting rid of them once and for all. We spent the better part of an hour discussing things before he called for the final vote. It passed without a problem. We'd be spending time over the next couple of days planning our runs. Today was Monday. We had a lot to do to get ready. I knew I'd have to tell Wren something because she'd know something was up. I just wouldn't tell her the details.

When I got back to the house, I cleaned up the kitchen and then took a shower. She was waiting in bed watching a movie. She put it on mute. I sat down with my back to the headboard. "What's happening? Terror doesn't just call church in the middle of the week," she said with a worried frown on her face. I shrugged.

"He got some news about the Savages and Bastards

he didn't want to wait to tell us." She slid closer.

"Don't think you can fool me. It's more than that. You're planning something. I know it. You don't have to tell me any details just tell me when you're going and are you going to be here for the wedding." I could see the fear in her eyes. I pulled her into my arms and gave her a hard kiss.

"Of course, I'll be here for the wedding. Nothing could keep me away. We're going to go on a run Thursday night. And we'll be having meetings for the next couple of evenings to get ready for it. That's all I can say. Please don't ask me more." She kissed me.

"I won't. Just please be careful and come back to me. I couldn't live without you. I need you. Our baby needs you."

"I promise. Now how about I make love to my woman." She eagerly threw off the covers. I'd been leery of touching her this past week because of the cramps. She'd told me more than once she was fine. I needed her tonight. We spent the next hour making love. I would do everything in my power to be sure I come back to her and our baby. She fell asleep holding onto me a little tighter than usual. I did the same.

The next evening, we met again. Terror and Smoke were going over aerial views, maps, and diagrams of the two compounds. We were leaving nine guys behind to guard the compound. This left twenty-two of us to be split into two teams. One would go to the Lansing, North Carolina clubhouse while the rest would go to the Arrington Mill, Virginia one. Gabe and Griffin would be in Arrington Mills with another one of their friends.

Sean and two others would be with the team in Lansing. They had access to more C-4. Several of our guys had experience with explosives from their days in Special Forces and the Seals.

We'd plant the charges which shouldn't take long and then remote detonate them once we were clear of the building. We were going in without anything identifiable marks or ID and in old, unmarked vans with stolen plates. We were lucky that both clubhouses set out in the open without close neighbors close to them. We didn't want to chance hurting someone else. Sean, Gabe, and Griffin would be here tomorrow so we could run through the plans and where we were planting the charges. Since they were a few hours away, we'd leave here at two for those going to Lansing since it was a three-hour drive. Those going to Arrington Mills would leave an hour later as it was only a two-hour drive. We wanted to have a couple of hours to get set and do our last recon.

After our meeting we spent time with our ladies, kids, and brothers in the common room. Things were rather subdued with the women. They knew something big was about to happen. The guys with wives and kids held them just a little bit tighter. I knew there'd be a lot of lovemaking going on tonight and tomorrow night. Just in case someone didn't make it back. I'd been raised as a Christian but also to believe in the old gods of the Apache. Our creator, Ussen, and the lesser gods who were protective mountain spirits. I prayed to both God and Ussen to bring me back to my woman and baby.

Wednesday came and with it, Sean, Gabe, and Griffin. They enjoyed spending time with Brielle and seeing how much Rowan had changed and to meet baby

Gabriel. They'd been the ones to rescue Brielle five years ago from her rapist. The women all made a big dinner for all of us which we ate after our last planning meeting. Our groups were decided. We'd finish packing our stuff in the morning.

That night after we made love, Wren cried before she fell asleep. I tried to reassure her, but she was scared. Us bringing Sean, Gabe, and Griffin in made it obvious we were planning something big and dangerous. I rocked her and whispered in her ear everything was going to be alright until she finally fell into a deep sleep. I stayed awake for another hour soaking up her scent and warmth.

Thursday morning found us all working to get our stuff packed and say our goodbyes. I ran through safety measures with Wren even though I knew she already knew them. No one would be leaving the compound while we were gone. The last couple of days had been hard. The stress had Wren vomiting more often. After tonight, she should be able to calm down and get it back under control.

I was going to the Arrington Mills clubhouse. Going with me were Rebel, Ace, Pope, Knight, Terror, Menace, Viper, Steel, Hammer, and Finn. Sean was going with my team and his guys would meet us there. Those going to Lansing were Tiger, Falcon, Mayhem, Lash, Savage, Ranger, Blaze, Tiny, Hawk, Devil Dog, Storm, along with Gabe, Griffin and their other guy who would meet them there. Saber, Ice, Crusher, Ryder, Smoke, Viking, Torch, Razor, Adam, Nick, and Tyler would stay behind to guard the women and children. We kissed our loved ones goodbye and loaded up in the vans and trucks with our equipment. The next two hours passed in mostly tense silence, as we drove to the rendezvous site.

We got to our meeting point and hooked up with Sean's guys. They led us into the area closest to the clubhouse. One of them was the guy who had been acting as a prospect for them. He said they wouldn't miss him, since he'd told them he had to go check on his sick mom today. We watched while one after the other streamed inside. This location had a total of eight guys. The other location had six according to intel. We counted and the prospect made sure to identify that all were present and accounted for. Once they were all inside and we saw it was seven o'clock, we headed in. We made sure to stay clear of windows and wired up the outside of the building. They had a garage right beside the clubhouse. We made sure to wire it as well. It took us roughly a half hour to get it done. We hurried back to our original rally point. It was seven forty-five. We didn't want to wait any longer and risk them getting out of church. Sean pushed the detonator switch.

The night sky lit up with the fireworks. Secondary explosions could be heard from the gas tanks and propane tank beside the garage exploding. That would be heard for miles. We got the hell out of there and back to our vehicles hidden on another access road. As we left the area, we could hear sirens blaring all over. Goodbye Savages and Bastards. Hopefully the others had it go as smooth as we had it. We were back by ten thirty at the clubhouse. Wren, Harlow, Harper, and Regan greeted us with hugs, kisses, and tears. The rest of the guys were asking if we had any trouble. We told them no. We'd get into more detail after Savage and his group got back. They should be rolling up in another hour. The guys at the clubhouse said they had gotten a text saying they were okay and would soon be on their way.

It was closer to an hour and a half before they made it back. Janessa, Alannah, Bri, and Sherry all greeted their men just as relieved as ours were. I saw Blaze had a bloody bandage on his shoulder. The ladies were swarming all over him checking him out especially Regan and Janessa. I decided to let them handle it. They'd let me know if they needed my help. They were cleaning and dressing his wound which, I heard him say was a gunshot wound. Savage confirmed they had accomplished their mission despite Blaze getting shot. Since it was already midnight, Terror decided to meet tomorrow to talk about our missions more in-depth. He told us to meet back here at ten in the morning. Feeling exhausted, everyone headed off to bed for a good night's sleep.

I took a long shower with Wren. She was drooping with fatigue and so was I. She kissed me. "Thank God, you came back in one piece, Talon. I love you, honey. So much."

"Not as much as I love you, Wren. You and this baby are my world, beauty. My fucking world." We kissed until we were breathless. When our heads hit the pillows, we were asleep.

When I woke up the next morning, it was eight o'clock. Wren was still snuggled in my arms fast asleep. I got up to use the bathroom. When I came out, she was awake. I slid into bed with her. She kissed me.

"Do you want some breakfast?" I nodded.

"I sure do. I want it right now." I whipped off the covers and started to kiss up her neck. She was laughing and trying to push me off her.

"No, that's not what I meant." She laughed. I growled.

"That's exactly what I meant." I attacked her mouth. I nipped at her lips and sucked on her tongue. She moaned and ran her hands down my chest to play with my nipples. Her breasts were full and topped by hard nipples. They were larger than they were just a week ago. I sucked her nipple into my mouth using my tongue to press it against the roof of my mouth while my fingers tweaked the nipple on her other breast. We were both too revved to spend much time on foreplay. I slipped my hand down and found her pussy was soaking wet. I rolled over onto my back.

"Get on top." She climbed on top and sank down on my rock-hard cock. Damn, she felt so good. Once seated, she began to ride me. She started out slow and easy but that didn't last long. She was as excited as I was. She was going faster and harder. I gripped her hips to hold her up so I could use my legs to thrust my hips hard into her. She whimpered and circled her hips again and again. After several minutes of this, I bit the spot between her neck and shoulder.

"Hold on, while I make us both come. I can't wait any longer," I growled. I hammered away thrusting my hips up and into her over and over. Going deep. Her heat surrounding me and her pussy gripping me tight. A dozen more strokes had us both coming and yelling out our releases. She collapsed onto my chest. I rubbed her back as we regained our breath. I eventually eased out of her so we could get cleaned up and grab a bite to eat. It was close to ten when we were done, and we headed to the clubhouse. She had decided she was going to go with me and see how Blaze was doing. We got inside to find Blaze being fussed over by the other ladies. Some of the guys were razzing him about being a pussy. He just grinned and nodded. Terror finally broke it up and called us into church.

We all sat down and went through our evenings. Apparently, Blaze ended up getting shot when one of the Savages came outside for some reason during church. He'd been bringing up the rear in the race to get far enough away to detonate. Luckily it had been a through and through and they were far enough away to detonate so the wayward Savage was killed by the blast anyway. This should be the end of the Satan's Bastards and the Black Savages motorcycle clubs. We knew there'd eventually be others moving in to take up their territories. Hopefully they'd be more like our club or at the very least, would stay far away from us and our areas. We spent the remainder of the day relaxing with our family. All of us thankful to be alive.

Epilogue: Wren

Today was the big day. Mine and Ghost's wedding day. The weather had cooperated, and the sun was out, and the temp was a high of seventy. The day before we had gotten the majority of the common room decorated. Ghost had been banned from entering because I wanted it to be a surprise. We'd have the dinner inside and then the tables would be pushed to the edges to allow for room to dance. When the Warriors had gotten this place, they made sure to leave a massive area for the common room. Usually, the middle of it was where the tables, chairs, and pool tables sat with lots of open space around them. Not all the guys from all the various chapters would be coming but everyone would send a delegation.

The ceremony was at four-thirty. The dinner part of the reception would begin at six and then the dancing at seven. The remainder of the decorating had been finished this morning with the various guys helping to get things done. I had stayed at the house so Ghost wouldn't see me the day of the wedding. He would get ready at Ranger and Brielle's house.

I started to get ready at two thirty. I wanted to be sure I had enough time. I soaked in a gardenia infused tub and then applied my gardenia body lotion. I'd been to the spa to have everything freshly waxed yesterday.

I got a manicure and pedicure at the spa as well where they painted my nails red. Brielle was helping with my makeup. I was going with dark gray, silver and black to give myself a smoky eye. I kept my cheeks pale with a minimal blush of pink on my cheeks. My lips were done in red to match the red in my dress.

The jewelry I'd found to go with my outfit consisted of a wide silver cuff with a bright turquoise center stone that had etchings all over the silver part. Around my neck was a three-strand choker necklace made of turquoise, red coral, black jet stones and white abalone shell. My earrings were long and matched the stones and shell in the choker. My hair was pulled to the left side and braided into a long rope braid. Wound in and around the braid was thin strips of rawhide leather adorned with beads that matched the necklace and earrings as well as feathers.

Brielle and the other bridesmaids were dressed in their outfits. They were wearing feminine tunic dresses made of soft, white leather that came to mid-thigh. The waist was cinched in with turquoise woven and beaded belts. Fringe hung from the deep V neckline, arms and hem and had red and silver beads on them. Their hair was done in the same style as mine but without the beads and feathers. Their jewelry was more understated. Their shoes were low-heeled sandals decorated with silver medallions that wrapped up their legs in thin leather strips to be tied.

They'd just helped me into my wedding dress. It had a red tight bodice with beading in a V along the neckline and yoke of the waist. Below waist and from my shoulders hung white fringe beaded with red, and silver beads. The skirt was alternating panels of red and white with embroidery of flowers on them in the opposite thread color. On my feet I had three-inch heels with three layers of fringe decorated in silver and red beads like the dress. The leather on the shoes was white as well.

The bouquet was the same for all of us just mine was larger. They consisted of red, peach, mint green, and lighter pastel flowers interspersed with small succulents. I didn't plan to wear a wedding veil. They were finishing getting me zipped up when there was a knock on the bedroom door. Brielle answered it. Bull was standing there in his outfit. The groomsmen and father of the bride were wearing white leather tunics over matching pants. The tunic was decorated with silver and turquoise beading. They had on moccasins done in the same beading. He came in to check out my dress. He was nodding and smiling. I gave him a huge. He stood back.

"You look gorgeous. I'll ask you what I asked the rest of these girls. Are you sure you don't want to run? There's still time," he teased. I laughed and told him no. "Well then I think this outfit is missing something." I frowned and looked down at myself.

"What?" He held out a box. I opened it to find a fabric headband that would go around my forehead, much like an Indian headband. On it were turquoise, rubies, diamonds and black onyx jewels. I gasped. I could tell they were real stones. I shook my head. "Bull, I can't accept this. This is too much." He smiled.

"I got every one of my girls something for their wedding—necklaces, bracelet, earrings and even tiaras. This is the first time I get to do a headband. Harlow told me the colors of your stones in the other jewelry so I could match it." I gave him a hug and kiss. The girls helped me to get it on without messing up my hair. It went perfectly.

The others soon left to take their seats. Five minutes later the music started, and my bride's maids headed out on the arms of their escorts. I was standing in the house and Bull would walk me to the teepee we'd set up for the ceremony. We were using the round arch that Brielle and Ranger had at their wedding wrapped in the desert flowers like my bouquet to stand under to repeat our vows. I heard the music I'd chosen to walk down the aisle. It was Apache tribal chanting music.

Outside, Bull helped me to the teepee and then down the short aisle to Ghost. He was dressed in in his white tunic and matching pants. It had fringe hanging from the sleeves and the bottom of the tunic and decorated with red, turquoise, black, silver beading. His moccasins matched the tunic. He wore his turquoise necklace I got him at Christmas and around his head was a headband. His long black hair was braided down his back. Eagle feathers decorated his braid. He was watching me not even blinking. When I reached his side, he took both my hands. Bear proceeded with the traditional wedding vows. However, he also added, at my request, the Apache wedding blessing.

He wrapped our hands in cloth and repeated the blessing. "Now you will feel no rain, for each of you will be shelter for the other. Now you will feel no cold, for each of you will be warmth to the other. Now there will be no loneliness, for each of you will be companion to the other. Now you are two persons, but there is only one life before you. May beauty surround you both in the journey ahead and through all the years. May happiness be your companion and your days together be good and long upon the earth. Treat yourselves and each other with respect and remind yourselves often of what brought you together. Give the highest priority to the tenderness, gentleness and kindness that your connection deserves. When frustration, difficulties and fear assail your relationship, as they threaten all relationships at one time or another, remember to focus on what is right between you, not only the part which seems wrong. In this way, you can ride out the storms when clouds hide the face of the sun in your lives - remembering that even if you lose sight of it for a moment, the sun is still there. And if each of you takes responsibility for the quality of your life together, it will be marked by abundance and delight." (The Knot, 2019). We exchanged wedding bands made of white gold that were carved with tribal designs. When Bear gave him permission to kiss the bride, Ghost swooped in and lifted me off the ground in his arms.

We led the wedding party procession back to the house to take pictures. The guys would likely change into more comfortable clothes after the pictures were done, but I wanted to keep mine on for a while. I was in the bedroom checking my makeup after the pictures were done when Ghost closed the door. He stalked me across the room. He grabbed me and growled.

"You fucking look so beautiful. My heart almost stopped when you came down the aisle on Bull's arm. I know if one of my ancestors had seen you, they'd have definitely kidnapped you and took you for his bride. I want to peel this dress off and make love to you for the rest of the evening." He captured my lips and kissed me until I felt drugged and weak. I pulled away.

"Talon, we can't. Our guests will be looking for us and I don't want to rush our lovemaking. Once we start, I don't want to have to stop. Let's get through the reception then we can ravish each other. I promise. All night if you want." He groaned and placed his forehead on mine.

"Okay. Let's get situated." He headed for the door.

"Aren't you going to change?" He shook his head no.

"Do you want to change, Wren?" I told him no. I made sure I was still put together and then we headed out to join the others at the clubhouse. Surprisingly, the groomsmen and bride's maids had all left on their outfits. Bull came over to congratulate Ghost. He told him he was keeping the moccasins. They were the most comfortable thing he'd ever worn.

Inside, the tables were set up. The wooden tables were left bare without tablecloths so you could see the beautiful wood. Placemats of turquoise were at each seat with white napkins wrapped in braided leather. The centerpieces had the clear glass candle holders of varying heights which we had filled partially with sand and then topped that with small stones in various shaded of brown. At the top of the holder was small cacti. Along the length of the tables were small tree branches that had been painted white with pieces of driftwood scattered around.

Dreamcatchers of various sizes, colors and designs hung throughout the space. Bare trees had been brought in and strung with white lights. Bright Apache rugs covered the floor and were hung on the walls. Set on a small table was our wedding cake. Alannah had outdone herself again. It was made of four-square tiers frosted white. The largest bottom tier looked like brown braided leather had been wound around it. The next tier had beautiful dreamcatchers on all four sides. The third tier had a replica of my choker necklace wrapped around it. The top tier had realistic eagle feathers all around it. On the top of the whole cake was a cake topper of an Indian man and his woman in full dress buckskins. The cakes had the colors of turquoise, red, brown, silver, and black. The cake he and I had chosen was a lemon-coconut cake with sweet mascarpone frosting. I hoped everyone else liked it. We'd loved it when we'd tasted it.

For dinner we'd decided to be eclectic and mix different foods we liked. We'd settled on roasted herb and garlic new potatoes, wild mushroom tartlets, spanakopita which was phyllo pastry dough filled with spinach and feta cheese, miniature crab cakes, pasta with roasted red pepper sauce and then a carving station of Cajun rubbed turkey breast and Tequila-lime marinated flank steak. In addition to the usual beer and mixed drinks we had red and white wine as well. The dinner went well, and everyone seemed to enjoy the food. Toasts were made and jokes abound. Most about how Ghost could have ever been lucky enough to catch me. I felt like I was the lucky one.

After the meal was over, tables were rearranged and pushed to the sides to make room for an actual dance floor. We'd hired a DJ for this part. We had our first dance as husband and wife then Bull claimed the father-daughter dance while Ms. Marie danced with Ghost as his "mother." She was heard to be lamenting losing another guy from her biker harem. We danced for a while before cutting the cake since everyone had been stuffed from the meal. We danced and partied for hours. I danced with all of Ghosts brothers and I think every other biker there. At one point, I had to throw my heels in the corner and slip-on flats.

Ghost and I danced and partied with everyone until ten. Then we left them to party until they couldn't party anymore. He whisked me away in one of the SUVs for our honeymoon. The girls had put my bag in the car earlier. He started driving east on Interstate 40. I kept asking where we were going but he kept saying it was a surprise. At midnight we pulled into the Biltmore Estate in Asheville NC. He'd reserved a room at the Carriage House B&B on the grounds. We were in the Honeymoon Cottage. Inside was very intimate and romantic with Victorian décor. There were two fireplaces, one of which was in the bathroom where there was a heart-shaped jetted tub perfect for two. Though it was dark, Ghost told me we had our own private rocking chair porch with views of the mountains. They had minx-lined plush robes. Set up were champagne on ice and strawberries.

I was blown away by it. He sat down our bags and started to unpack. I helped him get our clothes settled for the next few days. We'd be here thru Tuesday. I was looking forward to exploring the estate because I'd heard the other women talking about it. But right now, I wanted to explore my husband. He was putting the last of his clothes away when I wrapped may arms around him, hugging up against his back. I slid my hands down his front to rub across his crotch. I held my hands there and felt his cock growing hard underneath them. I lightly squeezed him. He groaned.

"You keep that up and I'll not be responsible for what happens."

I squeezed him again and said, "Good. Why don't you take a bath with me in that tub?" He turned around and kissed me.

"That sounds perfect. Let me help you out of that dress." He worked to get the back unzipped and then peeled it down my body. He carefully hung it in the closet. I was left standing in my corset and panties. Before he could remove those, I moved to help him strip off his tunic and pants. I hung his outfit in the closet with my dress. I wanted to preserve both of them. He took off his moccasins and now stood in front of me gloriously naked. Someone had prepped the room with candles lit all over the bedroom and bathroom. The candlelight made his bronze skin glisten. His tribal tats were even more mesmerizing.

He took my hand and walked me into the bathroom. He turned on the water to fill the tub while he slowly stripped off my corset and panties. He kissed my breasts as he revealed them. When I stepped out of my panties, he kneeled down and kissed my mound. He poured scented bath salts into the water. The scent of honeysuckle filled the air. I pinned up my braid so I could keep it out of the water. Then he scooped me up in his arms and sat us down in the hot water. He cradled me between his legs with my back to his chest.

His mouth was planting wet, hot kisses up my neck to my ear where he nibbled on my earlobe and licked the shell of my ear. "You look so beautiful and sexy, Mrs. Adair. So sexy. I've been in terrible agony all night waiting to have you all to myself. I plan to love you for hours. Before we leave here, I plan to take you in this tub, in the shower, on the bed, on our private porch and anywhere else I can find. If you weren't already pregnant, I could guarantee you would be after this honeymoon." I moaned.

I turned my head to the side so I could capture his mouth. I licked his lips until he opened up and I could slide my tongue inside to taste his mouth. Our tongues played with each other until we were both panting. He grasped my waist and lifted me up so I could turn around to straddle his thighs. His cock was hard and pressing into my stomach. I rocked against him. I ran my hands down his chest to play with his nipples and then I leaned forward to lick and suck on them. His hands were busy massaging my breasts and tweaking my nipples between his thumb and forefinger. My breath hitched and I threw my head back to groan. He took advantage to replace his hands with his mouth and torture me with licks, sucks, and nips. I was squirming on his lap. I could feel the wetness between my legs growing.

Ghost ran his hands down my back caressing everywhere as he went. His hands slid around to caress my stomach and then slipped down to fondle my folds. He rubbed his fingers back and forth along my slit and massaged my clit. Then his fingers slid down to thrust in and out of my pussy for several minutes. I moaned and chased his fingers with my hips when he withdrew. He slid his hands under my ass and lifted my hips. "I need you now, baby. I can't wait. Slide that tight little pussy down on my cock." I grabbed his hardness and guided it to my entrance and then sank down on him slowly. It was his turn to groan.

Once I had him fully inserted, he grasped my thighs to help me lift up and down on him. He made me feel so full. I held onto his shoulders to help me balance as I rode him. He was lifting up his hips and thrusting into me harder. I could feel my release already teasing my nerve endings. I rode him fast and hard. He picked up his pace as well. Soon we were coming together so hard and fast. His cock was touching deep inside. We were panting and the water was swishing around the tub. A half dozen more thrusts and I came crying out my release. He thrust two more times as I was coming, and he groaned out his. I could feel his warmth spreading throughout my core. I rode him until we both had stopped spasming. We rested for a few minutes and then cleaned ourselves off before getting out of the tub.

Back in the bedroom Ghost poured two glasses of champagne. I would take a sip or two since I was pregnant. He had me stretch out on the bed. I took a sip of the champagne while he took a drink of his. Next thing I knew, he was pulling my thighs open and clamping his mouth down on my clit. I jumped. I could feel the champagne bubbles tickling my clit. I shivered.

"Oh, that feels good." He held it there and then swallowed. He repeated this a couple more times. When he was finished with the champagne, he lifted his head and reached over for the strawberries. He slid one all over my lips before feeding it to me. He took another and rubbed it all over my nipples. The juice coated them, and he licked it off before he ate the strawberry.

The next strawberry he handed to me. I rubbed it along his lips and then held it between my lips and fed it to him. He licked the juice off both our mouths. His play was making me excited all over again. The next one he ran around my belly button and then dipped inside of it. He cleaned me off again making sure to thoroughly lick inside my belly button. He ate that one in one bite. I took the next one and outlined one of the tats on his chest. Once I had it completely traced, I licked him clean and ate the berry. We were both panting just a little. He picked up another one and kneeled down between my legs. He ran it up and down my slit teasing my folds and clit. He took it and placed the berry in his mouth. He moaned. "It tastes even better with your sweet juices on it." I sat up and crawled over to grab one. I looked at him.

"Let me see if it tastes even better with your essence on it." His cock had wept some precum during all this play. I ran the strawberry all over the head and then lowered my head to take the head of his cock in my mouth. He groaned. I licked him all over and then pulled away to eat my strawberry. "Mm, it does taste better with your cum and cock on it. I should eat my strawberries like this from now on." My words made him wild.

Ghost pushed me onto my back and dived between my thighs. He was lapping at my folds and sucking on my clit. He hummed in contentment the whole time as I laid back and got lost in the pleasure. His fingers slid through my folds and into my entrance. My hips bucked up off the mattress. He growled at me. "Don't move." I struggled to stay still while he tormented me with his tongue, teeth, and fingers. He teased me for several minutes then he gave two more thrusts of his fingers which had me coming. I could feel my juices running down my thighs. He lapped it all up. I sighed as I came down from my orgasm.

He got up off the bed. He stroked his cock as he stared at me. He was hard and his cock looked red and angry. "Stand up and bend over the side of the bed. Keep your feet on the floor and your legs spread," he ordered. I scrambled up to comply. I was breathless with anticipation. I knew he'd be making me come again. As I bent over the bed, he grasped my hips in his hands and slid his cock inside my pussy in one hard thrust. I cried out. He could go so deep in this position. His cock was nudging my cervix. He pulled back and slid back in. Things stayed nice and slow for a while. I was going to go insane if he didn't speed it up. I turned my head to look at him and beg.

"Talon, honey, please. I need you. Take me harder." He smacked my ass. I whimpered.

"Maybe I will and maybe I'll keep you like this all night. See how much you beg." I bit my bottom lip to keep from screaming. I knew if I protested, he would do it. He kept up the slow strokes for another minute or so then he began to thrust harder and faster. Soon his pelvis was slapping into my ass and his balls were hitting my pussy. I pushed back to see if he'd tell me to stop. He didn't but I felt him slide his fingers down to my soaking wet folds. As I thrust back to meet his thrust forward, I felt him touch my asshole and then slip a finger in my ass. I moaned and sped up. He was working his finger in and out of my ass as he worked his cock in and out of my pussy. When I came, I thought I'd pass out from the pleasure. He was grunting out his release with mine. We collapsed on the bed when it was over.

I laid in his arms and drifted. I must have fallen asleep because I jerked awake. I looked at the clock and saw it had been an hour since we'd had our last earth-shattering round. I looked over and found him staring at me. He was watching me intently and stroking his cock. He was hard again. I smiled.

"Are you looking for something there, husband." Ghost smiled and nodded his head.

"Oh yes, wife. I'm looking to take my beautiful wife again. Now roll over and let me play with that sweet pussy." I rolled onto my back. In no time, he had me soaking wet from his play. Ghost sat back on his heels.

"Roll over on your knees and keep them tucked under you with your head and shoulders on the bed." I got into position. I heard him opening something. I looked over my left shoulder to find him rubbing lube all over his cock. Jesus, he was going to fuck my ass! I loved when he did that. He raised up on his knees placing them on either side on my hips and began to ease his big cock into my ass. It was a tight fit and there was still some burning. He was not a small man. I worked to relax while he worked himself inside. Soon he gave a groan of pleasure as his pubic bone met my ass. He was fully imbedded.

He pushed down on my low back with one hand and grasped my hip with the other as he started to pump in and out of my ass. He worked me slow and then fast and then back to slow. I was pushing back to meet his thrusts and moaning. He kept this rhythm going for several minutes. Finally, I couldn't contain it.

"God, Talon, you feel so good. I love it when you take my ass. Make me come, please." His hips began to piston in and out, his balls slapping my pussy sending jolts of pleasure through my core. He was grunting and pounding my ass. The tingling started in my feet. It built there until suddenly, it shot up my legs into my ass and pussy. I came screaming his name. I clamped down hard on his cock and he growled and then started to grunt as his release filled my ass. I whimpered with every jerk of his cock. It seemed like we both went on forever before finally we stopped coming. He eased out of me. I rolled to my side. I heard him go into the bathroom and wash up then he came back with a wet cloth to clean me up. We curled up in the bed in each other arms.

"I love you, Talon Adair, my husband." He kissed me.

"And I love you, Wren Adair, my wife, my beauty." I fell asleep in his arms and dreamed about our life together and the baby we'd soon have. The life we were building together and with our Warrior family.

The End until Book 7: Viper's Vixen

https://www.theknot.com/content/wedding-vows-native-american-apache